D.K. HOOD

GOOD GIRLS DON'T CRY

bookouture

Published by Bookouture in 2025

An imprint of Storyfire Ltd.
Carmelite House
50 Victoria Embankment
London EC4Y 0DZ

www.bookouture.com

The authorised representative in the EEA is Hachette Ireland
8 Castlecourt Centre
Dublin 15 D15 XTP3
Ireland
(email: info@hbgi.ie)

Copyright © D.K. Hood, 2025

D.K. Hood has asserted her right to be identified as the author of this work.

All rights reserved. No part of this publication may be reproduced, stored in any
retrieval system, or transmitted, in any form or by any means, electronic,
mechanical, photocopying, recording or otherwise, without the prior written
permission of the publishers.

ISBN: 978-1-83618-729-5
eBook ISBN: 978-1-83618-728-8

This book is a work of fiction. Names, characters, businesses, organizations,
places and events other than those clearly in the public domain, are either the
product of the author's imagination or are used fictitiously. Any resemblance to
actual persons, living or dead, events or locales is entirely coincidental.

To Patricia Rodriguez, narrator extraordinaire for making my characters live.

PROLOGUE

Friday

Excitement vanished in one ugly second. The stretch limo taking them to the prom swerved suddenly and bumped over the curb. Horrified, Olivia Cooper gaped at the blood splashing across the divider window and running down the glass in crimson rivulets. What had happened to the driver? Her friends laughed and chatted as blood seeped through the tiny gap at the top of the window and trickled down inside, dripping onto the pristine white leather seats. Speechless with terror, she stared, transfixed as the vehicle stopped. Moments later, a door slammed and the limo took off again as if nothing had happened. She turned to her date. "Evan."

"I'm talking here." Evan sipped beer from a bottle.

Everyone laughed, totally oblivious to her gesturing toward the driver. No one noticed when the limo left the winding roads of Black Rock Falls and veered into the forest. Their minds were set on one thing: Prom night—the anticipated highlight of the year. Chills ran down Olivia's spine as branches brushed against the windows. "Evan." She grabbed his arm, but Evan was too involved with his friends. She shook him hard, unable to take her attention from the red drips. "Evan, something bad is happening." She pointed a trembling finger toward the blood-spattered window. "Look, that can't be a prank, can it?"

"Holy cow." Evan raised his voice as they bumped along a dirt track lined with tall pines. "Shut up, guys! This is bad."

"It's a joke." Graham Whitaker crawled up to the front of the limo and peered through the glass. He jumped back and the color drained from his face as he slid into the seat, staring blankly into space.

"What did you see?" Evan took him by the shoulders and shook him hard.

"Death." Graham turned to one side and vomited. He wiped his mouth. "The driver is dead. Someone else is out there but I can't make him out."

The stink of spew filled the back, and the other girls gagged and covered their mouths. Everyone moved to the rear of the limo. Trembling, Olivia turned to Evan. "Slide open the door. When he slows down, we can jump out and run."

Two of the boys tried to force open the door. The others tried the windows. "We're locked in." Evan slumped back in his seat. "Call 911."

"There's no bars." Liam Hawthorne waved his phone. "Anyone else?"

"Nope, nothing." Victor Langley pushed his phone back into his pocket. "We must be alongside the mountain." He shook his head. "What are we doing way up here? We're miles from town."

Eyes wide with horror, her best friend Chloe's face was streaked with tears. Pushing down her fear, Olivia went to comfort her. "It will be okay. It's probably just a stupid joke."

"Where is he taking us?" Evan peered out of the window. "Did anyone see where he turned off the highway?"

"No, but we're heading toward the river." Samantha

GOOD GIRLS DON'T CRY   3

Haimes cupped her hands around her eyes and looked out of the window. "I can see the full moon glinting on it. What now?"

"There are ten of us here, and whatever game this guy is playing, we should easily be able to overpower him." Evan scanned the back of the limo. See if you can find anything to use as a weapon." He looked around. "All you girls get to the back. He won't get through us."

They found nothing but beer bottles and as the limo got closer to the river, a knot formed in Olivia's stomach. Something was terribly wrong. She cried out as the limo came to an abrupt halt, tossing them from their seats. A door opened and then another, and Olivia watched someone moving in the darkness. The person appeared huge and humped as they disappeared into the trees. They waited, anticipation growing as the time ticked by. She looked at Evan. "We're locked inside with no phones. Do you figure, he's left us here to die?"

"If I discover some of our friends have done this as a prank, there will be hell to pay." Evan slapped a fist in one palm. "This isn't funny." He peered through the window to the driver's seat. "The driver is gone too. Maybe he wasn't dead after all. That might have been that blood they use at Halloween just to scare us."

Olivia froze and gaped at the huge shadow coming toward them. The door slid open and a big burly man in a balaclava holding a handgun aimed the weapon at them. He carried a rifle over one shoulder and a hunting knife in a sheath on his belt. His menacing dark eyes shone in the moonlight. He waved the pistol from side to side, taking in all of them. "Do as I say and nobody gets hurt."

Teeth chattering, Olivia froze. The interior light flooded over him and her attention moved over the blood dripping from his balaclava and covering one side of his coveralls. He wasn't the friendly man in a tux who had greeted them and then climbed into the driver's seat. Had he killed him? The boys formed a protective line, with Evan out front showing no sign of fear.

"You guys. Get onto the floor. Face down. Hands behind your backs." The man tossed a bunch of zip ties onto the floor. "Now!" He moved his gun across the line. "Girls, tie their hands and feet, nice and tight now. I'll be checking."

"No!" Martin Caldwell raised an empty bottle. "You can't shoot all of us."

Bang!

The force of the shot sent Martin flying backward. He bounced off the seat and slid to the floor. He clutched his chest, his eyes wide with pain and shock. Blood bubbled from the corners of his mouth and his eyes fixed in a death stare. Hysterical screams came from the girls, but Olivia couldn't move. Her gaze locked on Martin and then swiveled to the shooter. The boys fell to the floor their arms behind them. She held up her hands. "Don't shoot. We'll do as you say."

"You learn fast." The man held the pistol steady. "Get on with it."

With trembling fingers, Olivia tied up the boys one by one. She went to stand with the other girls when finished, but the man waved a gun at her.

"Now the girls. Hands behind their backs." He waved each one to a seat. "Don't move. What's your name?" He glared at Olivia.

Panic had her by the throat and she needed to push out the word. "Olivia."

"Come here, Olivia." He beckoned her with his gun. "Kneel down with your back to me, just in the doorway here."

Too afraid he'd kill her, she complied, and he savagely tied her hands behind her back. He lifted her up and tossed her back with the girls.

"Don't anyone move. I've got a full clip of bullets." He went to the boys and hogtied them. "Now, ladies, this way." He waved them outside. "Do anything stupid and I won't hesitate to put a round in you."

Fear clawed at Olivia's throat as the girls staggered from the limo. Cold mountain air seeped through her thin dress as he marched them along a wide trail through the dense forest. Their high heels made walking difficult and branches reached out to tangle their elegant gowns in the underbrush. Each step threw another obstacle in their path. When Madison tripped over a tree root and fell flat on her face, the man pressed the gun to her head and dragged her to her feet. The terrified sobs of her friends echoed through the forest.

"Shut up." The man pushed Olivia hard in the back. "One more sound and I'll dispose of you."

Smelling the heavy male sweat close behind her, Olivia stumbled forward and followed the trail. The corsage Evan had given her drooped on her wrist, the crushed petals pressing against her flesh. Panic had her by the throat as they approached an old dilapidated van parked on the fire road and the man slid open the door and ordered them inside. The door shut with a sickening *thunk*. They were trapped.

Shaking with fear, she stared out of the window and watched the man walk back to the limo as if he had all the time in the world. She could make out the white vehicle clearly in the moonlight, parked on the steep bank of the river. Their captor leaned inside and then came out and tossed an object into the air. It reflected the light and resembled a shell casing. He closed the door and then went to the driver's door, pulled it open, and slid inside. The engine roared and the windows of the limo slid down. The next moment, the long sleek dream machine jerked forward. The man rolled out of the door and Olivia screamed as the limo and her friends rolled over the edge and plunged into the river.

She banged her head against the dirty window. Horror twisted her insides. He'd drowned her friends. The girls screamed in terror as the man slid behind the wheel of the van. Angry, she stood and walked to the front. The man turned to look at her, pointed the gun at her face, and laughed. He stood and tipped his head to one side observing her. Olivia no longer cared what happened. She glared at him. "What have you done?"

"I killed them all." The man's eyes hadn't left her face. "Do you have a problem with that, sweetheart?"

Horrified, she stood her ground. "You're a monster."

"Oh, I haven't started yet." He chuckled. "Now go and sit down before I forget my manners."

Glancing over her shoulder, she shook her head. "Let us go or we'll scream so loud someone will hear us."

She didn't have time to react when his fist moved as fast as a snake and punched her in the stomach. Shocked, she fell to her knees gasping.

"Now, anyone else wanna play?" He pressed the gun into Olivia's temple and time ticked by as his unwashed scent crawled up her nostrils. "No? Good. Now shut up with the sobbing and wailing. Don't you know that good girls don't cry?"

ONE

Stuck in a claustrophobic nightmare, Olivia groaned in pain as she scanned the back of the van. No one had ever hit her before, and her teeth chattered with fear. Her friends sat huddled together in the gloom, either staring blindly ahead or sobbing. Their cheeks were wet with tears and mascara ran in lines down to their chins like grotesque clown masks. The stink of mildew and old leather thickened the air, making it hard to breathe, and beneath her, a filthy rusty floor scratched against her legs. Grime caked the tinted windows, allowing only small slivers of moonlight to peer through, but made it light enough to see. Not that she could do anything. The zip ties binding her hands dug deeply into her flesh. Her numb hands throbbed and her stomach ached. As the van bounced and rattled over the uneven road, each jolt sent a fresh wave of fear through her.

Debris littered the floor. Leaves from falls long ago sat in drifts along each side mixed with discarded wrappers, broken glass, and an odd assortment of filthy torn clothing. Olivia wanted to speak to her friends but was too scared to say anything with the driver so close. Her mind raced, trying to make sense of the situation. Where was he taking them and what was his intention? They were going deeper into the forest and darkness seemed to close in around her. The man was whistling now as if he didn't have a care in the world. The sound sent shivers down her spine. How could they escape this maniac?

In a squeak of brakes and a grind of metal, the van bounced to a stop so suddenly it sent everyone sprawling across the filthy floor. Struggling to her knees, Olivia looked from one to the other and kept her voice just above a whisper. "Do as he says for now, but if there's a chance to get away, run for your life. Don't wait for anyone. The sooner someone knows where we are, the sooner we'll get out of this mess."

"He's got a gun." Madison struggled to rise from the floor. "If one of us runs, he'll shoot us in the back. He's probably one of those serial killers we've all been warned about. We mean nothing to him. I figure we do as he says and maybe we'll be rescued."

The back doors of the van creaked open, and moonlight glistened on the weapon in the man's hand. Using the side of the van, Olivia staggered to her feet. Behind her she could hear the others doing the same. She stared at the eyes of the man, like black coals in the sockets of the balaclava. "What are you going to do with us?"

"Whatever I want." He chuckled and pointed the gun at them. "Get out of the van." He waved them along a pathway that led to an old abandoned mineshaft.

Shivers ran down Olivia's back as she gaped into the black depths of an open maw. As they stepped inside, tripping over the old railway lines, it was as if the darkness had swallowed the moonlight. She sighed with relief when the man aimed a flashlight down the hole. They staggered onward, moving down a slope into the unknown. Cold bit into her flesh as a moaning wind whistled past them, bringing with it the stench of damp and decay. They shuffled past a thick metal gate, along another

GOOD GIRLS DON'T CRY   9

passageway, and then turned into a lighted area that looked like some type of office, with a desk and shelves.

Along each wall, open doors led to six small cells. Outside the cells, she made out a large shower cubicle, a pile of towels, and a metal rack containing clothes. She swallowed hard at the sight, hoping she wasn't hallucinating. What was a shower doing at the bottom of a mineshaft? One by one, the man locked them into the small, cold cells and asked them their names. It was so dark Olivia couldn't see her hand in front of her face. The sound of metal doors clanging shut echoed through the cavern. Terrified, she trembled and turned toward the door, seeking the only flicker of light. She peered through the bars on the top of her door. The man had one hand on Madison's shoulder. Her friend stood like a zombie, round-eyed and frozen with fear. What had he planned for her friend?

"You're perfect for my needs." The man stared down at Madison. "Take off your shoes." He stared at her, his mouth twitching into a sinister smile. "You're a very special girl. We're going back down the tunnel. I'm taking you for a little ride." He grabbed her arm and dragged her away into the darkness.

TWO

Madison cried out as the man tossed her face down onto the front seat of the van. He drove off at high speed, giving her no time to sit up. Her head ached and she wanted to spew as the van bounced and swerved along dirt roads. Trembling with terror, she lay as still as possible, too afraid to move or say a word. Eventually the van came to a stop. She didn't move when the man slid out from behind the wheel. Moments later, he grabbed her, dragged her out, and tossed her to the ground. She caught sight of the knife in the moonlight and screamed, but he didn't stab her. He bent to cut the zip ties on her wrists. She staggered to her feet and her long blue ball gown tangled around her legs. The forest closed in around her, the trees so dense no moonlight penetrated the gloom. Shivering as the man ran his gaze from the top of the head to her feet and back again, she hugged her chest. What did he want from her?

"Run." He aimed the rifle at her and a sinister chuckle escaped his lips. "I'll count to twenty."

Hesitating for just a second, Madison lifted her gown and ran into the dense forest. Unable to find a trail, she stumbled over tree roots and dashed between the trees. Branches clawed at her dress, but she kept going, driven by sheer terror. All around, shadows played tricks on her mind, creating bears and men waiting to jump out at her. With each step her feet sank into the soft ground, and pine needles and twigs cut into her bare flesh. Desperate to escape, she scanned the trees, searching for a trail to follow, and finding nothing, she dashed on. It hurt so bad to breathe. The cold mountain air burned her chest and cut through her thin gown, chilling the sweat on her skin. She'd always been afraid of the forest, and when an owl shrieked above her, she turned and ran in a different direction.

How long had she been running? Was he still behind her, stalking her like prey? She looked left and right at the lines of pines. They all looked exactly the same. Indecision crept over her. Had she run in a circle? Hearing a crunch close by, she turned and glanced over one shoulder, convinced the man was right behind her. Heart pounding, she bit back a sob and stared into the darkness. As a freezing breeze rustled through the forest, shadows twisted and morphed into hands reaching out to grab her. Where was he? Had he decided not to chase her after all? Her teeth chattered with fear but she kept going.

Where was the trail? A deer path—anything. She stumbled to a halt and bent over, hands on knees, panting. The break was a luxury she couldn't afford. She straightened and turned in a slow circle to peer through the labyrinth of trees and shadows, not knowing which way to go. The maze of trees disoriented her and Madison sank into the depths of despair. Cheeks wet with tears, she sucked in ragged breaths and headed toward the moon, but it seemed to move with every step. A noise in the underbrush stopped her midstride. Staring into the darkness as leaves rustled and twigs snapped, she gaped in horror as something huge crashed through the trees. Flattened against the trunk of a tree, the rough bark cut into her skin, but she didn't care. The next second, a proud head with antlers moved into a shaft of moonlight. Trembling, Madison sagged and sucked in freezing air. It was so cold in the mountains her breath came out in a white cloud. Behind the buck, she made out a fire road and lifted her filthy torn gown and ran. Fire roads led to highways and people.

Muscles screaming with fatigue, she kept moving. She couldn't stop—wouldn't stop until she'd found safety. Ahead, moonlight illuminated the gravel-covered road and she burst out of the forest and slowed. Which way—left or right? She heard a sound, and stomach clenching with terror, turned slowly to stare at the man in the balaclava. He stood not ten feet away from her, casually leaning against a tree, with his gun pointed at her. She took three steps back, gaping in disbelief. How had he found her? She'd run for miles. Exhausted, her mind fogged, she didn't know what to do. If she ran, he'd shoot her just like he did Martin. *There's nothing I can do.* She wanted to scream but her throat closed and she fought to breathe.

"Well, hello there, Madison." He eased away from the pine tree and strolled toward her. "What took you so long?"

THREE

BLACK ROCK FALLS

Saturday

A call woke Sheriff Jenna Alton a little after three. The 911 calls went to Chief Deputy Zac Rio, so being disturbed in the middle of the night when she was currently nine months pregnant meant something bad had happened. She reached for her phone but her ex-special forces deputy and husband, Dave Kane, plucked the phone from her hand. She sighed. "Dave, it's okay. It must be an emergency."

"Go back to sleep. I'll deal with it." Kane answered the call. "This better be good, Rio." He sat up in bed and switched on the bedside lamp. "You know darn well not to disturb Jenna."

"I know the sheriff would want to know if kids were missing." Rio's office chair creaked. *"I'm back at the office. I've had reports that a limousine filled with high school kids has gone missing. It's the new stretch limo company that's been doing the weddings around town. The wife of the driver said he hadn't returned. Usually, he goes home until it's time to pick up the passengers. He was due to pick up the kids at eleven and should have been home by one o'clock at the latest. She's been calling*

14   D.K. HOOD

*him for hours and drove the route he would have taken in case
something had happened. At one-thirty she started getting calls
from the parents. They've all called 911. None of the kids have
returned home. They were heading for the high school prom.
Some of the parents have called others on the PTA, who were
either on the door or chaperones. They know their kids and none
of them recall seeing them, and Olivia Cooper and her boyfriend,
Evan Blackwood, didn't show to be crowned prom king and
queen."* He sighed. *"I don't figure they made it to the high
school."*

"It's a bit late in the year for a prom, isn't it?" Kane frowned.
"As far as I know, they're in May."

*"Apparently the school postponed it due to the flooding. So it
was last night."* Rio yawned. *"I've visited all the parents and
they said the driver had a name tag. His name is Carl Winslow
and that checks out with his wife. He fits the description they
gave me."* He cleared his throat. *"On the way to the kids' houses,
I checked alongside the roads in case he wrecked the limo, but all
the kids were carrying phones. It makes no sense not one of them
called if there was a problem."*

Jenna sat up in bed and gave Kane a long look. "Update the
files and we'll take it from here. Go home and get some sleep."

"You got it." Rio yawned again. *"I'll be back in a couple of
hours."*

Taking her phone from Kane, Jenna called search and
rescue. "Sheriff Alton here. We have a white stretch limo
missing filled with high school kids. The location is sketchy, so
we need to search from Bear Peak in the north and Maple in the
south and all along the route to the high school. I need a
chopper in the air with searchlights. Deputy Rio has conducted
a preliminary search and found nothing. No calls from the kids,
so we need this pushed to high priority."

*"It will take maybe two hours to get a chopper and crew in
the air. Do you need a search party on the ground at daybreak?"*

GOOD GIRLS DON'T CRY 15

Glad to hear his enthusiasm, Jenna nodded. "Yes, we need to locate the limo and find ten kids, so any help would be appreciated."

"I'll have teams standing by at daybreak. We'll use the forest warden's office at Bear Peak as a command center. They always help out."

Jenna looked at Kane and smiled at his bleak expression. "Thanks." She disconnected. "What's that sour look for?"

"You're honestly not considering heading out on a case today, are you?" Kane shook his head. "The obstetrician told you to rest. Dashing out at four-thirty in the morning isn't what I call resting. I'll go. I can handle this with Rowley until Rio gets back into the office. There's no need for you to come."

Having started a new life in Black Rock Falls as Jenna Alton with a new face and hair color, she'd left DEA agent Avril Parker long behind, but the grit and determination she had then had never left her. Becoming sheriff and marrying Kane, she'd grown tougher than ever. Being pregnant hadn't stopped her taking down serial killers, so she didn't believe it would get in the way of her finding ten missing kids. She leaned into Kane and gave him a hug. "I know you worry about me, but trust me, I'm not going to break. The chopper won't be in the air for the next two hours. It's too dark to hunt down the limo ourselves, so we'll have time to eat breakfast and settle Tauri with Nanny Raya before we leave." She gave Kane a side-eye. "Moving around some might bring the baby on, and to be perfectly honest, I can't wait to get this over with and see who the little person is inside. I've been waiting long enough."

The baby had been a wonderful surprise. Jenna had given up hope of having a child of their own and they'd jumped at the chance to adopt a four-year-old Native American boy. They both doted on Tauri. Big for his age and very smart, with eyes like an eagle and blond streaks in his dark hair, he'd filled their life with so much joy. He was coming up to six now and Jenna

16   D.K. HOOD

had hired a live-in nanny, with her own self-contained apartment, to care for him when they were on a case. The bonus was Nanny Raya slipped into the family like a grandmother and was able, along with their dear Native American friend Atohi Blackhawk, to teach Tauri about his culture.

"Well, you can rest until five." Kane sat on the edge of the bed and stretched. "I'll put on the coffee and go and tend the horses."

Jenna watched him dress and wondered how he came immediately awake and ready to go in an instant. She never had that luxury; it took her a few minutes to get her head straight after waking—like normal people. There was nothing normal about Kane. Six-five and two hundred and sixty pounds of muscle, her ex-special forces husband had skills she hadn't seen yet, and after knowing him for coming up to seven years, he still surprised her. She stared at her phone and then checked to see if Rio had loaded any information onto the server. Rio was gifted with a retentive memory, which meant he rarely wrote any notes. He could recall facts from cases years ago, which made him very useful to have around. She just knew he'd have the case file ready for her to view.

The seriousness of the situation hit home when she read the list of the missing kids, five boys and five girls, all between sixteen and seventeen years old. The boys—Evan Blackwood, Graham Whitaker, Liam Hawthorne, Victor Langley, and Martin Caldwell—they'd all congregated at Evan Blackwood's house on Maple and the limo had arrived at seven. The girls—Madison Reed, Samantha Haimes, Isabella Coleman, Chloe Bennett, and Olivia Cooper—were collected separately. The last stop was for Olivia, who lived on Pine Cone Drive. All the kids were accounted for up to that point. The driver and part owner of the limo company, Carl Winslow, had opened the door for all the passengers. None of the parents who'd watched them all drive away had noticed anything amiss.

GOOD GIRLS DON'T CRY 17

Wondering if this had been a prank gone wrong, Jenna meticulously ran all the names through the system. Being Black Rock Falls, aka Serial Killer Central, she insisted her team made files on every incident, no matter how small or who they involved. She'd seen so many terrible murders in her time in Black Rock Falls, and realizing not all psychopathic killers were drifters, she needed records she could trust. When she'd first arrived in town and won the election for sheriff, the files were practically nonexistent. She sighed in relief when all the names came back clean, including the driver. What had happened between Pine Cone Drive and the high school?

FOUR

THE MINE

Olivia crawled to the old mattress along one wall and sat on it hugging her knees. What was happening to Madison? Would she ever see her again? Shivering, she peered into a black void, too afraid to move. Trapped in an abyss of darkness, she could smell the scent of damp earth and decay. The only light came from a flickering bulb outside, but it was enough for her to see the cockroaches scattering across the floor and words scratched into the walls of a cell. Like her, the previous occupant had been terrified. Names written and crossed out reminded her of her Christmas list, but there was nothing jolly about being locked in a cell deep in an old mineshaft. Had this man kidnapped girls like her before and kept them here before murdering them one by one? Why hadn't Sheriff Alton caught him? The sheriff and her deputy had taken down all the threats that came into their town. How could she have possibly missed this one?

Her mom would be missing her. As her only daughter, she hated her going out anywhere and stranger danger had been drummed into her since she could walk. Her mom would blame herself and she wondered if she would ever know the truth about what happened. She rocked back and forth hugging her knees. Since the man had dragged Madison out of the mine, the only sounds had been from her friends crying. As the captain of the cheerleading squad, she needed to try and keep up their morale. There must be a way to escape, and she just needed to discover it. She went to the door, pressed her hands against the cold metal and peered through the tiny barred window. "Can anyone hear me? It's Olivia. I believe the man has left for a time. We need to talk before he comes back and make a plan so we can escape."

The small light barely penetrated the darkness, but she made out the pale faces of Isabella and Chloe at the two windows opposite her, and she could hear movement from the cell beside her. "I can't see you, Samantha, are you beside me?"

"Yes, I'm here." Sam's voice was barely a whisper. "What do you think he wants with us and where did he take Madison?"

Trying to keep her own fear at bay, Olivia swallowed hard. "I don't know but we need to stay calm. Sheriff Alton will find us. You know she'll never give up searching." A shiver went through her. Deep down she knew the truth. A crazy man had kidnapped them, and from the evidence scratched into the wall, he'd done this before.

"She has no idea where we are." Chloe shook the bars. "There's no escape from this place, is there? Have you noticed there's a toilet and a sink in one of the corners? I've been feeling all around. There is a shelf above the mattress. I found two blankets up there. They're filthy but it's better than freezing to death."

Olivia reached out, searching the damp, moss-covered walls. She found the toilet and sink and crawled across the filthy floor to the mattress, stood and found the shelf. Dust and animal droppings fell all over her as she pulled down the blankets. The cold had seeped into her bones and even a filthy blanket would keep her warm. Ignoring the smell of urine and rats, she draped

20   D.K. HOOD

it around her and went back to the door. "I found the blankets. They stink."

"I figure they're all the same." Chloe's head popped up at her window. "How can we get out of here?"

Olivia stared out at her friends. "I don't know, but I figure no matter what, if anyone gets a chance to escape, run and get help. It might be our only chance."

"I don't think we have a chance." Chloe peered back at her, only her large round eyes in view. "If he plans on killing us too, I'm not going without a fight."

In the cell beside Olivia, Samantha Haimes burst into tears and started to wail. "Sam, keep it together. We don't need to antagonize him."

"He killed Liam." Sam wailed and punched the door. "I loved him. We'd gotten into the same college. Can you imagine what it was like for them, tied up and unable to get out of the limo? It would be a terrible death." She sobbed and shook the bars. "I can't stop thinking about it. I don't care what happens to me. I want to die."

Footsteps sounded along the passageway, slow and deliberate. Tall shadows followed a flashlight beam and then the man appeared. Shocked at the sight of his blood-soaked coveralls, Olivia gaped at him. He stood staring at her and then smiled. His teeth white in the gloom. More lights came on and the extent of the blood spatter became evident. Shaking with fear, Olivia lifted her chin. "Where's Madison? What have you done with her?"

"I released her in the forest." The man shrugged and peeled off wet gloves. "I need to take a shower and head into work. I guess I'd better feed you first." He went to a closet and collected armfuls of silver packages. "These are Army surplus rations. You get three each and a few bottles of water. Make them last all day. I don't know when I'll be back." The man swept his gaze along the cells as he dropped in the supplies, followed by blood-smeared bottled water. "Which one of you wants to die? Was it you, Sam? Ah, yes, I can see it in your eyes. You hate me for killing Liam. He was weak. He didn't even try to protect you, did he?" He looked at her. "Still want to die?"

"I don't care what you do to me." Sam sobbed. "I don't want to live without him."

"I've never had requests before." The man chuckled. "This will be interesting."

FIVE

Jenna stared out of the window and drummed her fingers on the counter. The mist had lifted from the mountains over an hour ago, and before her the forest stretched out in various shades of green against an endless blue sky. She turned to look at Kane working at his desk. They had spent all morning organizing search parties and anyone with a helicopter was in the air, including the medical examiner, Dr. Shane Wolfe. "How could we possibly lose a white stretch limo? It would be one of the hardest things possible to hide and the fact that it's filled with ten high school kids makes it even more impossible."

"I called Bobby Kalo." Kane stretched out his long legs and leaned back in his chair. "Now everyone is saving their CCTV footage to the cloud, he can gain access to everything that's happening around town."

Jenna pushed away from the counter and sat down slowly in her chair. Her back ached constantly and the weight of the baby was starting to become uncomfortable. She couldn't wait for it all to be over but having a case to solve made the wait easier. "So what did our FBI computer whiz kid discover? Did he actually find them on the footage or has someone gone and

GOOD GIRLS DON'T CRY   23

mysteriously managed to change everything? With the AI capabilities at the moment, I'm not discounting any possibility."

"He has footage of them leaving town, but nothing outside the range of the cameras." Kane twirled a pen in his fingers. "Rio just issued a media report to ask anyone with dash cam or any visual sightings of the limo last night to call. Many people were heading toward the prom around the same time. As the limo service is new in town, its car gets a lot of attention, so we're hoping someone noticed it, especially if it left the route it was supposed to be heading." He ran a hand through his hair and looked at her. "I hope we find it soon or it will become another legend of Black Rock Falls and people will start seeing ghostly white limos traveling through town every prom night." He shook his head. "Honestly, I've never lived anywhere with so many weird stories. The people who live here just live for this stuff. I hope the limo going missing isn't a prank. Kids are doing weird stuff these days and posting it online. If it is, when we find them I'll mention that I don't appreciate being woken up at three in the morning, especially on my day off."

Jenna turned to him. "I'm sure they wouldn't put their parents through the torture of believing they'd been abducted."

"I guess not." Kane rubbed his chin. "It doesn't make a whole lot of sense, right now."

Concerned for the young people, Jenna checked her phone for messages again. "There are many aspects of this case that don't make sense. The main one is that kids of that age always have their heads in their phones. If something was going down, why didn't they contact their parents? Even if they couldn't call them because they had no bars, they could have sent texts. They would know that once the phones came back into range, they would send the texts. There were ten kids in the back of that limo, you would have thought one of them would have tried to make contact or called 911."

"Which makes me wonder if it's a prank." Kane tossed the

24   D.K. HOOD

pen into a mug on his desk with AUNT BETTY'S CAFÉ written on the side. "Although I don't believe kids would give up their prom for a joke, especially when Olivia and Evan were nominated for prom king and queen. It's a big deal, isn't it? I recall my prom. I even made it to a couple of reunions, but being in the service I didn't get much downtime." He smiled at her. "I bet you were prom queen."

Jenna shook her head. "Nope I wasn't. At that age, I was tiny and very scrawny. My natural color is blonde, as you know, but at that time it was a dirty blonde. I went to the prom with a nerd called Nigel. He was a very nice boy. What about you?"

"Well." Kane ran a hand down his face. "Although bringing up past girlfriends is something I never want to do with you, we did promise to tell each other the truth. My date was a cheerleader by the name of Mia. We were prom king and queen." He held up a hand to prevent Jenna from asking questions. "I left for college just after. I wanted to enter the Marines with a degree."

Intrigued, Jenna leaned back in her chair. Talking about Kane's real life was fraught with danger. Like her, he had a new name and face after terrorists placed a bounty on his head. She knew very little of his past life and he'd never revealed his true name. As far as anyone was concerned, that person died in a car bombing that took him and his pregnant wife, Annie. Kane was left with a metal plate in his head, which still troubled him in winter. "I won't ask any more questions, but I'm intrigued to know what subject you studied. You seem to have so many skills, especially speaking nine languages."

"Criminal justice." He grinned at her. "Maybe someone up there"—he pointed to the ceiling—"knew I'd need it one day."

Jenna's phone chimed. She stared at the caller ID and then placed the phone on speaker. "Hi, Shane. Any news?"

"Yeah, it's bad news I'm afraid. We spotted the limo at the bottom of the river near Bear Peak." Wolfe's footsteps could be

GOOD GIRLS DON'T CRY   25

heard as he walked through the morgue to his office. *"I need a team to get out there and recover the bodies. Do you have anyone on your team who are divers? Only one of the search-and-rescue team is qualified. I'll need Kane and I've called in Carter and he's on his way. As luck would have it, he was in the air over Blackwater when I contacted him. He'll be landing here in about ten minutes."*

Jenna nodded. Agents Ty Carter and Jo Wells worked out of the Snakeskin Gully FBI field office. Carter was a Navy SEAL before joining the FBI and came with a K-9 Doberman explosives-detection dog by the name of Zorro. His partner, Jo, was a world-renowned behavioral scientist.

"I'm here, Shane." Kane stood and walked to Jenna's desk. "I'll go and check my diving gear. It's stored here at the office."

"I have extra gear and spare tanks, but I need people who will cope with dead bodies." Wolfe sighed. *"One of the search-and-rescue guys went in for a look and confirmed the fatalities. He won't be going back down. There's no way I can see of retrieving the limo."*

Shocked and desperately sad, Jenna forced her mind to stay focused. She needed to lead her team and not allow her pregnancy hormones to take over. "How did this happen? Any signs of it being an accident?"

"I was in the air, Jenna." Wolfe was moving again. *"There's no room to land a chopper there. It's close to the fire road, so that must have been the access point but from what I could see, the limo left the fire road and went along a trail before running into the river. The bank is steep there, if the driver lost control at speed, it's very possible. Blackhawk is on his way to the scene. He'll backtrack the limo's trajectory and we'll have a better idea of what happened. I'm getting my team together now. I'll send you the coordinates. Wait for Carter. He'll need to go with you. You'll be able to drive right there."*

"I'm on my way." Kane headed for the door as Wolfe disconnected.

Jenna glared after him. "Just a minute. I need to get our team organized." She'd call in Johnny Raven a new deputy and K-9 handler and trainer. Being a chopper pilot and a medical doctor, he made a great addition to the team. "I want Raven and his dog out there and I'm coming too." She pressed her fists into her hips and stared at him. "It's close to the fire road and there's a track. Hardly any walking. I'll be fine. I need to know what's happened to those kids, Dave. I'm the one who'll be speaking to their parents."

"Really?" Kane wiped a hand down his face. "This isn't a serial killer and you promised to leave all the other cases to the team. I don't want you delivering our baby in the forest."

Jenna rubbed her belly and smiled at him. "I don't want you to be miles away from me either. This way, you'll be able to drive me to the hospital in the Beast—the fastest most tricked-out ride in town. I need to be at the scene—with you."

"Okay." He walked to her and pulled her into his arms. "But promise me you'll take it easy and don't overdo."

Jenna looked up into his caring eyes. "I promise. Now can I organize my team?"

"Sure." Kane kissed her on the forehead and then hurried from the room.

SIX

Kane drove along Stanton in the direction of Bear Peak, but his mind wasn't on the beautiful green forest lining the highway or the zebra-stripe shadows dancing across the blacktop. His full concentration had centered on why a limo would leave the highway and go along a forest fire road. The location Wolfe had given him was miles from the turnoff to the high school. One thing was for certain: teenage girls wouldn't risk messing up their hair or makeup to make out before the prom. The driver had been checked out and had no priors. Many people had used his company for special occasions and everyone he'd called had mentioned his professionalism.

"What's cooking in your head?" Jenna turned in her seat to look at him.

Kane smiled at her. "I was trying to make out why the limo driver would drive to this remote area in the first place. As you mentioned before, if there was something unusual happening, one of the kids would have called their parents before they got to the mountain range. Most of the kids who live in this town are fully aware of the areas where there's no bars. Agreed, they might have been chatting and having a good time and not

28   D.K. HOOD

noticed. If this is what happened, I figure someone was with the driver and kidnapped them."

"Why would anyone kidnap ten kids?" Jenna opened a bottle of water and took a few sips. "Some of those seniors are big guys. You'd think five of them would be able to overpower one man."

Kane turned to look at her. "Unless he was carrying. Most kids wouldn't take a chance with an armed man. Many of them are fully aware of the dangers of firearms." He slowed to take the turn from the highway onto the fire road.

"I'd like to know what made him drive into the river." Jenna stared out of the window. "Do you figure one of the kids tried to overpower him and he lost control of the vehicle?"

The same thought had occurred to him, and Kane shrugged. "Maybe, but only a fool would open the glass partition behind the driver. The kids would be trapped. He could lock the doors. A limo is no different from most vehicles."

"The fact this reliable man, who has no priors, suddenly decided to commit a murder-suicide makes no sense at all." Jenna chewed on her bottom lip. "It must have been an accident. Maybe he had a heart attack or something?"

"We may never find out. I'm guessing the search and rescue contaminated the scene?" Carter leaned forward in his seat. He had a dog on each side of him: his K-9, Zorro, on one side and Duke, Kane's bloodhound and tracker dog, on the other. "They wouldn't know it was anything but an accident."

"Maybe." Jenna blew out a sigh. "They came here on quad bikes. So there's every possibility if the limo left tire tracks, they would have been obliterated." She pushed her hand through her dark hair. "Keep going. We must be close by now."

As they moved slowly along the fire road, their friend Blackhawk stepped out of the tree line and waved them down. Kane slowed the Beast to stop beside him. "Need a ride?"

"Nope." Didn't you see the murder of crows? The trees are

GOOD GIRLS DON'T CRY   29

black with them." Blackhawk's serious expression alerted Kane to a major problem. "There's a body just behind me in the trees. Stab wound to the neck, from what I can see. I'm guessing he's the limo driver. He's wearing a tux." He sighed. "I haven't seen Wolfe. Is he following behind you?"

The smell of death wafted on the breeze. It was going to be a rough day. Kane nodded. "He was organizing his team when Carter left. He shouldn't be too far behind me." He turned as Jenna opened the door. "Hey, wait for me." He slid from behind the wheel and hurried after her.

"When did you find him? Phew, it stinks around here. Wait up." Jenna pulled examination gloves and masks from a small bag she carried over one shoulder. She handed some to Kane and Carter before pulling on her own.

"Just a few seconds before you arrived, I was checking for life signs when I heard the Beast." Blackhawk looked from one to the other. "This means the limo in the river was no accident. Why would someone want to kill ten kids?"

"I'll never try to understand the mind of a psychopath again. They all work on a different plane." Jenna bent over the body to examine the wound in the man's neck. She opened his coat and glanced over his body before straightening. She pressed one hand in the small of her back and groaned. "I can see only one wound."

Moving away from the ant and fly-infested body, Kane turned to Blackhawk. "There's no way he fell out of the vehicle or was pushed to end up here. This body was dumped." He turned slowly and bent to examine the ground. "Did you find any drag marks?"

"No." Blackhawk pointed to a depression beside the body. "He was carried here and dropped. See the square impression just here in the soil?" He bent beside Kane and pointed to a mark on the forest floor. "I figure that's where the killer turned on his heel, dropped him, and went back to the limo."

"That's assuming there was someone in the limo with him. None of the kids' families mentioned seeing anyone." Jenna stared at Blackhawk. "The driver must weigh at least two hundred pounds. Whoever carried him would need to be strong."

"Well, he didn't walk here." Blackhawk indicated to the ground. "There's no blood spatter trail and with that injury he'd be spurting blood. Chances are he died in seconds."

Running through the limo driver's timeline that Rio had mentioned, the driver went to each residence, knocked on the door, and waited for his passenger. Kane turned to Jenna. "The killer could have accessed the vehicle at any one of the stops. The last one is in a wooded area and perfect. The attention of the kids would be focused on the last passenger. Or he might have been inside all along. If he insisted the interior light was turned off, no one would have seen him behind the tinted windows." He turned at the sound of an engine. "That should be Wolfe. I'll go and meet him."

"I'll go. Why don't you stay here with Jenna? We don't know who's watching us. I'll wave him down." Carter headed back to the fire road.

"I'll track the killer back to the road." Blackhawk rubbed Duke's ears. "Can I take Duke? He'll follow any blood spatter I can't see."

Kane smiled at him. "Yeah, sure. Duke will enjoy that. He loves being in the forest." He turned to Jenna. "Do you have any crime scene tape in your bag? I figure we need to preserve the area."

"Yeah, I have the usual." Jenna pulled out a roll of tape. "It's just the things I usually keep in my pockets. It's easier this way for now."

Voices came through the forest as Kane wrapped the tape around trees. He looked up as Wolfe arrived with his daughter Emily and assistant and badge-holding deputy Colt Webber,

GOOD GIRLS DON'T CRY 31

along with Wolfe's fiancée, forensic anthropologist Norrell Larson.

"A single body?" Wolfe frowned as he pushed his way through the trees.

"It's the limo driver." Jenna held up an image on her phone. "He matches the MVD photo on his license."

Kane nodded to the others and then went to Wolfe's side. They'd worked together for many years and only Jenna was aware that Wolfe was his handler. His time as a black ops sniper was ongoing and he never knew when he'd be called back into service for his country. He'd become a fixer and worked alone with Wolfe overseeing his top-secret missions. "Blackhawk believes his killer carried him here. He's backtracking with Duke to discover exactly where he came from."

"Okay." Wolfe crouched down to examine the body but didn't move him. "I assume you haven't had time to process the scene."

Kane shook his head. "Not yet. I taped the area, is all."

"Webber." Wolfe turned to his assistant. "Record the scene —images and video. We'll stand back." He turned to Jenna. "Have you been to the crash site yet?"

"Nope." Jenna frowned. "We just arrived. Blackhawk waved us down. He found the body. He checked for vital signs, is all."

"It didn't rain last night, did it?" Wolfe stared at the man's clothes. "He looks reasonably dry and there's no interference by animals, which seems very strange. There's no blood spatter." He turned, slowly scanning the immediate area. "I can't even see any spatter on tree branches. So we must consider that this is a dumping area. How far away is the river from here?"

Kane pointed north. "From the coordinates that you gave us, I would say the limo turned off the fire road approximately two to three hundred yards in that direction. I'm not sure how far from the fire road he drove to reach the river's edge."

32   D.K. HOOD

"I couldn't make out the trail he used from above." Wolfe waved Emily toward the body. "What do you see, Em?"

"From what I've observed from past crime scenes, someone who is attacked from the front, which the wound would indicate, usually grabs their throat and stumbles back. Death is within a minute or so, so the victim is usually found either flat on his back with his arms spread wide or flat on his face still clutching his neck." Emily tied her long blonde hair behind her neck in a ponytail. "From the position of this body, it appears as if someone carried it here over one shoulder and dropped it. I'd say the victim was dead before he hit the ground. There is no indication of him moving around in the long grass. There is no blood spatter, as you said, Dad. I figure this guy was dead at least ten minutes before being dumped. From this kind of injury, the maximum amount of blood loss would have happened immediately after the injury. The victim doesn't have very much blood down the front of his shirt, which would indicate he was fighting his attacker. His elevated heart rate would have caused the blood to gush out, away from his body. I doubt, from the length and depth of the wound that I can see from here, he had time to press his hands against the wound to stop it bleeding."

"There you go." Wolfe moved his gaze to Jenna. "I couldn't have said it better myself." He nodded to Webber, who'd finished recording the scene. "Let's take a look."

Kane turned at the sound of another vehicle. He stared through the trees as a Black Rock Falls Sheriff's Department vehicle pulled up alongside his black truck. He looked at Jenna. "I thought Rio and Rowley were on scene already?" He was referring to Chief Deputy Rio and Deputy Rowley, the latter trained from a rookie by Jenna.

"It's Raven." Jenna stared into the trees. "I asked him to come. We'll have people moving bodies through the forest all day and his K-9, Ben, will be an asset." Her satellite phone

GOOD GIRLS DON'T CRY   33

chimed and she looked at Kane, worry etched on her face. "Yes, Maggie, what's up?"

Kane moved closer as she placed the phone on speaker. It was unusual for their office administrative assistant, Maggie, aka Magnolia Brewster, to call when they were on a case unless it was pertinent.

"Hikers have found what looks like a tree decorated with body parts. They figure they're human but didn't get close enough to examine them. It's near the Glacial Heights Ski Resort." Maggie took a deep breath. *"They said they'll wait there until someone comes but I don't have anyone to send."*

At that moment, Raven walked through the trees. Jenna looked at Wolfe. "Could you spare Emily or Norrell if I send her with Raven to check out a possible body sighting?"

"Yeah. It's good experience for Em." Wolfe straightened. "I'm done here. We'll pack up this guy and get him into the van." He turned to Emily. "Take what you need from the van. It's probably an animal hung after field dressing. If not, call me and be as quick as you can. I need you here." He gave Raven a long look. "Take care of my girl."

"You have my word." Raven touched the front of his Stetson. He looked at Emily. "I'll help you grab your things."

Kane turned as Blackhawk walked back with Duke leading the way. "Find anything interesting?"

"Yeah, tire tracks about twenty yards along the fire road and a pool of blood." He indicated through the forest. "I marked all the spots of blood I found." He frowned. "This is a strong man. He carried his victim all this way. Why didn't he stop closer? We are only a few yards from the road."

Kane rubbed his chin. "I have no idea. Why did he drive into the river? He'd know it was certain death."

"Maybe he isn't inside the limo." Blackhawk grimaced. "Maybe he's close by enjoying the show."

SEVEN

THE MINE

After a freezing night, Olivia fought to breathe. If it weren't bad enough being kidnapped and held in a stinking cell underground, she had asthma and it had chosen now to make life difficult. Without an inhaler, an attack could be fatal. Her purse and inhaler had gone down with the limo. She choked back tears. He'd killed her friends, shot one and drowned the others without a second thought. He'd taken Madison. In her mind, she could still hear her screams echoing through the caves and his laugh. The thought of him sent shivers down her spine. Her chest tightened and she tried to concentrate on just the next breath, but breathing the thick air in the neglected mine was like trying to inhale in a dust storm. The only air seemed to be outside of her cell. She pressed her face against the bars in the cell window at the top of her door, gasping in the breeze that came from the outside.

In the faint glow of a swinging dust-covered light bulb, eerie shadows danced across the cold stone walls, but for now they were alone. Their captor hadn't returned all night. She stepped away from the window and ran a hand down her once beautiful prom dress. After a night sleeping on the dust-caked mattress, the expensive gown was too damaged to even use as rags. She'd washed her face and hands in the sink but there was nothing to dry them on, apart from a few sheets of toilet paper pulled from a roll that she discovered on the cistern.

The darkness inside the cell suffocated her and she went back to her position in front of the door. The cleaner air helped and her breathing improved. Cold seeped into her bones and her stomach growled with hunger. The old military rations that the man had given them had been disgusting. She'd forced them down not knowing even what they looked like and she imagined them covered with maggots with every bite. She shuddered. Sobbing came from the other cells. All of her friends were terrified just the same as her. Would they die trapped in these cells? Or would he come and get them one by one?

She'd hoped Madison would have returned by now, but after the initial screaming, they'd heard nothing. He'd probably killed her. Panic gripped her and she wanted to scream, but no one was coming to help them. She needed to calm down. There must be a way to escape. She just hadn't thought it through. "Hey, are you all okay?"

"Alive." Sam coughed. "I won't last much longer in the cold."

Everyone was at their window, and the sounds of their shallow rugged gasps filled the quiet. Olivia waved at the two she could see. "Keep moving if you're cold. Remember what they told us about survival in camp when we were kids?"

"I don't figure that included being locked in a cell at the bottom of a mineshaft with a maniac intent on murdering us all." Chloe's large round frightened eyes peered at her. "That's what's happening here, isn't it? We need to face facts: we're not going home anytime soon—if ever."

Olivia wanted to at least try and keep their spirits up. She'd never been a defeatist. During competition as the leader of the cheerleading squad, even when the chips were down she'd managed to encourage them to give their all and they usually won. "We have to think positive. There must be a way to escape this man. If he takes us out one by one, there's a good chance that he's going to make a mistake sooner or later, and when he does, we act on it. For now, if he comes back, we should try and get some decent food and some clean blankets. Just starting to negotiate with him will make him see us as human beings and not toys for him to play with."

"I figure you're all batshit crazy if you believe this guy's going to let us escape." Isabella shook the bars. "We're all going to die. If he doesn't kill us, we'll die here. Have you seen his eyes? It's like looking into the eyes of the devil. He is enjoying seeing us frightened. He's a monster."

Olivia heard something and hushed them. She listened intently as footsteps echoed through the cavernous space. She looked at the others staring open-mouthed toward the source of the noise. Her stomach churned with dread as the footsteps grew louder. She wanted to run, hide, do anything to get away, but the steady deliberate footfalls kept coming. The beam of a flashlight cut through the darkness and illuminated the girls' terrified faces.

"Did you miss me?" He moved the flashlight across each girl's face.

With him hidden behind the balaclava and wearing gloves, all that Olivia could make out was the glint of black eyes peering at her. Terrified, her breath caught in her throat as he approached her cell. She trembled but stood her ground as he came closer. Determined to give the others encouragement to remain strong, she sucked in a few deep breaths. Without warning, the man reached through the bars and touched her face, stroking her cheek. Her skin crawled at his touch and she recoiled, but too late. He'd grabbed her by the throat and the smell of blood on the leather gloves crawled up her nose. His fingers tightened and the cell blurred. Fighting for her life, she grasped at his arm, pulling it down hard, and the grip released. She staggered back, gasping for air and wheezing.

"I like that you're afraid of me." His voice sent shivers down her spine. "But this is only the beginning. I have great plans for you." He pointed at each door. "Eeny, meeny, miny, moe, which of you is next to go?"

EIGHT

As Raven's SUV patrol vehicle climbed high into the mountains, Emily gazed out of the window, enjoying the lush beauty of Black Rock Falls in summer. Being apprehensive about going alone to a potential crime scene had eased a little with Raven beside her. After all, Jenna did this all the time and her dad would never send her into danger alone, and yet as the dense forest enveloped them, knowing a killer was out there sent cold chills down her spine. She concentrated on the spectacular view to push away the fear threatening to spoil everything. She'd never live down the embarrassment of losing her nerve in front of Raven. She stared into the trees, searching for a glimpse of wildlife. The various shades of green, bathed in sunlight filtering through the dense canopy, seemed surreal, almost magical. Why did someone always spoil it by committing murder in the forest?

"Are you concerned about what we might find?" Raven looked at her.

She turned to him. "Not at all. I've spent my fair share of time at body farms and at some nasty crime scenes and I haven't puked yet." She shook her head. "It's just—well—it

GOOD GIRLS DON'T CRY   39

would be very unusual if someone has tied human body parts to a tree."

"How so?" Raven flicked her a glance.

Emily waved a hand dismissively. "We've already had a killer using that MO in Black Rock Falls. I don't recall his name, but the dismembered bodies were left during the winter. I recall Jenna and Kane were on vacation at the ski resort when the body parts were discovered. The case was solved and the perpetrator would either be dead or in prison."

"That's good to know." Raven kept his attention on the winding road ahead. "I don't recall ever visiting the ski resort in summer. It's very peaceful here and the scenery is magnificent, isn't it?"

In truth, dread at what they might find hung over Emily, but she brushed it away and forced a smile. "It sure is. I've been in the mountains before in summer but never this high. It won't be long before the place is bustling with skiers. The ski lodge has certainly had its share of serial killers, but the tourists keep on coming, year in and year out." She turned around in her seat to peer down the mountainside. At this position, she could see all the way to town, including the rivers and the lake, all springing from the falls. "This would be a wonderful place for a picnic, don't you agree?"

"Absolutely." Raven rubbed his short beard and glanced at her. "Although you might think differently when we arrive at the crime scene—it could be a field-dressed animal hung in a tree to keep it away from the bears."

Her thoughts drifted momentarily to the crime scene they were heading toward and she turned in her seat to look at him. "Dad mentioned you were in the military before joining the sheriff's department. Were you deployed overseas?"

"Yeah, I served as a medic." Raven gave his head a little shake as if talking about his service was a problem. "I flew a medevac chopper and saw a lot of action, but it prepared me well for this kind of work. Before you ask why I left before my twenty years, I suffered from PTSD and decided that being involved with K-9 training would be a good way to rehabilitate. That's how I come to have Ben. I believe that saving rescue dogs and training them for personal protection is a good community project that also makes me a living."

Emily enjoyed his company and getting him to open up about his past was surprisingly easy. She'd spoken to Dave Kane about him, after her dad had informed her that Raven had asked if he could take her on a date. The idea had both thrilled and annoyed her. To think that in this day and age a man figured he needed to go to her father to ask his permission. So after giving her dad the stink eye and refusing to discuss Raven with him, she'd gone to her ally. Kane had informed her that in his opinion Raven was an open book. A "what you see is what you get" kind of guy. However, she'd made a point of keeping him at arm's length. As an independent grown woman, she didn't need her father interfering—or choosing her dates. He'd been overprotective since she'd attended kindergarten, and if he approved of Raven or not, who she dated was none of his business.

Dragging her mind back to the conversation, she smiled at him. "I imagine everything was going really fine until you found my sister in a plane wreck."

"Indeed." Raven barked a laugh. "My life has completely changed since then. I will still train the dogs, and now that I have Atohi Blackhawk as a partner, their training and well-being will continue when I'm working for the sheriff's department."

Emily nodded. "That's good to know. It must have been quite an adjustment coming back to civilian life. Dad mentioned that you fly a chopper and that one is available for you now."

"Yes, and with all the additional training I've received, I'm one of the team now." Raven cleared his throat. "I figured with everyone being so close and all, acceptance would be a problem, but everyone has been amazing and Kane is like my big brother. I was resistant to join society again. I liked living in solitude with my dogs, but I've found a new purpose here." He slowed to take a tight bend. "What made you want to follow in your father's footsteps?"

It wasn't a difficult question, but Raven didn't know how the family had suffered before moving to Black Rock Falls. Watching her mother slowly die of cancer, and seeing how her dad carried the burden for everyone and then respected her mom's wishes by creating a new life for them, had been all the inspiration she needed. She looked at Raven. "He started off like you, you know, flying medevac choppers under fire. Then he became a handler for a special forces operative, who unfortunately died. He decided the only way to keep himself busy during the long nights he stayed awake nursing my mother was to finish his studies in forensic science and then apply for certification as a medical examiner. The one thing that made up my mind to follow him was that he always told me he did the job because there was no one else to speak for the victims of crime."

"That's very noble." Raven whistled through his teeth. "Now he has found Norrell. They seem like a perfect fit for each other."

Emily remembered her mother, a day or so before she died, insisting that she encourage her dad to move on with his life. It should come like a slap in the face to think that anyone could ever take her mother's place—they couldn't, of course, and she knew that now. Norrell was more like a really good friend and it had taken her father a long time to get the courage to ask her out. She'd seen Norrell with her little sister, Anna, and the way she encouraged her to remember their mom. She turned to look at Raven. "We all believed they'd be perfect together but my father is old-school and took forever to take the first step. He had some stupid notion that he was too old for her. There is

42 D.K. HOOD

only seven years difference between them and they were best friends long before they got involved."

"I'm kind of old-school too." Raven flashed her a smile. "I don't see anything wrong with respecting women and their families. I'm more of a slow and easy kind of guy, rather than jump in boots and all."

Laughing, Emily looked at him. "You sound too good to be true, but then I believed Dave was hiding behind a mask for a long time, but he's the real deal. It must be military brat syndrome. I don't need to ask if you were raised in a military family. It's kinda obvious."

"Yes, ma'am." He grinned. "I followed in my dad's footsteps as well."

Emily's smile froze on her lips as they turned the next bend to see a couple of hikers, pale and wide-eyed, sitting on a boulder beside the dirt road. They pointed to the trees on the opposite side of the road. She looked past them to the tree adorned with body parts. The victim was a young woman. The head faced the road. Her long dark hair flowed in the breeze, making her appear almost alive. All around her, body parts hung from the branches of a pine tree. Emily swallowed the bile rushing up the back of her throat. She hadn't prepared herself for a sight as barbaric as this. The killer had wanted them found and placed them so they were visible from the road. She squinted her eyes and made out a message cut deep into the flesh of the torso: NOT MINE.

"Oh, that's not good." Raven drove under the cover of trees alongside the mountain and pulled the vehicle to a halt. He turned to her. "Stay sharp. We don't know who's out here. Call your dad and update him. I'll go and speak to the witnesses. They need to be anywhere but here. I'll get their story and then cut them loose. Jenna can follow up later."

Grabbing her phone, Emily sighed with relief when Jenna answered her phone. Her dad would be in the river with Kane

GOOD GIRLS DON'T CRY   43

and Carter recovering bodies. "I'm on scene. It's a homicide. Do you recall the serial killer who cut up his bodies and displayed them in the forest. It was during winter?"

"*Vividly.*" Jenna blew out a long sigh. "*It can't possibly be him. So we have a copycat.*"

Emily stared at the body parts shifting macabrely in the breeze. "Yeah, and this one is leaving us notes."

NINE

Shaken by Emily's call, Jenna sat on a rock beside the fast-flowing river and replaced the phone in her pocket. She kept her back to a clump of trees, always concerned someone might creep up on her. She had two dogs close by and Norrell, Webber, and Blackhawk a few yards away. Her position was well away from the edge. She'd learned her lesson after falling in the river and being washed miles downstream. Kane, Carter, and Wolfe had tied ropes around their waists and then anchored themselves to trees before diving to recover the bodies. Although she'd seen Kane dive before, seeing the three men vanish under the rapids frightened her. She'd been stuck in those rapids and understood the danger from the incredible force of the water.

It seemed to take forever before Kane surfaced with one of the bodies. He informed her that four of the five boys had been hogtied, one shot in the chest, and all the girls were missing. Without being asked, Blackhawk left at once to hunt down the girls' trail. She chewed on her bottom lip as Kane dived again and her heart ached as, one by one, they hauled pale lifeless corpses from the icy depths to the riverbank. Norrell went to each one and bent down, brushing the hair from their faces and closing their eyes. A lump formed in Jenna's throat as Webber took photographs and her eyes stung with unshed tears. The boys, all dressed in tuxedos, were so young. *What a waste.*

Trying to take control of her emotions, she stared at the river, trying to grasp the implications of what had happened. These murders were another class of brutality. Five dead boys, the driver, and now five missing girls. As the reality that another serial killer had arrived in Black Rock Falls hit her like a tsunami, she rocked back and forth, running everything through her mind. First this and now a young woman found dismembered and hung in a tree. Could she be one of the missing girls? If so, did this killer kidnap the girls so he had a batch of potential victims to choose from? The copycat murderer had left a message on his victim—why? What did it mean? Jenna shook her head trying to look at the crimes from every angle. If these two crimes were connected what game was he playing?

She shivered and pulled her jacket tighter around her. Beside her, Duke sat with his head resting on her thigh. Sitting a little way away, Zorro, Carter's Doberman, sat like a statue, his gaze fixed on the water, but he was alert. Carter had given his dog orders to guard her, and every so often, his proud head turned toward her, as if checking. She turned and scanned the forest. The dense pine trees spread out for hundreds of miles. The killer might have four or five girls hidden somewhere out there. They'd be terrified and wearing nothing more than thin prom dresses, all potentially suffering from hypothermia. Horrified, she stared into the distance. How could she possibly find them, before he killed them all?

Jenna turned at the sound of voices. Rio and Rowley headed toward her through the forest. She looked up as they approached. "It's good to see you. Raven has gone with Emily to look at a potential crime scene close to the Glacial Heights Ski Resort, and Webber needs help getting the murder victims into body bags once Norrell has done a preliminary examination. We found only the missing boys in the limo and now Blackhawk is hunting down tracks of the girls in the forest."

"Murder victims?" Rio's brow creased as he peered past her at the bodies laid out on the grass. "Have they been shot?"

A pang of deep remorse gripped Jenna as she nodded. "One of them at least. The others were found hogtied and left inside the limo to drown."

"Have mercy." Rowley ran a hand down his face and his eyes filled with sadness. "Do you believe that the murder at the ski resort has anything to do with this?"

Jenna handed them gloves and masks she'd taken from Wolfe's forensics kit. "Emily is on scene now and I'm waiting for a report, but she said the victim is definitely female. I don't like her up there alone with Raven. We don't know who is hanging around watching us. The only reason I agreed to her going was the fact that Raven has Ben with him and that dog would smell a stranger a mile away."

"Then you'll need Wolfe's team up there as soon as possible." Rio indicated to Rowley. "Let's get this show on the road."

Splashing in the water caught Jenna's attention just as Kane and Carter broke the surface with a body of a young man between them. The young man was strong and muscular. His pale handsome face and staring eyes brought a lump to Jenna's throat. She stood as Kane and Carter fought against the fast-flowing river. The swirling currents made it difficult for them to maneuver the body to the bank. As they were wearing wet suits, diving tanks, and flippers, lifting the body across the rocks and up onto the bank was almost impossible. Rio and Rowley ran to the edge to take over and hauled the body onto the grass. There was no time to talk or give her team encouragement. Kane flicked her a glance and then turned and dived back into the swirling current as Wolfe broke the surface with the final victim. As they struggled with another victim, she stood and stumbled over the uneven surface toward the river's edge.

"Don't come any closer, Jenna." Carter dropped onto a boulder to remove his flippers. "The rocks down here are slippery. Just wait, we'll move them onto the grass." He stood and walked to the water's edge and assisted Kane and Wolfe with the last body.

Wanting to see the extent of the victims' injuries, Jenna moved slowly to Norrell's side. In her time as sheriff she'd seen so many horrific murders, but the sight of these young men lined up wearing their finest clothes tore at her heart. She couldn't imagine the heartache of losing a child like this. Their deaths were senseless. The serial killers she'd dealt with over her career always had a crazy reason or a fantasy to fulfill. She couldn't imagine anyone creating a fantasy of drowning young men in the river. The killer had used them to get to the girls. To him, they were nothing more than collateral damage. He needed them out of the way and drowning them was quick and easy. Driving the limo into the river made it hard to find and gave him time to move the girls to a safe location.

"I'd say the last four are death by drowning." Norrell straightened from bending over the final victim. She turned to Webber. "Bag them up, we need to get them to the morgue as soon as possible, but the chances of finding any evidence on them is practically zero."

The drivers removed their wet suits, dried off, and dressed. None of them said anything and all had a faraway expression. Jenna looked from one to the other. She needed to keep up morale. "I have coffee in the Thermoses for when you're ready, and then we need to head to the next crime scene. Emily confirmed it's a female victim."

She went back to the pile of their belongings and Kane came to her side, pulling his T-shirt over his head. She handed him a cup of coffee. "This is bad, isn't it?"

48   D.K. HOOD

"Yeah. I sure as heck won't get the sight of those boys floating inside that limo from my head for a long time." Kane sipped the coffee and then handed back the cup before pulling on a sweater and jacket. His lips had turned blue. "It was dark down there and seeing them floating under the roof of the limo hogtied like that was nasty." He took the coffee from her and rubbed his hair vigorously on a damp towel.

"That coffee sure smells good." Carter came to her side, his blond shaggy hair dripping down his suede jacket. "It was like the Arctic in that river. The only good thing is that it would've preserved evidence." He sighed. "The limo is under a rock shelf way down at the bottom. It will never see the light of day again."

Jenna poured a cup, added the fixings, and handed it to him. As Wolfe joined them, she updated them on the Glacial Heights Ski Resort murder. "I figure it's a copycat of one of our old cases, but why the message? Who is it to? The killer obviously murdered the girl, so why carve 'not mine' into her torso?"

"Unfortunately, I guess we won't know unless he murders another victim." Kane observed her over the rim of his coffee cup.

"We can't assume the mutilation is the same killer." Wolfe swallowed half his coffee and then looked at Jenna. "There could be significant clues all over the body parts, for all we know. Although, it would be very unusual for someone to have an argument with his wife or girlfriend and then cut them up and hang them from a tree."

"Where are the energy bars?" Kane's teeth chattered as he hunted through one of the backpacks. "I packed a ton of them."

Unable to believe he had an appetite after what he'd just witnessed, Jenna raised one eyebrow and reached for the bag resting beside the rock. "The energy bars are in the Beast. Sit down. I have enough sandwiches here to feed an army."

"From Aunt Betty's Café?" Kane peered into the bag and smiled at her. "You amaze me." He gave her a long look. "I know

GOOD GIRLS DON'T CRY 49

you want to get to the next crime scene but I'm cold. I need to eat and so do the others. It's a necessity to survive after being in freezing temperatures. Get warm first and then eat."

"I agree. We need the calories and then we'll carry the bodies back to my van. I'll be able to fit them all inside. Although we'll have to make a couple of trips." Wolfe reached for a sandwich and then looked at Jenna. "I'm guessing it will be a waste of time asking you to return to the office and leave the rest of us to deal with the other crime scene?"

Rolling her eyes, Jenna stared at him. "An absolute waste of time. I'm not leaving Dave's side. If I do, I'll end up having our baby without him and that's not going to happen." She sighed. "I'm happy for the team to deal with the day-to-day running of the office, but I'll handle the serial killer cases. I'm feeling fine, and trust me, you'll be the first one to know if I'm not."

"What's up?" Norrell came over and sat beside Wolfe. "Mmm, coffee and sandwiches. I'm starving." She glanced at Jenna and read her mind. "I'm afraid that if dealing with corpses affected my appetite, I'd be dead by now. I know it seems insensitive, but like they say, someone has to do it."

Understanding, Jenna looked from one to the other. "I know none of you are heartless, far from it, but it breaks my heart seeing those young boys like that. I'm the sheriff and I'm responsible for taking care of the people in my town. They voted for me, trusted me"—she poked at her chest —"to keep them safe. How am I going to tell these people that their sons are dead and victims of a mass murderer?"

"No one will blame you, Jenna." Kane put his arm around her shoulder and pulled her close. "They'll expect you to bring their killer to justice."

Jenna leaned into him. Determination surged through her. She suddenly understood why the notorious and almost mythical Tarot Killer delivered their own brand of justice to unstoppable serial killers. She'd come across the Tarot Killer by chance when her prime suspects in unsolvable crimes had been found dead with a tarot card beside their bodies. The Tarot Killer's vigilante form of justice had removed some of the most horrendous serial killers from existence. Jenna didn't agree with vigilante justice but she understood the reasons why some people were pushed to find justice in any way possible. Right now, she'd been pushed to the edge and needed justice for these young men. "Oh, I'll catch him, but deep down I'll be hoping the Tarot Killer gets to him first."

TEN

GLACIAL HEIGHTS

As Raven approached the two hikers, they ran to meet him, both talking at the same time so fast he couldn't understand either of them. He held up a hand. "Okay, slow down. I'll talk to you one at a time. Who would like to go first? How about we start with your names?"

"Michelle Holland and this is my dog, Moxie. I'm at 8 Aspen Grove." She indicated to her friend. "This is Vilma Chancy and her dog, KC, out of 11 Glacier Point."

Raven made notes. "Okay, and do you often come here to walk your dogs?"

"Yeah, it's a beautiful place in summer." Michelle shuddered. "Until now. We've seen hunters' kills strung up in trees but not around here. We didn't go close, but when I noticed the hair I figured something was up. I called 911 right away."

"I said we should wait here." Vilma opened her jacket to display a shoulder holster. "We both carry protection here in the forest. You never know who is lurking about."

Nodding, Raven looked from one to the other. "Did you happen to see or hear anyone?"

"No." Vilma pointed to the trees. "I noticed the crows, so

we took this trail, but we can see right across to the body. We both listened and kept moving until we were undercover here in the trees. That poor woman. Who would do such a thing?" She rubbed her arms. "I can't stop shaking. Do you figure the killer is hanging around?"

Folding his notebook and pushing it into his pocket, he looked from one to the other. "I doubt it, but would you like me to give you a ride home?"

"Nope, we're fine. Our vehicles are parked at the ski resort. It's only a short walk from here." Michelle's mouth turned down. "Whoever did that won't dare to come near us. We're armed and the dogs will alert us if anyone is near." She looked at Ben. "That's a mighty fine dog you have there. I've never been this close to a K-9. He seems placid. I figured they were on attack mode twenty-four/seven."

Raven rubbed Ben's ears. "No, only when he meets the bad guys. They react to orders, and the rest of the time they're normal super-intelligent dogs." He heard Emily clear her throat and flicked her a glance. "Okay, I'll call if I need anything else." He handed them a card each. "If you see anyone suspicious on your way home, call me."

"We will." Vilma headed along the trail with Michelle close behind.

"Those women are braver than I am." Emily scanned the forest. "I'm seeing men behind every darn tree."

Raven shook his head. "If anything moves out there, Ben will bark. He can hear much better than we can, so don't worry." He led the way through the trail to the tree decorated with body parts.

The stench of death reached him on the usually fresh alpine breeze along with a high humming sound. The hairs on the back of his neck prickled and he glanced at Ben. The feeling of being watched concerned him but the dog hadn't reacted. Perhaps it was the barbaric murder that was getting under his

GOOD GIRLS DON'T CRY   53

skin. He scanned the area for the umpteenth time and then reached into his pocket for a face mask. He noted that Emily had already covered her face and was keeping close behind him. He stopped a few yards away from the carnage and grimaced. The blackened body parts appeared to be moving in undulating waves and then a crow dived down to hang on one of the ropes sideways to peck at the rotting flesh. A black mass of angry flies rose up in a swarm. Raven took a few steps back as they flew into him. "Ugh, that's disgusting."

"They're just flies." Emily marched past him. "Dead bodies always have flies on them in summer, some are crawling with maggots. You'll get used to it."

Shaking his head and waving the flies away, he stared after her as she marched in, boots and all, without a moment's hesitation. He admired her attitude, she had grit. "No, I won't, and I'm not sure I want to."

He stood back, intending to watch her do her work and assist if required. She walked around the scene in a businesslike manner, taking photographs from every angle and then swabbing the open mouth of the victim. The horrific scene didn't faze her at all. "You handle death very well. I admit seeing this poor woman brings back memories I'd rather forget."

"She'll be forgotten if I don't tell her story." Emily took out her phone again and took more photographs. "Right now, my dad and I are the only people who can bring her killer to justice. We'll discover the proof to put the man who did this behind bars. My dad will stand up in court and speak for her. This is why I do this job. It's not nice and I could be helping the sick, but she needs me. No one else will tell her story."

His admiration growing, Raven nodded slowly. "I can see why you're so dedicated, but it is an awful job. Seeing so much carnage. Do you get bad dreams?"

"As in, do I believe the dead haunt me, demanding justice or something?" Emily gave him a long look. "You need to speak to

54   D.K. HOOD

Dave about his angle on the dead. He will tell you; it's not the dead you should be worried about—it's the living." She turned away to continue with her work.

Unable to ignore the flies that crawled up his face and tried to get into his eyes, he brushed them away. Beside him, Ben gave a low growl just as a red spot danced across Emily's back. When it moved slowly to her head, he reacted on muscle memory, as if he were still on the college football team. He lunged forward and grabbed her, taking her to the ground with all his body weight behind him. He heard the breath whoosh out of her just as a bullet thumped into the torso of the victim hanging right where Emily's head had been.

"Oomph" Emily wriggled below him. "What exactly do you think you're doing?" She snorted. "Let me up now. Trust me, I know how to protect myself."

Finding her insinuations a little insulting, Raven rose up enough for her to turn to face him and then covered her with his body. "Shooter. Lie still." He indicated to Ben to drop and the dog shuffled along on his belly to lie beside them. "It must be a sniper. I didn't hear a shot."

"Fine, but I can't breathe." Emily moved her head slightly. "Can you move just a little?!"

Shaking his head, Raven stared into eyes gray like storm clouds. Anger flashed in her eyes and her hand came up to push him away. He grabbed it and grimaced. "I don't have time for this. I don't need to knock women down to get their attention and I have more respect for you than to try anything so darn stupid."

"So you say." Emily wriggled. "You're squashing me. Move now!"

Raven sighed. "I will if you roll over and be ready to move." He rolled to one side but kept one hand firmly on her back. "We need to belly-crawl deeper into the forest. Understand?"

Another bullet hit the tree and showered them with bark.

GOOD GIRLS DON'T CRY 55

Raven stared at her. "Happy now? Head into the deepest underbrush. Move! Now!"

"Fine, but I need my phone." Emily shook her head. "You're overreacting. They're probably stray shots from a hunter, stop overreacting. Who'd want to shoot me?"

Rolling his eyes and praying for assistance, Raven shook his head. He needed to take charge of the situation before somebody died. "You had a red dot on you. You were the target. Someone wants you dead. Now move. I'll get your darn phone. Keep down as low as you can to the ground."

As she moved away, he rolled across the ground, grabbed her phone and then followed her. When they reached inside the tree line, he handed her the phone. "Stay down, keep behind the tree, don't move a muscle." He called Kane. Hopefully he'd be out of the river by now. He sighed with relief when Kane picked up. "I need Wolfe and the team up here ASAP."

"Something wrong?" Kane cleared his throat. *"We found all the boys—one gunshot wound, the others hogtied and drowned. What other bad news do you have for me?"*

Raven narrowed his gaze. He wanted to ask about the missing girls but he had his priorities. "We're under sniper fire aimed at Emily. We've hunkered down inside the tree line. The crime scene is barbaric—young female, maybe seventeen. Em only had time to collect a few swabs and capture a few pictures when I noticed the red dot on her back. I tackled her to the ground and a shot hit the victim, another followed. I'm afraid Emily isn't too happy with me right now."

"That's Em. Stubborn like her dad." Kane cleared his throat. *"Did you get eyes on the shooter? Do you figure he's still hanging around?"*

Scanning the hillside, Raven hadn't seen any movement at all. "No and I doubt it. Shooting would be difficult with the tremors. I figure he's gone but I'll be careful. What's your ETA?"

56   D.K. HOOD

"We have the bodies in the van. I'll head straight for your position." Kane's footsteps crunched through the undergrowth. *"You'll need to be vigilant. If this is the killer, he doesn't want you around. What direction did the shot come from? I'll need to be on my guard once we reach the area."*

Raven flicked a glance at Emily. "Above us and to the left. I figure the shooter must be at the northern end of the road to the ski resort. He could very well be at the ski resort. The crime scene is in a direct line from there. The tree with the body parts is close to the road, in plain sight of anyone passing by. I figure it was intentional. The killer is using it as a lure."

"Okay, hang tight. I'll head to the ski resort with Rio and Rowley via the highway and see if we can flush him out. I'll send the rest of the team to assist you."

Raven disconnected and looked at Emily. "Help is on the way."

"Why is everything so complicated?" Emily hugged her chest. "What is it about Black Rock Falls?"

As if the mountain had heard her, the ground shook and Emily's face drained of color. The mountains had suffered numerous episodes of seismic activity over the last six months. Landslides and mudslides had caused many roads to be closed for weeks. Wanting to ease her mind, he smiled. "Let's worry about the shooter. It's just a tremor."

"I don't think so." Emily shook her head. "I can still feel it. Something bad is happening."

The ground shook again with intense violence. The forest trembled and crows rose in squawks and took off into the sky. Ben let out a long whine and crawled close to his side. Emily was correct, something bad was coming. Frowning, Raven scanned the area. Through the trees, a cloud of dust darkened the deep blue sky. He sprang to his feet. No shooter could take a shot with the ground vibrating. "Get up! We need to get back to the truck—now!" He grabbed Emily by the arm and they sprinted through the trees with Ben at their heels. He'd parked his vehicle in the shadows under the trees at the side of the mountain. As they ran, tremors shook the ground, hurtling them into trees. When Emily tripped and fell, he scooped her up, tossed her over one shoulder, and ran. She yelled something at him and hammered his back, but he kept running.

Gasping for breath, he reached the truck and tossed her unceremoniously inside. Ben followed and Raven slid behind the wheel intending to drive away as fast as possible. His heart pounded as the screams of trees being ripped out by the roots and cracking of trunks filled the silence. The ground shook with violence and thunderous rumbles deafened him. At first a few small rocks pinged over the hood of his truck and then he gaped in horror as massive boulders crashed through the forest, flattening everything before them.

"Oh, my God!" Emily ducked, covering her head. "We're going to die."

ELEVEN

Vehicles stopped along the highway as tremors rocked the mountainside. With lights and sirens blaring, Kane weaved around the traffic, heading the Beast toward the Glacial Heights Ski Resort. The decision to take the highway route rather than the back mountain road, where Emily and Raven hunkered down, was to take note of any vehicles coming from the closed ski resort. The owner remained there in a huge log-built cabin all year round and the manager lived in one of the staff cabins, along with a small group of employees. The ski resort also engaged various contractors during the summer to maintain the buildings and equipment. All these people and their vehicles could be accounted for. The ski resort had CCTV cameras, and the manager would soon pick up anyone suspicious hanging around.

Another tremor shuddered through the truck and Kane increased his speed as they climbed high into the mountains. Up to now most of the rockslides had occurred in the areas that had been damaged by either fire or flood. The higher they moved up the mountain the safer they should be. There was also another road they could take to get home if necessary. It

GOOD GIRLS DON'T CRY   59

would take some time, following the lowland road, but they could get to Louan and then loop back to Black Rock Falls. He glanced in his rearview mirror to see Rio close behind him and then Jenna let out a small cry. A boulder rolled down the side of the mountain across the road in front of them, bounced like a bowling ball across the blacktop, and then disappeared down the other side of the highway. "That was close." Kane looked at her. "I've never seen rocks bounce like that before."

"This doesn't look good for Emily and Raven." Jenna peered up at the mountain. "They're directly below the ski resort. That road was cleared only recently after the floods. The odds are if there's going to be a slip, it's there."

Although Kane had been considering the same thing, he flicked her a glance as they turned from the highway and headed along the mountain path. "Don't forget that Raven is an experienced mountain man after living there for so long. He'll know where to go to get out of any rockslides. I would say he'd start moving as soon as he felt the first tremor."

"I'll call Emily." Jenna pulled out her phone and made the call. "She's not picking up. It went to voicemail." She gave Kane an anxious stare and left a message. "Emily, call me right away. We are just above you at the ski resort."

Kane glanced at her. "Call Wolfe and give him the heads-up. He is heading up the mountain and he needs to change course and get off the mountain. Tell him to use the highway not the back road."

"Okay." Jenna made the call and then looked at him. "Are we safe at the resort?" Her hands went protectively to her belly.

In truth nowhere was safe in an earthquake but Kane didn't believe it would come to that. He nodded. "It's at the top of the mountain, so the chances of a landslide there would be remote, plus they placed all kinds of protection around the resort to prevent avalanches. I'm sure we'll be okay. The worst-case scenario with the tremors is rock or mudslides. The chance of an earthquake is remote. I believe there hasn't been anything really bad since the nineteen fifties, but I guess anything is possible."

"Why is this happening now?" Jenna stared up at the mountain.

Kane had been reading up on just that topic. The sudden changes in the weather, including the weird storms and hard winters had made a difference. "From what I've read, the damage by the prolonged winter and then the floods have made parts of the mountain unstable. That's where the slips are occurring and the forestry can't get the trees to grow fast enough to fix the problem. Without the tree roots holding everything together, this will keep on happening."

As they reached the resort, Kane scanned any suitable area where a shooter might be hiding. Seeing nothing of interest, he concentrated on the main building. A high window would be his choice, but all the shutters were closed and no vehicles sat in the parking lot. The place appeared completely deserted, perhaps the owner and employees had taken their vacations at the same time. He noticed the CCTV cameras swiveling toward them as they drove into the parking lot. He climbed out and gave them a wave. Obviously the company they employed for security was doing its job. He'd need to ask FBI whiz kid Bobby Kalo to check out the feed and see if it picked up the shooter. He handed Jenna a Kevlar vest from the back seat. "Put this on. I doubt the shooter is around, not after the tremors, but it's better to be safe."

"Okay." Jenna climbed out, pulled the vest over her head, and headed to the entrance to the back road that led down the mountain. "I'll just take a look."

Rio pulled his truck to a halt beside the Beast and as the deputies climbed out Kane turned to them. "I'll get Duke. You guys stick to Jenna like glue. There's a shooter on the mountain and he's likely in this area."

GOOD GIRLS DON'T CRY 61

"Copy that." Rio took off at a jog with Rowley on his heels.

As Kane opened the back door to allow Duke to jump down, Jenna's cry of anguish broke the silence and he ran to her side. The three of them were staring down the back road. It was the one used by staff during the winter and easily cleared by the snowplows. It was also the road where he'd found body parts hanging from a tree during his vacation there with Jenna, some years ago. It wasn't body parts he could see this time, but right before the first bend, the road had vanished under a rockslide. Dust still hung in the air and the mountain shuddered as if complaining. The Native Americans would insist that it was angry for all the deaths that had occurred there. Blackhawk told him that when bad things happened the mountains created the landslides to cover the scars, made by the stupidity of man.

"The road is blocked." Jenna paced up and down. "They're stuck down there with an active shooter." She reached for her phone and then looked up, anxiety etched in her face. "They're not answering their phones and she hasn't activated her tracker." She turned to Rio and Rowley. "The satellite phones should work here."

"Not if they sheltered in a cave. I doubt her tracker would either." Rowley lifted one shoulder in a half shrug. "Raven knows the forest. He'd get up close to the mountain. He'd know that part of the mountain is stable. There are caves all along that side. I don't figure he'd risk driving down. Once you get past the first bend, there's a drop right down to the valley."

Kane grabbed his field glasses from his pack and moved them across the area. "The slide looks concentrated to the back road almost as if it channeled it. I'm hoping once the tremors stop, Raven and Em will venture outside and then you'll be able to contact them. Why don't you send them a message? There's a good chance that will go through and they'll be able to reply." He rested his arm across her shoulder. "There's no way down.

We'll need to wait until the dust settles or get choppers out here."

"We have two pilots here now and choppers ready to go." Jenna frowned at him. "I'm guessing you'll be the one going down to help them?"

Not wanting to concern her about the complexity of doing a rescue beside a mountain range in high winds, Kane nodded. "Carter is the most experienced in mountain areas and I'm trained to do this in my sleep. First, we try and communicate and then get the choppers up." He glanced up as dark clouds rolled in from over the mountain. Lightning flashed and thunder echoed through the mountains. "Oh, now that's all we need." He took Jenna's hand and raised his voice. "Everyone back in the trucks. It's not safe out here in a storm."

A loud crack and a blue flash came so close it raised Kane's hair. He pulled open the door for Jenna and helped her inside. He turned to check that Rio and Rowley were running for their truck. Another loud crack and the mountain shook as thunder rolled around them. Beside him Duke whined and pressed against his leg. He bent to pick him up and drop him onto the back seat and then ran around the hood as rain pelted his back. As he slid behind the wheel, he looked at Jenna's stricken face. "I'm sorry, we can't risk a rescue until the storm passes."

"They haven't responded, Dave." Jenna stared at her phone and then lifted her gaze to him. "I hope they're okay."

He'd never admit it, but hope was fading fast. Even the elements were against them. It was getting late and he could see no way of reaching them. In the dark in this weather, risking the shifting rocks in a storm would be suicide. They had no choice but to keep trying to contact them and hopefully organize a rescue at first light. Kane squeezed her hand. "So do I."

TWELVE

THE MINE

Pain shuddered through Samantha Haimes' body and the tight belt around her neck made it hard to breathe. The disgusting man had forced himself on her in the shower, deep underground in the old mineshaft with her friends ordered to watch through their barred windows, except Olivia, who refused to witness her humiliation. Exhausted and way past screaming and crying now, she stood under the warm flow, scrubbing every inch of her flesh. Her attacker leaned against the wall with his arms folded across his chest staring at her through the mask he wore to cover his face. The fact that he kept his face covered gave her some modicum of hope that he was afraid of being recognized, which meant there may be a chance of escape. He'd made her wear examination gloves throughout the ordeal, no doubt afraid that she might scratch him. After, he'd sprayed her all over with a chemical before allowing her to shower.

"Turn off the water." The man tossed her a towel. "Dry off and put on those clothes over there." He indicated to a small pile on what had been an old desk against the wall. "When you're done, we're going for a ride."

Trembling so hard her teeth chattered, Samantha found it

difficult to do anything with the tight belt around her neck. Well, it wasn't a belt, more like a leading rein for a horse, looped at one end to tighten easily and he'd never let go of the end. He seemed to get great pleasure out of seeing her choke as he tightened it.

Samantha dried quickly and pulled on old but clean blue jeans. She reached for a pink T-shirt, and the man held a gun on her and then dropped the leash to allow her to feed it through the neck of the T-shirt and a yellow sweater. All had been neatly folded and set on the top of a surprisingly clean wooden desk. As she glanced across the top of the desk, she searched for anything she could use as a weapon. She found nothing, not even a pen or a pencil she could use to stab him. Fear and anger mingled as she glanced at him over one shoulder. She wanted to hurt him so bad.

"Give me your leash." He held out one hand and she reluctantly passed it to him. "There's a good girl." He tugged hard and dragged her toward him. "You've amused me. Don't spoil it."

The talk between the girls in his absence had been about how to avoid making him angry. Olivia had said that people like him feed on fear, so no matter what happened they should all try and not react when he threatened them. That was all right for Olivia to say, but she hadn't been tied up, gagged, and raped. Her stomach heaved. The way he'd chuckled all the way through and insisted the girls watched what he was doing made her sick to the stomach. She would do anything to get away from him—anything.

"Find a pair of slippers that fit you from that box over there at the end of the desk." He pulled on a thick jacket and a clean pair of examination gloves. "Okay, it's time to go."

When he gave her the flashlight to carry, Samantha wanted to turn around and smash him in the face with it. Her mom had always told her she had a bad temper and it was starting to come

GOOD GIRLS DON'T CRY 65

to the surface. She considered her situation as he nudged her along the passageway using the muzzle of his pistol pressed into the middle of her back. She stumbled across the old railway tracks as the flashlight bobbed along in front of them. Things moved in the shadows, on the ground and above. Reluctant to take another step, she slowed her pace and the pistol dug hard into her spine. She glanced back at him but couldn't see his face in the gloom. He resembled a grizzly looming in the shadows, big and hulking. She shuddered. "Where are we going?"

"We're heading into the forest." He pushed her so hard she stumbled forward. "There's a special trail I want you to see and then I'm going to let you go. Do you figure you could survive in the forest overnight?"

Nodding, Samantha moved faster. The sooner she could get out of this place the better. There were plenty of places to hide in the forest where the wildlife wouldn't find her. If he left her alone, she would just lie low until he'd gone and wait until morning. She had been raised in Black Rock Falls and understood that if she ever became lost in the forest, she should locate a river and follow it downstream until she came to the town. All rivers in Black Rock Falls led to some form of habitation.

When they arrived at the van, he'd covered it with a camouflage tarp and gave her the job to remove it, which was more than a little difficult. She climbed inside and he handcuffed both her hands to the door handle. She realized as they took off in the darkness that they were well away from the town and on the edge of the lowlands that contained many of the old gold mines. She knew where he was keeping the others, and if she could get to safety, she'd be able to get help for them. It took a while for them to get back into the mountains. The first road he took had been blocked by a rockfall. Instead, he negotiated the fire roads until they were deep in the forest. When he pulled the van into a small clearing beneath a canopy of trees and turned off the headlights, darkness surrounded them, and suddenly afraid, Samantha looked at him. Emotionless, dark eyes hidden within the holes of the balaclava stared back at her.

"This is where we say goodbye." He leaned toward her and removed the belt from around her neck. "Sit still and do exactly as I say or I'll change my mind."

Samantha sat absolutely still as he removed the handcuffs. She'd remained alert the entire time and could find her way back to the highway. All she needed to do was follow the fire roads. She tried not to flinch when he stroked her cheek but she couldn't stop her knees trembling. Her heart pounded when he leaned in closer and gazed deep into her eyes as if daring her to move away from him. She froze in the seat, wondering what he intended to do.

"It's a shame, I know, but I must let you go." His gloved hand moved over her face in almost a caress. "There are so many other things we could have explored together. It would have been fun, but right now, I'm going hunting while the moon is high." He plucked a bow from behind his seat as he climbed out of the van. He leaned inside again to pick up a quiver of arrows and slung them over one shoulder. He waved a dismissive hand at her. "You can go now, Samantha. There's a trail right in front of you."

Samantha jumped from the van and took off at a run. No footsteps followed behind her and the moonlight illuminated a long straight trail directly ahead. She dashed forward, ignoring the tree branches reaching out to tear at her face and hair. She'd sprinted almost one hundred yards when a strange noise came through the air. Something hit her between the shoulder blades and the pain sent her sprawling on her face. Pine needles pressed into her cheeks, and the damp smell of rotting leaves filled her nostrils. Panic gripped her so hard she couldn't breathe. The metallic taste of blood filled her mouth, and the forest moved in and out of focus. Under her a patch of warmth spread out. She must get up but her arms and legs refused to move. Footsteps came on the trail, snapping twigs and crunching pine needles. She swiveled her eyes to look at him staring at her, a bow hanging from one hand. He'd shot her with an arrow. She opened her mouth to say something but nothing came out. She stared past him to the moon peeking through the canopy, bright and beautiful. She must try and get up and run from him.

"It won't be long now." He tossed two coins in his hand. "Money for the ferryman."

Samantha lifted her head but her heavy limbs refused to respond. *I'm dying.* As the forest faded around her, she turned her gaze back to the heavens and then closed her eyes.

THIRTEEN

GLACIAL HEIGHTS

Emily tried her phone again and then looked at Raven. "This is the best satellite phone money can buy and it's not working. I've used my tracker and we haven't seen or heard anyone for hours. It's after midnight. What is happening?"

"First up, you need to stay calm." Raven had pushed his seat back and was lying with one arm over his eyes. "Secondly, you should know that during bad weather sometimes the satellite connection is sketchy. We're very close to the mountain, which also interferes with the signal, and that includes your tracker device. To be perfectly honest, I don't believe you need to worry about contacting your dad because he knows where you are and will be doing everything possible to get us out of this situation."

The tremors hadn't stopped, which made being exposed to the thunder and lightning even worse, and she'd never liked being in a storm. In fact, storms and earthquakes had become her worst nightmares. "How can you just lie there and do nothing? Shouldn't you be trying to climb out of here and get help?"

"Nope." Raven opened one eye to look at her and then closed it again.

GOOD GIRLS DON'T CRY   69

Baffled by his nonchalance, she gaped at him. "So you expect me to sit here forever?"

"Emily." Raven clicked his chair and the back came up to a sitting position. He rubbed one hand down his face and stared at her. "There is absolutely no point in going out in a storm to get soaking wet and try to climb loose boulders. If I made it to the top, which would be highly unlikely, where would I possibly go for help? The ski resort is closed for the summer and it would take me most of the night to hike to the highway." He held up one finger when she opened her mouth to say something. "Another thing. Do you really want me to leave you alone here? There is a good chance that grizzlies live in some of the caves and they'll be hungry. It will only be a matter of time before they rip off the door or smash a window to get to you."

The reality of what was happening suddenly sank in and she nodded. "I can see your point but how long do you expect us to be here?"

"I figure they'll have a chopper up by morning." Raven tossed her a blanket. "We're lucky it's summer, but it does get cold in the mountains, so rug up and try and get some sleep. Ben will alert us if anything tries to creep up on us."

Emily took the blanket and added it to the one she had wrapped around her legs. "Not even you will be able to stop a grizzly."

"I'm not planning on killing anything, Em." Raven yawned and tipped back his chair. "But I have the firepower in this truck if we need it, and by morning we might find a way to drive out of here. We don't know the extent of the rockslide. There's a good chance we can get through alongside the mountain, even if it means moving a few rocks." He gave her a long look. "To ease your mind, at first light I'll hike away from the mountain and try to make contact with the office."

Concerned, Emily shook her head. "No, call my dad. He'll be frantic with worry. He'll let everyone know we're okay."

"Sure." Raven closed his eyes. "Try to get some sleep. You'll need your strength if we need to dig the truck out." He lifted one of her hands and smiled. "Ah, good. No long nails." He chuckled. "I wouldn't want you to break one."

Bristling, Emily reclined her chair and glared at him. "What do you mean by that? Do you figure I'm not tough enough?" She snorted when he grinned at her. "I've faced down serial killers—and survived. Dave and my dad instructed me and my sisters how to protect ourselves."

"Yeah? That worked well when that guy on the snowmobile tried to grab you last winter, didn't it?" His white smile glowed in the moonlight. "If I hadn't been there, you figure you'd have survived?" He chuckled. "Don't get mad with me. I'm just teasing you, Em. I must admit I admire you. The way you walked onto that crime scene and didn't flinch or puke would put most people to shame. You'll make a fine medical examiner. Wolfe will be a very proud daddy."

It was hard to be angry with Raven, when he took everything in his stride. His placid easy-going nature was something she admired about him. He'd saved her and her sister's lives—but sometimes he infuriated her. She recalled talking to Jenna about her early days with Kane. She'd never met anyone who would take a bullet to protect her, and at first Jenna had found Kane's overprotectiveness suffocating. Later she'd told her that often men who'd been raised in the military had an old-school respect for women. She figured that Raven was like Kane in that way, but only that way.

She'd seen how Kane's expression changed when he faced down a killer. The look had frightened her. It was as if he became a brick wall, and no one was getting through him. Raven was more like the dogs he trained—he'd be a best friend until given a command to attack—and she liked that about him too. She snuggled under the blanket and looked at him. "Thanks. I'm working hard to get through all the requirements.

It will be a dream come true to work alongside my dad. He needs a vacation so bad. Although, when he gets married, he'll arrange for another ME to cover for him if needed. I hope we have a death-free week when he's away. It would make life so much easier."

"I wouldn't worry." Raven yawned explosively. "Between us, we'll manage normal deaths, and homicides we can put on ice until he returns. You can run the necessary tests, and my license is current, so it's all good. Go to sleep, Em. We'll talk in the morning." He sighed. "Goodnight, Ben."

The dog barked and Emily giggled. The dog's long tail was wagging a few inches from her face. Damp dog and a man that smelled like pine trees. She sighed. It was going to be a long night.

FOURTEEN

BLACK ROCK FALLS

Sunday

Jenna dragged herself out of a dream at the sound of Kane's voice. She opened her eyes and looked at the clock on the bedside table. It was a quarter after seven. The smell of freshly ground coffee wafted toward her from a cup sitting beside her as she looked up at Kane sitting on the edge of the bed. "Why didn't you wake me earlier? I need to know what's happening with Emily and Raven."

"Trust me, so do I." Kane sipped from the cup in his hands. "The only problem is we can't get a chopper up at the moment. The mountain is cloaked in low clouds and visibility is down to practically zero. The moment the sun burns it off, I'll be heading off with Carter and Wolfe to see what's happening."

Wanting to protest, Jenna opened her mouth to say something, but Kane gave her his combat face and she frowned. "What's that look for? Is there a problem?"

"No, I just wanted to finish what I was going to say, is all." He smiled at her. "I have good news. Raven managed to get a call out to Wolfe. It dropped out a few times but he said they

GOOD GIRLS DON'T CRY   73

were fine but trapped by the rockslide. He's planning on trying to get back alongside the mountain, but he believes the way will be blocked with boulders. I called the mayor and he's organizing a work crew to get up there and inspect the damage. They'll have the machinery to clear a path for them and anyone else trapped up there."

Sitting up and pulling pillows behind her, Jenna reached for her cup. "Thank God they're okay. So why do you need to head up in a chopper if the mayor is handling the situation?"

"If they can't get back today, we'll need to haul them out." Kane frowned. "We can get the truck later when the road is cleared but they'll run out of water by then. I figured we could drop them supplies but Carter insists he can't risk getting that close to the mountain. If they can walk out to a clear area, he can get his chopper in close enough for a rescue. I'll need to rappel down and bring them up one at a time, including the dog."

She swallowed hard. Windy conditions high in the mountain made a rescue mission close to the rock face very dangerous. The thought of Kane hanging from the chopper buffeted by the high wind terrified her, and he'd need to do it three times. Her concern must have shown on her face as Kane shook his head slowly.

"Jenna, every time I do something like this, you worry." He placed his cup on the bedside table and frowned. "You shouldn't. I'm never afraid. In fact, I enjoy it. I'm very close to Emily, and you know I could never risk her safety with anyone else." He sighed. "A rescue might not be necessary, but if it is, I'm going. We'll take supplies as well, just in case we can't get them out for a time." He stood and smiled at her. "Breakfast is just about ready. Carter is helping this morning and Tauri is already at the table waiting to eat. How long do you need?"

It never ceased to amaze her how her team worked seam-

74   D.K. HOOD

lessly together. Kane had organized a rescue in a few minutes. Impressed, Jenna nodded. "Is ten minutes okay?"

"Ten minutes is fine." He collected her empty cup and headed out the door.

At the kitchen table, Jenna grinned at Carter, wearing Nanny Raya's apron and with flour on his cheek. Although the batch of pancakes he'd made were delicious, the added pile of crispy bacon Kane had fried made the meal perfect. She looked at her son. "What exciting things are you doing at kindergarten today?"

"Painting, I hope." Tauri beamed at her. "I hope Ms. Smith will show us more dinosaur bones. She said she had a movie to show us all about them too."

"That will be great." Carter nibbled on a strip of bacon. "One day maybe your mom and dad will take you to visit the tar pits in LA."

"Uncle Ty is referring to La Brea Tar Pits in Los Angeles." Kane poured maple syrup over his pancakes. "It has a dinosaur exhibition. I recall seeing mammoths, saber-toothed cats, dire wolves, and many more. I figure it's a great place to take kids."

Nodding, Jenna smiled. "I'll need to have the baby first, okay?"

"Hurry up, baby." Tauri rested his ear against Jenna's belly. "He says, blub, blub, blub."

"It might be a girl." Kane chuckled. "Would you like a baby sister?"

"I'm not sure." Tauri stared at his plate. "Girls can be icky. I figure he'll be a boy like me. Big and strong."

Jenna's phone chimed and she stared at the caller ID and shook her head at Kane. It was a private number. She stood and walked into the passageway to take the call. "Sheriff Alton."

"Ma'am. My name is Edgar Finch. I'm with the work crew checking the damage from the rockslide. We've found the body of a woman laid out on a boulder with copper pennies on her

GOOD GIRLS DON'T CRY   75

eyes. Seems like the wildlife has nibbled on her some. Poor kid."

Stiffening, Jenna walked back to the kitchen. She went to the pad on the counter and pulled out a pen from a cup beside it. "I'll need your details and the coordinates. Did you touch anything?"

"No, ma'am." Finch blew out a long breath. *"I can leave two of my men and a truck on the fire road to keep the critters away until you get here. We need to keep movin'. There are people wanting our help. I know you require more details, but no one has gotten too close. It was a shock, seeing her laid out like that. I'll text you the coordinates, but it's along the fire road, close to the forest warden's station."*

Heart thumping, Jenna made rapid notes. "Thank you. I'll send my deputies right away." She disconnected and called Rio. "Are you heading to the office? Grab Rowley and head for the forest. I believe someone has located one of the missing girls."

"Alive?" Rio's engine roared.

Jenna frowned. She couldn't be specific in front of her son. "I'm afraid not. I'll send the coordinates. It's the fire road close to the forest warden's office. I'm having breakfast with my son, so I'll give you the details later."

"Dead body, likely one of the missing girls. Is someone on scene?"

Blowing out a long sigh, Jenna nodded. "Yeah, two guys in a work truck. They'll be waiting for you. I'll call in the ME and follow you ASAP."

"Copy that." Rio disconnected.

The moment Nanny Raya came to collect Tauri for kindergarten, Jenna gave the others the bad news. "We need to head there now."

"Pennies on her eyes?" Kane pushed plates into the dishwasher. "Don't tell me this is another copycat murder? Did they leave another note?"

Anxious to get to the murder scene, Jenna stood. "Not that I'm aware but the first on scene kept clear of the body, so I don't have any more details." She turned to Carter. "Would you call Wolfe? I'll grab my things."

"Sure." Carter frowned and ran a hand through his shaggy blond hair. "If this is another copycat, maybe we need to run it past Jo. With her insight into the criminal mind, she'll be able to give us a profile."

Having an FBI behavioral analyst on the team was a bonus and Jenna nodded. "I'll upload all the details when we get back from the crime scene and then give her a call. I need to know exactly what we're dealing with. We need to find this monster before he strikes again."

FIFTEEN

As they headed into town, Jenna turned to Kane. "We'll need to split the team. I'll go with Wolfe to the crime scene and you'll need to go with Carter to spot Raven and Emily. You can at least get their coordinates so we know what to tell the road crew heading that way to clear a path through for them. It will also give us an idea of just how much damage the landslide has done to the roads. I suggest you drop them provisions for a few days, just in case we can't get to them."

"They are our priority." Kane flicked her a glance. "The problem is I need someone else in the chopper to work the winch and lower me down and then pull them up."

"In normal conditions I could do that from the cockpit." Carter leaned forward in his seat and Duke licked his face. "The problem is the wind and the low cloud cover is causing havoc at the moment. The wind alone is a reason why I can't be distracted for a second while I'm that close to the mountain." He stroked both dogs and leaned back in his seat. "I say we have a look-see and then work out a plan to rescue them. Dropping them supplies is a good idea because we have no idea how long the cloud cover is going to cause a problem. Low clouds come

78   D.K. HOOD

and go, which makes matters worse." He sighed. "We don't need to be flying a rescue mission in dense clouds. It would be suicide that close to the mountains."

Understanding the risks that chopper pilots took when undergoing rescue missions, Jenna nodded. "I'll call Aunt Betty's and ask them to make up a few boxes of supplies. If we're going to be on the move most of the day, we're going to need them as well. We can pick up energy bars and bottles of water from the office. Will Raven need a first aid kit? Not speaking to them personally is a big problem." She sighed. "I wish I could talk to Emily and find out if she's okay. I also want to know if they believe the crime scene was obliterated by the rockfall or not and if Emily managed to take enough photographs and swabs to identify the body."

"Wolfe did say that Raven needed to climb some distance up the rockfall to get a signal, so I doubt you'll be able to speak to them unless they've found a way through the forest, which in that area is just about impossible." Kane stared ahead as they turned onto Main. "They'll need a lot of water, maybe a purifying kit as well. I'll see what we have in the store closet. We can't waste any time. The moment the cloud cover lifts we need to be in the air."

Jenna pulled out her phone and called Aunt Betty's. She placed a huge order and then looked at him. "They'll have it ready as soon as possible. I'll pack energy bars and chocolate as well as military provisions just in case they're there for a time. We'll drop by Aunt Betty's on our way to the crime scene to collect it."

After making a few phone calls while Kane and Carter collected everything they needed, she stood the moment they walked back into her office. "Ready to go? I've spoken to Rio. This case is familiar. In fact, it is exactly the same as one we've solved before—a copycat of James Earl Stafford—but they only mimicked his crime scenes. This one is different. I know that

GOOD GIRLS DON'T CRY   79

killer is either dead or in prison. It's another copycat." She leaned back and pressed her hands into her spine and moaned. Sitting had become a problem today. "Wolfe has just arrived. We need to get there ASAP."

"We'll be right along." Kane gave Carter a meaningful stare and he slipped from the room with Zorro on his heels. "Jenna, I can handle this if your back is aching. It might mean the baby is coming. You really need to be close to town."

Jenna smiled at him. "I love that you care, but I need to be close to *you*. I'll have my doctor on scene and my coach if needs be. Right now, I'm not having contractions, just an aching back. Your baby is very heavy, Dave. By the way it's kicking right now, I'm starting to believe it's a boy dressed in tactical gear and Army boots and wearing night-vision goggles."

"Well, they do say the baby goes quiet before delivery, so maybe it's going to be a few more days yet." Kane chuckled. "Army boots, huh? Now wouldn't that be something?"

SIXTEEN

Mist hung over the mountain, the wisps of water vapor blackening the trunks of the tall pines and coating everything, enhancing the colors. Water droplets glistened on leaves and flowers like millions of diamonds, and the entire forest looked magical. The fire roads into the forest were surprisingly busy. Road crews and heavy machinery made their way toward the rockfall in a long convoy. Jenna gripped the side of her seat as Kane switched on lights and sirens and barreled past them on the wrong side of the road. Bounced all over the seat, Jenna breathed a sigh of relief when they finally drew up behind Wolfe's van. Rio's truck was parked in front, blocking the trail. She turned to Kane as he opened a door to lift Duke down. "Do you mind helping me down? I don't want to risk turning an ankle on that uneven ground."

"Yes, ma'am." Kane swept her into his arms and carried her to the trail. He set her down gently beside a tree ringed with crime scene tape and scanned the area. He looked at Carter. "It's déjà vu all over again." He walked beside Jenna as they approached the body. "Do you figure he shot her with an arrow?"

GOOD GIRLS DON'T CRY   81

"That would match the copper pennies over the eyes of the last victims who were left like this." Carter wrinkled his nose and coughed. "I guess a wound from an arrow would clinch it."

Grabbing a face mask as the bittersweet stench of death crept toward them like an otherworld entity, Jenna pressed the mask to her face. "I hope not. It would make this case more difficult."

This part of the forest was beautiful. The trail was a favorite of hikers in summer. The forest here held an abundance of wildflowers and over the years they'd spread into a carpet of colors. Normally the air would be filled with fragrance but the smell of decomposition overpowered everything. Crows circled above like vultures or sat clumped together on any available branch just waiting for a chance to fly down. From the marks on the victim's clothes, a few critters had already chewed on exposed parts.

Jenna's gaze slid over the body, mentally taking in the victim's position. Most times murderers left their victims where they fell, or where they'd tossed them. A few made a point of laying them out, either in crude poses or to make them appear asleep. This was the latter. The girl's arms were folded over her chest, her legs straight. The victim's clothes were intact and she wore blue examination gloves—why? She couldn't recall any other victim wearing gloves. After moving closer to peer at the victim's face, she pulled out her phone and scrolled through the images of the missing high school girls. She nodded to Wolfe as he talked into a small recording device and peered at the victim's face. Although bright copper pennies covered the eyes, it was still obvious this poor girl was Samantha Haimes. Jenna swallowed hard and took in the scene and then went to speak to Rio and Rowley. They stood some distance away staring at Wolfe as he conducted a preliminary examination. "Okay, what have you got for me? The victim resembles Samantha Haimes. What did the first on-scene witnesses see?"

"Not much." Rio stood hands on hips and feet apart. "They noticed the body as they drove past and stopped to take a look. One of the men, I have his details, came closer but didn't go past the head of the trail. He knew by the smell the victim was deceased and called it in. They waited until we arrived to make sure nothing happened to the body. They've been sounding their horn repeatedly to keep the crows away." He lifted his chin. "I've sent them on their way as they're part of the crew heading up the mountain to unblock the road to the ski resort." He sighed. "Any news of Em and Raven?"

Jenna gave her head a shake. "Nothing new, no. I'm guessing they're trying to find a way through the forest. Raven mentioned staying with his vehicle, but worse case, they'll try and hike out but it's dangerous with the tremors and the rockslides."

"They'll be fine." Kane rubbed his chin. "Raven knows the forest, and he won't take any chances." He looked up at the heavy low clouds. "Once the visibility improves, Carter will take up his chopper. When we locate them, we'll drop them food and water and a few other supplies. Hopefully the road crew will make a path for them, but if not, they'll need to get away from the rock face, and we'll be able to get them out."

"I'm checking visibility every ten minutes or so." Carter looked up from his phone. "Once it's safe, my chopper is ready. I only need a few preflight checks and we can leave."

"Rowley." Wolfe beckoned him. "I need your eyes on this wound."

Jenna followed him and they all peered at a single puncture wound in the victim's back. She watched as Rowley bent closer, with one hand clamped to his face mask.

"I'll need to look closer once I get back to the morgue but that doesn't resemble a gunshot." Wolfe frowned and glanced at Kane.

"A bullet large enough to make a hole like that would have

GOOD GIRLS DON'T CRY 83

gone right through and blasted a hole the size of my fist out the front." Kane shook his head. "Not a bullet."

"Nope, that's the typical wound I'd see in bowhunting." Rowley stood slowly. "This guy went overboard. From the size of the wound, the victim was hit with a broadhead arrow with a head size of 125 grains."

As Rowley's passion was bowhunting and competition, Jenna had an expert standing beside her. She looked at him. "What kind of arrows are we looking at, Jake?"

"A few types but I'd say maybe the FMJ Dangerous Game or the Carbon Express Piledriver Pass Thru Extreme, although I figure the FMJ would be closer to what I'm seeing." He glanced around at the trees. "I don't see any marks from retrieved arrows and these would leave a decent hole. This guy is a marksman if he took her down in a single shot."

"You'd assume she was running for her life." Kane looked at him. "It's a straight trail but has roots all over, so I'd imagine she'd be moving from side to side. You'd be able to make the shot, right?"

"That would depend on the light." Rowley frowned. "It was a full moon last night and this is a wide trail, so yeah. I'd make the shot, but it wouldn't be easy." He indicated to the body. "That is a kill shot. The arrow would have passed straight through the heart and embedded in the sternum. Getting it out wouldn't have been easy."

"Look at this." Wolfe rolled the body onto its back and lifted the front of the T-shirt.

Jenna moved closer. The killer had scratched the words "not mine" deep into the skin. She looked at Kane. "Another message. What does this mean?"

"I figure he'll kill them all until he makes his point." Kane shook his head. "We need to be looking at the cases he's copying and search for anything that could possible connect them."

Frowning, Jenna shook her head. "This time, I figure you're

wrong, Dave." She stared into the forest and then her attention rested on Wolfe. "These are our cases, right? Most of our cases are multiple homicides, so I'm guessing this guy is telling us we made a mistake with at least one of the victims." She chewed on her bottom lip. *Did I make a mistake? Did I have the wrong man convicted for murder?*

SEVENTEEN
GLACIAL HEIGHTS

"Don't you dare turn around." Emily's voice came through the rush of water.

The night with Emily had been interesting and Raven wondered if she knew she made these cute noises when she slept, like sighs of contentment. He kept sweeping his gaze across the forest searching for bears. He'd noticed bear scat alongside this stream and behind him Emily was bathing in a small waterfall—naked and vulnerable. He shrugged. She'd insisted on bathing and changing her clothes. He'd been more interested in finding a way out. He'd explained they might be trapped here for days, and she washed her underwear and hung them from the windows in his truck.

They'd only moved a few hundred yards when he'd spotted the stream. It wasn't deep but the small waterfall feeding it came from high in the mountains. He collected water and treated it with one of the pills he aways carried with him. He had a few supplies, and had added to them before he'd left, but they wouldn't last more than a day. He'd need to hunt for food, and although Emily enjoyed meat, she refused to kill anything. He could hear her argument buzzing in his ears.

86   D.K. HOOD

Do you want to put the stores out of business?

He'd explained that every hunting season most men in town would go and bag an elk or similar to last them through winter. It was what people did in Black Rock Falls. Her argument was that Kane had all his meat delivered from a cattle ranch. He ate only prime beef, and she believed it was the right thing to do. He tried to concentrate on anything but Emily and stared at the white cloud still blanketing the tops of the trees. It was a little better. An hour ago he couldn't risk driving it was so thick.

"Ah... Raven. Don't turn around." Emily's voice came out in a squeak.

He stared at his boots. "What?"

"I don't have a towel." She cleared her throat. "Do you have anything I can dry myself on?"

He bit back a grin. "Nope. When I'm out alone, I just let the wind dry me." He strolled to the back of the truck and opened it. He did have rolls of paper towels in a box with his camping gear and he did have a towel, but he'd used it a few times and she'd rather die than have his smell all over her. He dug out a roll of paper towels—he had three—and backing up, placed the roll on a flat rock beside the stream. "I'll leave this here. I'm going to climb up the rockpile again and call Kane. He might be able to tell me what's happening and how far the slide extends."

"What if the bear comes back?" Emily's voice quivered. "Do you really need to go right now?"

So she did need his protection. Raven shrugged. She'd been giving him a hard time all day. "You're armed. Shoot into the air and it will run away—unless it's a grizzly. You know the difference, right?" He snorted. "That's right, they don't have them in Texas, do they?"

"I know what a grizzly looks like." Emily tore off sheets of paper. "I've lived here for seven years."

Raven went to turn around and heard her squeak behind

GOOD GIRLS DON'T CRY 87

him. He stopped and kept his eyes to the front. How long would it take her to dry herself and dress? "One thing, if you refuse to eat anything I kill, we'll need to ration the supplies. It might take days to get out of the forest and we have one day's supplies and no coffee."

"I need my cup of coffee." Emily sighed. "Now I'll be grumpy all day."

He shook his head. "You'll be fine. I'll leave Ben to stand watch." He gave his dog a hand signal. Ben dropped to the ground and whined. He hated being left behind, but Raven couldn't risk taking him up the rockslide.

Striding away and heading for the pile of mangled trees, boulders, and loose soil, Raven picked his way around the edge, moving up away from the rock face. Small pebbles moved underfoot and his heart raced. One wrong step and the entire pile would slide again and bury him alive. It took ten minutes to get high enough to get a signal. The low cloud cover wasn't helping either, but eventually Kane answered. "Hey, am I glad to hear your voice."

"Everyone will be relieved you called again." Kane blew out a sigh. "Keep sending your coordinates. As soon as the cloud cover lifts, Carter will be up in the chopper. If we can't rescue you in the chopper, we'll drop down supplies. Do you need medical supplies as well?"

Balancing between two boulders, Raven shook his head. "Nope, we have them. We need food and maybe coffee? Bottled water. If we're here for a time, Emily will need clothes and towels. Me too, really, but I can manage as long as she can put up with my stink." He chuckled. "We found a small waterfall this morning and she took a cold shower and then realized we have nothing to dry on. She's currently using paper towels."

"Emily has never enjoyed camping." Kane cleared his throat. "Don't kill anything in front of her either, or she'll go ballistic."

88   D.K. HOOD

Raven's heart skipped a beat as rocks moved under his boots. "I gathered that. I could hunt. I've seen a few critters and I have all my camping gear in the truck. We'd be fine living off the land for a time if needs be, but she'd rather starve to death." He rebalanced his weight. "I hear heavy machinery, but I can't see what's happening. Do you know if the road crews are anywhere close by? I could walk out, but it would take days to get to the highway from here. I'd likely make it alone but not with Emily and carrying supplies. I don't know where the next water might be located."

"The road crews have been working since daybreak, but the slide is extensive and unstable. Move down the mountain as far as you can." In the background he could hear the team's voices. *"We'll be leaving here soon. I'll follow the road crew and see how much farther I can get toward you. I know a few old hikers' trails and I might be able to fit the Beast through. If you only need to walk a mile or so around the slide to our position, leave your truck and hike to us. We'll get the truck out later. You can always use Jenna's cruiser until we do."*

Raven let out a sigh of relief. "That sounds like a plan. We'll keep moving as long as I can fit the truck through the trees. At least no one is shooting at us right now. I'll contact you again within the hour."

"The tremors will make life difficult for a shooter. They'll also be in danger of rockfalls. He's likely gone." Kane's boots crunched through the pine needles covering the forest floor. *"Try and keep moving. The cloud cover looks set in and we can't get supplies to you just now. If it's any incentive, we have coffee and fresh food from Aunt Betty's Café."*

Chuckling, Raven shook his head. "We're leaving now."

EIGHTEEN

THE MINE

Shivering, Olivia pulled the dusty blanket around her as she sat on the stinking mattress and stared at the moss on the damp wall. Overnight, water had leaked through a small fissure high in the roof of the cave and trickled down, making large wet patches across one of the walls. The water spilled across the floor and vanished down a crack. She wished she could follow the water and escape. Two of her friends had vanished, and deep inside, she understood their fate. The weird man had murdered them. He had no conscience, no remorse, and seemed to find their predicament funny. She made up games to pass the time. In the dim light the moss resembled a map and she tried to fit countries to the shape of the green patches. She picked up a tiny speck of a leaf and allowed it to flow across the floor and vanish down the hole. Did it join an underground stream that rushed all the way to the river? Or did it keep on going down to fill a subterranean cave with stalagmites and stalactites?

No sounds came from other cells and yet Isabella and Chloe hadn't been taken away. They'd all talked until they had nothing left to say. Depression set in and hopelessness was written all over their faces. They'd both given up fighting and had accepted that they'd be murdered. Olivia had tried to talk them around, giving them hope that they'd be rescued, but after seeing what had happened to Samantha, they'd shut down completely. Olivia pushed to her feet and went to the barred window in her door. She shook the door but it wouldn't move. All that achieved was to make the spiders run around trying to get away. "Hey, you two. Why are you so quiet? Maybe we should sing or something. If anyone was searching for us, they might hear us."

"You've finally lost your mind." Chloe's pale face appeared at the window, and her eyes looked too big for her face. I'm trying to prepare myself for when that animal drags me out of here and rapes me before whatever end he has planned for me."

Olivia shook her head. "We don't know he killed our friends. He keeps his face covered and wears gloves. He doesn't want us to recognize him. He might have let them go."

"Pigs might fly." Isabella barked a cynical laugh. "You're the smart one. You must know he's killed them. He has an agenda like he's proving a point or something. He only wants females to humiliate, doesn't he? That's why he murdered the guys. Somewhere in his twisted mind he's living out a fantasy. I've watched shows about serial killers and they all have some kind of story to validate killing people. The dog barking made me do it. Every time I hear the name Jill, I want to murder someone, things like that. He's no different. I bet we're a few in a long line of girls he's murdered. It's just a game to him."

"See, we're never getting out of here alive." Chloe blew out a sigh and pushed her matted dark hair behind her ears. "None of us are strong enough to fight him. He's huge. If we could get out of here, it might be different. Three of us could run at him in the hope that one escapes but he's never going to risk it."

Olivia pursed her lips, thinking. "Maybe we can ask him if we can have a shower. He'll complain about the hot water and we can say we'll all shower together. He's a pervert. He'll likely

GOOD GIRLS DON'T CRY   91

find that interesting." She looked from one to the other. "We'd need to select our clothes beforehand so we can grab them and run. We wouldn't survive outside naked."

"You wouldn't survive outside without water either." Isabella sighed. "I'm in if you can convince him. If it doesn't work, at least we'll be clean."

A short time later, footsteps echoed through the mineshaft and the beam of a flashlight bobbed in the distance. The metal gate squeaked and the man walked in, leaving the gate open. He carried supplies and dumped them on the desk before moving his gaze across the cell doors. Heart pounding, Olivia pressed her face against the bars. He didn't like it if they spoke, so she waited. He'd usually ask them questions.

"Look at me." The man stood in the center of the cave and swiveled his head to look from one to the other. "This time you choose. I want a very cooperative girl to come with me. You must be nice to me. If you do exactly what I say, I'll leave you on the bench outside the old library." He moved his black gaze from one girl to the next and back again slowly.

Nobody said a word.

"We'll be real good if we can have a shower. We know the hot water is precious so we'll shower all together. You can choose then which one of us to take to the library." Chloe blinked at him, her eyes like an owl's.

"Ah, no." He shook his head. "That just ain't gonna happen. The one I take will have a shower after she shows me just how obedient she can be."

A shiver of mind-numbing dread slid down Olivia's spine. She cringed away as he came closer. It was plain to see, he only had one thing on his mind.

NINETEEN

GLACIAL HEIGHTS

Over the time Emily had lived in Montana, she'd never experienced the humidity of being in the mountains under heavy cloud cover. She pulled her shirt away from her sticky flesh and inhaled air thick with the scent of pine resin and wildflowers. Her stomach rumbled with hunger and she stared through the dense forest searching for an opening wide enough to get the truck through. Raven had gone ahead along a narrow animal trail. Although they had found themselves in a life-threatening situation, this part of the forest was particularly beautiful. Above her, the forest canopy created a patchwork of dappled sunlight and cast intricate patterns across the forest floor. She stared in the direction that Raven had taken, hoping to hear his footsteps returning, but all she could hear was the occasional call of a distant bird.

She returned to the truck and dragged out their backpacks. She'd listened with interest when Raven had passed on Kane's instructions to dump the truck and walk rather than starve to death in the forest. The survival packs that her father had insisted on adding when she left for the crime scene still sat untouched in the back of the truck. She opened one and

GOOD GIRLS DON'T CRY   93

glanced through the supplies. There should be enough to last them a couple of days if they were careful, but water would be a problem. This must be the reason that Raven had stuck to the rock face. The chances of finding a small stream running down the side of the mountain increased tenfold. They had containers to collect the water and pills to make it safe to drink. Although, heading into the forest, without a known water supply could be a problem.

She added water bottles to their personal backpacks and any food she could find. Like Kane, Raven consumed many energy bars during the day and she found a box of them wrapped in plastic behind his seat. She pushed them into his backpack and then stowed both packets in the seat well and the survival packs between the front seats. They would be ready to grab in an emergency. A dog barked, and she looked up to see Ben bounding out of the forest with Raven not far behind. She slid out of the truck and went to meet him. "Please tell me you found a way out of here?"

"I've found a trail to another part of the forest, but it's uncertain if it's going to do us any good. I can't see where it goes from this end. It would have been a waste of time and energy walking the mile or so to find out. I figure we should risk it. Once we move away from the signal interference from the mountain, we'll be able to use the GPS to find a way out of here."

Emily nodded. "It would be better than walking through the forest. Without a GPS signal we could be walking around in circles forever."

"That wouldn't happen. I know my way around the forest, but I don't know how far reaching the rockslide is right now." Raven opened the back door for Ben to hop inside and slid behind the wheel. "The thing is, I navigate from different points in the forest. Like the two boulders on top of each other alongside the river, or the bare space where the mudslides

94   D.K. HOOD

ripped a path. We don't know what landmarks the rockslide took out."

Emily climbed into the passenger seat. "Until they can get a chopper up, I guess we're on our own." She sighed. "Although we do know Kane and Jenna are heading in our direction." She stared out of the window. "What if the killer is the shooter? He might be stalking us."

"I'd say he hightailed it out of here at the first tremor." Raven grimaced. "No one is stupid enough to follow us with rocks slipping all around."

A sense of foreboding washed over her as they pushed the truck between trees and deep underbrush. Beside her, Raven gripped the wheel and scanned the path ahead as he navigated through the dense forest. They had traveled about three or four hundred yards, when the GPS screen lit up. Emily searched the map, trying to find an alternative route. She turned to Raven. "I believe there's an old logging road ahead. If we can find it, we might be able to get around the rockslide."

"Which way do we go?" Raven shot a glance at the screen. "Left or right at the end of this trail?"

Emily leaned forward and ran a finger across the map. She could easily follow the truck's path, but according to the map, it was just moving through the forest. The small trail that they were following wasn't there. "When we get to the end of this trail maybe I can tell you, but for now, we need to just keep going forward. According to the GPS, we're not on a road."

The truck suddenly jolted as the ground beneath them shook violently. She clung to the side of the seat as Raven fought to keep the truck on the narrow path. All around them trees swayed and bent over, threatening to break off at the roots and crash down in front of them.

"That's another tremor. Hang on, Emily." Raven leaned forward over the wheel, staring at the mountain. "We need to keep going." He accelerated. Tree branches cracked and splintered as he pushed the truck through the narrow trail.

The shaking intensified. Loose rocks and debris tumbled from the sky, bouncing off the roof of the vehicle like gunshots. Terrified, Emily gaped in horror as a large boulder smashed into the hood. The windshield shattered and glass shards flew through the air like a thousand scattered diamonds. She ducked, covering her face. "Don't stop! We need to get out of here, fast."

"I can't see." Raven stopped driving and pulled an ax from beside his seat. "Get down and cover your eyes." He swung it at the windshield, forcing a hole in the shattered glass. "Okay, put on your sunglasses or the glass will get in your eyes." Raven's jaw set with determination as he pressed down the accelerator and urged the truck forward. "Have you found the logging road yet? We can't go back now."

Cold damp air surrounded Emily and fragments of glass bounced across the hood. Trees swayed as the mountainside continued to tremble. She enlarged the map on the GPS and tried to estimate the distance between their position and the easiest way to the logging road. It was proving difficult because the map represented them as a small blue arrow in the middle of nowhere. "We are heading in the right direction but none of these old trails are listed on the GPS map. I'm just guessing if we're on the right trail or not."

As the tremors continued and the front of the truck bounced up and down, Emily swallowed her rising fear. Beside her, Raven fought to keep the track in the right direction. As he maneuvered the truck around fallen rocks, the sides of his shiny new truck scraped against the trees. The path was getting narrower and more difficult to navigate by the second. Emily lifted her gaze from the GPS and stared into the forest, trying to get her bearings. "There is a wider trail on the left. We've got no choice but to take it. This one is going nowhere."

"Okay." Tires skidded on loose gravel as Raven swerved the truck onto the trail.

Sighing with relief, Emily stared ahead as the trail opened out. It was much wider than the one they'd been on previously. The next moment, a massive boulder rolled down the hillside and crashed through the trees, leaving behind it a trail of destruction. Bracing herself against the impact, Emily cried out as the boulder hit the back of the vehicle and spun it around. The engine roared as the truck came to a sudden halt wedged between two massive rocks. When Raven slammed it into reverse, the wheels spun but it didn't move an inch.

"Dammit!" Raven smashed his palms down on the steering wheel. "We're stuck and we need to get out of here now. Grab what you can. We need to get out of the impact zone." He grabbed two of the backpacks and slung one over each shoulder before whistling to Ben to jump out of the truck.

Shaking with fear, Emily collected her backpacks and scrambled out of the truck. Underfoot, the ground vibrated as they dashed into the forest dodging falling debris. "Which way? It all looks the same to me."

"Follow me and stay close." Raven ran into the dense underbrush.

Terrified, she dashed after him. The sound of crashing rocks and trembling earth was a constant reminder of the danger. The smell of dust and freshly cut timber filled the forest as each boulder destroyed another line of trees. They kept moving and each step became a battle against the rugged terrain. Gasping for breath and arms aching from carrying two backpacks, Emily fell behind. She slowed, unable to get enough breath to call out to him, but as if sensing her missing, he stopped and turned around. She stared at him. "Wait!"

"Give me one of your backpacks." Raven put his down, shrugged one onto his back, one on his front, and slung the other over one shoulder. "Try and keep moving."

GOOD GIRLS DON'T CRY   97

At that moment, the tremors slowed. Emily stared all around, conscious of the eerie stillness in their wake. So quiet. It was as if they were the only people alive on earth. "Is it over?"

"I sure hope so." Raven pulled out his phone and checked the signal. "Okay, I have the GPS screen. We're not far from the old mining road. We keep moving." He stared at the sky and then smiled. "The mist is clearing. We can get a ride out of here. The mining road will be far enough from the rock face to fly a chopper." He scrolled on the screen and made a call. "Kane, we've found an old mining road. I'll send the coordinates. My truck is wrecked. It was smashed by a boulder. I hope it's insured."

"It's all good." Kane sounded relieved. "I'll call Carter and then head back to town. We'll get there within the hour. There are flares in the survival pack. Set one off when you hear us coming. Is anyone injured? Any sign of the shooter?"

"No, and we're both fine." Raven frowned and looked at his dog. "We'll need a harness for Ben. Do you have one available?" He cleared his throat. "He's heavy and it's too risky to try and hold him in the wind gusts."

"Carter has one in his FBI chopper for his dog. It will be fine." The engine of Kane's truck roared in the background. "We're back on the highway now. Brief Em on the rescue protocol. I figure I'll come down for her and you can come up with Ben. He'll feel safer with you."

"That works for me." Raven pushed a lock of hair from his forehead and smiled at Emily. "We'll see you soon." He disconnected.

A slight tremor bounced the ground under Emily's feet and she gasped. She grabbed Raven's arm and moved closer. When he gave her a long silent stare, she cleared her throat. "Sorry."

"Don't be." He indicated ahead. "This way, let's keep moving." He turned to look at her. "Don't worry, I'll keep you safe."

Emily hurried to keep up. In that second, the attraction Jenna had for Kane was explained. Jenna had always complained that Kane was overprotective but she married him anyway. Of course, she'd always had her dad to protect her, but this was different. She stared at Raven's wide back and sure steps through the forest. In all this time, she'd never seen him scared. He'd been strong when she'd fallen to bits. She blinked. *Oh, get a grip, now you're suffering from hero worship. This guy is way out of my league. Stop acting like a dizzy female.*

She followed, stepping in his footprints. They wound through dense forest and sidestepped fallen rocks. The next moment, a ripping sound slashed through the silence. The ground under Emily's feet bounced and trees swayed and groaned. Terrified, she cried out. Ben barked and Raven swung around, clasped her by the waist, and dived to one side. As they fell, Emily gaped in horror as, in a roar, the path split into a wide chasm so fast she didn't have time to react. Raven held her tight and Ben was rolling over. They all tumbled out of control into the screaming forest. She clung to him as the mountain tore apart right in front of her eyes.

TWENTY

THE MINE

Isabella so wanted to get away. All she could think about was her mom and dad. Her little sister would be missing her so much and she'd promised to help her buy a dress for her birthday. She needed to go home. There was nothing else left for her. Her boyfriend had died in the limo along with the others. The murderer was playing a cruel game with them. It didn't take a genius to understand him, really. He'd threaten her and hurt her and then he'd let her go. If he hadn't planned to set them all free, he wouldn't have covered his face. Olivia was correct, but if the others had been set free, why were they all still locked in the cells? Unless he blindfolded them and they'd have no idea where he'd taken them. She moved to the front of the cell and stared at him. His smug posture made her want to spew. How could she give herself willingly to this animal? Her little sister's face loomed across her mind again and she cleared her throat. "I'll do whatever you say as long as you promise to set me free."

"I promise, you'll be sitting outside the old library tonight as soon as it gets dark." He moved closer to the cell, his breath ragged. "The old library, the one that blew up a few years ago out near the Triple Z Bar. You'd be able to walk to the roadhouse and call your mom. The deal is, if anyone asks, you say you don't remember anything."

Confused, Isabella stared at him. "How would you know if I keep my word?"

"I know where you live. I was in the limo when we dropped by to collect you." He moved so close she could smell his rank sweat. "Say one word and I'll break into your house and slit your parents' and little sister's throats." His chuckle was low and menacing. "Yeah, I know about your little sister. I know everything about all of you." He moved closer. "Do we have a deal?"

Terrified and knees trembling, Isabella nodded and waited for him to open the door. She cringed when he chained her to the wall, took out a knife, and sliced off her clothes. Unable to stop shaking, she closed her eyes tight. She couldn't look at him. He'd become violent when the others screamed, as if it excited him. Her teeth chattered and goosebumps rose on her flesh. She could survive this—she must. Biting down hard on her bottom lip, she turned her head away. *I'll never scream.*

TWENTY-ONE

Wolfe pulled on gloves and covered his face with a mask. He stepped into the examination room. Webber had prepared the victim for the autopsy and everything he needed had been laid out on silver trays. Cold fluorescent lights cast an unearthly glow on the body lying on the stainless steel table. It should be clinical and yet it never was for him and never had been. Even though the air around him was heavy with the familiar scent of antiseptic that never completely covered the smell of death, he'd learned to deal with it—and did without a problem. He'd never become accustomed to the sight of a young girl whose life had been taken so viciously. He needed to get the evidence to bring her killer to trial and spent the next half an hour collecting samples from under her nails, feet, and various places on her skin. He combed her hair. Even dust particles could be useful in determining where she'd been since she left the limo. Any trace evidence he could find could be valuable.

The preliminary examination of a victim prior to the full autopsy was often long and tedious but it revealed so many important facts in a murder case. He pulled down the microphone to make notes as he went along. He'd noticed bruising on

102   D.K. HOOD

her wrists and on the inside of her thighs. He took photographs of each of the bruises from different angles and then cursed under his breath when he discovered she had been sexually assaulted. He collected swabs and went over her body with a magnifying glass to check for any pubic hairs left by her attacker. He found nothing.

He turned the body over to examine the wound in her back. On arrival he'd used epifluorescence microscopy to take images of the sharp forced trauma to determine what arrow caused the injury. He'd leave the full autopsy until he had the results needed for comparison. The information about the type of arrows used in the previous murders had never been released, so only the killer would know which brand of arrow he used. From the information that Rowley, a keen crossbow hunter, had given him, most bow hunters had a particular favorite and he could use this information to identify the killer. He'd sent Webber to purchase the arrows that Rowley suggested, along with a side of pork to test them. Every weapon used usually left a signature behind and it was no different with arrowheads. Each wound would be microscopically examined in the same way and compared to determine the exact arrowhead used to kill the girl.

From the moment he'd arrived on scene, the murder had brought back memories of a previous case. Jenna had recognized the MO as well. He went to his files and pulled the images from the previous case and went back to look at the body with interest. He glanced back and forth from victim to screen. There was no doubt in his mind that in front of him was a copycat kill of James Earl Stafford, a notorious serial killer. The case they dealt with previously had also been a copycat killer of this famous murderer. Jenna and Jo Wells had gone to the prison to interview him but he hadn't been very forthcoming, but they had caught the killer. Although it was impossible for this murder to be attributed to him. The copper pennies placed on the eyelids were Stafford's signature, as was this method of

GOOD GIRLS DON'T CRY 103

murder. He compared the wounds made from the arrows, placing them side by side on the big screen and then superimposing one over the other. As he suspected, none of the previous cases involving arrows matched this one. This copycat had no knowledge of the arrows used, which made this case unique. He sighed and covered the body with a sheet. He had little doubt that the victim's name was Samantha Haimes. Her face hadn't been damaged and he would forgo a DNA match if one of her parents were willing to identify the body.

Trying to keep busy and convince himself that Emily would be in Raven's safe hands, Wolfe went back to his files. Having no remains to examine for the first victim, he compared the writing on the torso of the dismembered remains with the same message he found on Samantha. They appeared to be identical from the photographs Emily had uploaded onto the server—the writing being the only evidence that connected the two murders —but he had no doubt the way the *T* on the "not mine" message was angled down, making it resemble an *X,* was a match. The first murder was another copycat and resembled the same MO of a serial killer who decorated trees with frozen body parts during winter. Apart from the message, there was nothing else to link these two murders. In both previous cases Jenna had solved the crimes. It should be case closed. He removed his gloves and mask, tossed them into the garbage, and then headed to his office. Jenna had asked Jo Wells, the FBI behavioral analyst, for assistance, and knowing Jo, she would have the answers they needed. He made the call and she picked up right away. "Hey, Jo. How are things in Snakeskin Gully?"

"It's quiet here without Carter." Jo sighed. *"I'm guessing you're calling about the recent cases in Black Rock Falls?"*

Wolfe put his phone on speaker, went to the coffee machine, and pushed in a pod. "I am. I've just finished my preliminary examination of the second female victim. It's tragic. Raped and then shot in the back by what I believe is an arrow.

It's a copycat for sure and so is the first victim, from what I can tell without a body, but Em did a fine job making notes and taking images. She took swabs as well. When we can rescue her from the mountain, I'll know more, but the messages carved into the torsos are identical."

"Since Jenna contacted me for my opinion, I've looked over the old case files and I agree with you this is definitely copycat murders. The message 'not mine' would make me believe that he intends to leave a body with 'mine' written on it."

Wolfe stirred sugar and cream into his coffee and frowned. "How so?"

"There is only one explanation, Shane, and that is one of the victims who was attributed to another killer over the last few years or so was his." She blew out a long breath. *"This is the thing with serial killers: they like to own their kills. In fact, they don't suffer remorse. They're proud of them. If they're attributed to somebody else, I'd say they'd want to put things right. I would be looking at any violent criminals who have been let out of prison recently. They might not have been imprisoned for attacking someone, but for some reason, they were unable to put this misconception right. He may have done this type of murder previously in a different state, for instance. If he's been away for a long time, it could have happened way before Jenna took office. Maybe he'd just got out of prison, committed his first murder, and then been arrested for something else. Maybe seeing his murder triggered the guy who you arrested. In all likelihood, he committed the others. It's a very unusual situation, but I don't believe his focus is on Jenna. I figure it's on you."*

A cold shiver went down Wolfe's spine. "Me? Why on earth would he blame me?" He thought for a beat and then ran a hand down his face. "I do recall there was very little evidence in both the cases, but I meticulously check every detail before I make a decision. For instance, the second killer couldn't possibly know what arrowheads the first killer used. I've proved the arrowheads are different."

"It seems he's sticking close to the original murders." The chair squeaked as she slid it across the floor in a familiar sound. *"I figure he is taking his information from the newspapers or internet. But I can tell you one thing: he's trying to prove a point. He won't leave any evidence for you to follow. You didn't catch him the first time, so he's well aware of forensics. The problem is, how many girls will he murder before he informs you which one is his?"*

Wolfe leaned against the counter and sipped his coffee. "I have faith in our team. Every killer makes a mistake sooner or later and it won't slip by Jenna or Kane."

TWENTY-TWO

As they made their way back to town, Jenna made all the calls necessary to get the chopper into the air as soon as possible. She listened with interest as Wolfe brought her up to date with what Jo had told him about the killer. It made a lot of sense. "These monsters have been trying to outwit us for years and we still get them in the end. I wouldn't worry too much about it. You don't make mistakes. We've all discussed the previous cases and none of the killers who we've sent to prison have ever mentioned that one of the kills wasn't theirs. As their egos are so big, you would imagine they would kick up a stink if we tried to convict them of a murder they didn't commit." She pushed hair from her face. "Once we have Raven and Emily safe, I'll go back through my files and check on any recent releases from prisons throughout Montana. I'll also see if I can discover any similar cases to ones that we've been involved in in Black Rock Falls." She chewed on her bottom lip. "Rio is working on a list of possible suspects, and we'll talk again to the parents of the kids in the limo. Someone must have seen a second person in the vehicle or noticed something wasn't right with the driver.

"Don't worry too much. I'll get to the bottom of it." Wolfe's

GOOD GIRLS DON'T CRY   107

chair creaked as he moved. *"Carter is doing the final preflight check. We'll be ready to head out the moment Kane arrives."*

"We're five minutes away." Kane accelerated along Stanton. "You should be able to hear us by now."

"Copy that." Wolfe disconnected.

Wanting time to move faster and see the chopper in the air, Jenna flipped a glance at Kane. "I'll call Rowley to give me a ride to Glacial Heights Ski Resort. I should be able to watch the rescue mission from there."

"I've no reason to believe the shooter has left the area, Jenna." Kane frowned at her. "I'm not sure if that's a good idea."

Determined to be there for Emily, Jenna waved away his concern. "We've no reason to believe the shooter is involved with the murder. They could easily have been stray shots from the other side of the resort."

"With a scope rifle?" Kane frowned. "No way, and hunting season is over until fall. I doubt the killer is hanging around shooting at people, but this means we might have another crazy in the mountains." He drove around back of the morgue and stared at her. "Do you really want to take the risk?"

Unease crept over Jenna. She had more concern a sniper would shoot at him and the others during the rescue, but she bit her tongue. His job would be hard enough without worrying about a shooter taking potshots at him. She shook her head. "I doubt a shooter would be up there during the tremors and rock-slides. No one would be that stupid. In any case, Raven said that after the initial shooting, they haven't experienced any problems. I figure we can safely say that the shooter has left the area." She returned the glare Kane gave her. "I'll wear a Kevlar vest and my riot helmet. I'll watch from the vehicle, so you won't need to worry about me. Rowley's truck has tinted windows. If there is a shooter, they won't even know I'm inside."

"Tell him to take the Beast." Kane shrugged. "I trust him to drive it and I know the Beast will keep you safe—if you remain inside." He wiggled his eyebrows at her. "It doesn't have a force field—yet."

Jenna took in his expression. He'd tried to appear amused but hadn't hidden the worry in his eyes. She didn't want him going on a dangerous mission worrying about her safety. "I'm sorry I'm causing you so much concern, Dave." She squeezed his arm. "It wasn't my intention to be so stubborn. I promise to take due care and I can assure you Rowley is used to pregnant women. Sandy is six months along now. He'll make sure I'm okay."

"Yeah, but his wife takes things easy." Kane hunched his shoulders. "I'm married to a superhero."

They met Wolfe and Carter gearing up in the hallway outside Wolfe's office. Jenna nodded to them and then pulled out her phone to call Rowley. He picked up right away. "Hey, Jake, can you come to Wolfe's office? I need you to give me a ride to the ski resort. Well, actually, I need you to drive the Beast to the ski resort. I want to observe the rescue mission and Dave is concerned about a possible shooter in the area."

"I've never driven the new one." Rowley sounded apprehensive. *"Kane actually nominated me to drive it?"*

Jenna laughed. "Yeah, he said he trusted you. Just hang on a minute." She walked to Kane. "Any instructions for Jake?"

"Hey, Jake, it drives like a dream. Don't stress, you'll be fine. It's bombproof, so as long as you don't drive off the side of the mountain, you should be fine. Just try and keep Jenna inside the vehicle."

"There's one piece of advice I can give you." Rowley sucked in a deep breath. *"It's best not to argue with your wife when she's close to delivery. Trust me, it never ends well."*

"I'll keep that in mind." Kane raised both eyebrows at Jenna. "I don't believe Jenna has any intention of arguing. We're good. I'll see you back at the morgue when we're through here."

"Okay. I'm on my way." Rowley disconnected.

GOOD GIRLS DON'T CRY   109

Keeping it casual, Jenna smiled at Kane. "I'll go and grab a Thermos of coffee, then wait for Rowley. I'll see you when you get back." She went on tiptoes to kiss him. "Have fun."

"I will." Kane shot her a brilliant smile.

"We'll get the gear stowed in the chopper." Carter looked at Jenna. "I'm leaving Zorro in Wolfe's office. Would you mind leaving Duke with him? Zorro stresses when I leave him behind."

Jenna nodded. "Sure, he likes the treats Wolfe leaves for them." She patted her thigh. "Come on, Duke." She headed for the office.

By the time she'd filled the Thermos with coffee, Rowley had arrived. She handed him her set of keys and then followed him out to the Beast. "They'll probably beat us to the ski resort, although they won't be leaving for another ten minutes or so." She noticed Rowley's white-knuckle grip on the steering wheel. "Just pretend it's your truck. I know you see Dave as overprotective with his belongings, but when anything happened to the old Beast, he fixed it in a couple of days. It's fully insured, so just drive and forget all about who owns it."

"That's easy for you to say, Jenna." Rowley hunched his shoulders. "I figure if I do something wrong, this truck will yell at me. It's got so many gizmos and gadgets it's like driving an aircraft."

Biting back a grin, Jenna nodded, understanding his concerns. "Trust me, if I could fit behind the wheel, I would drive myself. I'll honestly be glad when this is all over. These last few weeks have been a nightmare."

"Yeah, but the moment you see the baby you'll want to start another one right away." Rowley grinned at her. "I figured when Sandy had the twins she wouldn't want any more kids, but by the time they started walking, she was already talking about having more. I've always wanted a big family and getting the substantial raise you gave me last year made it possible. Kids are expensive and we don't want them to go without anything they need."

As Jenna glanced at the multitude of rocks piled up along the guardrails to the highway, she nodded. "Well, last year I made an agreement with the mayor that everyone in my department will receive a cost of living raise each year. The motion was passed at a council meeting, so even if I'm not voted in as sheriff next term, it is set in concrete. Plus, the overtime rate has increased, so always put in for overtime and expenses. I have a very generous budget to cover everything."

"That's good to know." Rowley smiled at her. "Are you concerned about the rescue mission?"

Shrugging, Jenna looked at him. "I don't want to be, but the idea of seeing my husband hanging over the side of a mountain in high winds trying to rescue Emily makes me want to puke." She shot a glance at him. "But Dave must never know that. I don't want to be his Achilles heel and he loves doing anything risky, believe it or not."

"I wouldn't worry too much. He sure knows what he's doing." Rowley accelerated along the mountain road. "I'll never forget when he rescued me. It was like, 'Hi there, Jake, wanna ride in a chopper?' Man, I was terrified, but he kept me safe and talked to me all the way. He's so cool."

Relaxing a little, Jenna leaned back in her seat as the wind buffeted the Beast. Alongside the highway, trees bent and turned as the wind changed direction. Her stomach twisted. No matter how confident Kane was acting, this rescue mission was going to be life-threatening.

As they climbed the mountain, Jenna scanned the horizon for the chopper. Moments later, Rowley drove into the parking lot at the ski resort and turned the Beast to face the rugged, unforgiving mountain terrain. Fierce winds battered the surrounding forest, lifting dust in the parking lot and swirling it into will-o'-the-wisps that danced in front of the truck. She

GOOD GIRLS DON'T CRY 111

made out the chopper circling in the distance, swaying precariously in the howling wind as it moved closer to the jagged mountain peaks. Heart pounding, Jenna gripped the edge of the seat, her gaze fixed on the small figure dangling from the chopper and descending fast.

She had seen Kane rappel from a chopper before and it never ceased to amaze her the speed at which he seemingly slid down the rope. She pulled field glasses from the glove box to get a better view. Her stomach dropped as the chopper lurched and shuddered as it fought against the relentless gusts of wind. Her breath caught with every dip and sway as her gaze fixed on Kane. His muscles bulged as he let out the rope and yet his face appeared almost serene. A human pendulum, he twisted and turned as he fought against fierce gusts threatening to smash him into the jagged rocks. The descent had only taken seconds and Jenna sighed with relief when he dropped below the tree line and she lost sight of him. "He's down."

"He'll bring Emily up first." Rowley was peering through his own field glasses. "I'd say then they'll send down the ropes for Raven and Ben. Raven would have done this a hundred times, same with the dog."

The chopper swayed and turned, buffeted by the relentless gusts. She could see Wolfe standing by the open door, his hair whipping around in the wind. His expression was grim. Seeing Wolfe worried when Kane was involved in anything concerned Jenna. She gripped the field glasses tightly and then noticed the dark clouds rolling across the sky toward them. She figured Wolfe had seen them too. Now they had minutes to get everyone to safety. "The weather is changing. Carter won't be able to hold the chopper in that position for much longer. He's drifting closer to the rock face with every gust of wind."

TWENTY-THREE

Enjoying the spectacular view from the chopper, with the wild swinging and turning all the way down to the ground, Kane frowned when Wolfe's voice came through his headset. He glanced up and noticed the sudden change in the weather. Knowing how thorough Carter was about everything surrounding a mission, this sudden change had not been in his weather report. The unexpected weather events had become more frequent of late and added another level of danger to the high winds. As Kane hit the forest floor, he looked at Emily's sheet-white face as she leaned against Raven. He nodded to himself. Raven would have explained the procedure but it hadn't allayed her fears. She trusted him. Maybe he should ask him to escort her to the chopper? She'd watched his descent, and from her expression, wasn't thrilled about being hauled up into the wind. He smiled to give her confidence. "Are you happy with coming with me or do you want to go with Raven? I can take Ben."

"I'm not happy going with either of you." Emily winced. "Don't take it personal. I'm scared to death."

"I won't, but we need to move fast, Em." He unclipped a

GOOD GIRLS DON'T CRY   113

harness and helped her climb into it. "Do you have the evidence you collected in your backpack, the images and samples?"

"Yeah." Emily looked up at the chopper high in the sky and shuddered. "Is my dad up there?"

Kane nodded. "He's sitting on the edge of the door. He'll grab you and so will I. You'll be very safe. Come here and I'll attach your harness to mine. Hold on to my straps and I'll wrap my legs around you. You can't possibly fall. Okay?"

"No, not really." Emily trembled so much her teeth chattered. "I'm terrified and I'll probably scream like an idiot."

Trying not to laugh, Kane rubbed her back, like he did Duke's when his dog was frightened of the storms. "It's a maybe once-in-a-lifetime experience. Keep your eyes open and look at the scenery. Think about it as a ride at a fairground. People would pay a fortune to do what we're going to do." He looked into her scared eyes. "I love doing this. I'm never scared because I know my team will keep me safe. Take deep breaths and enjoy the ride. It will leave you wanting more."

Unclipping two harnesses and handing them to Raven, Kane indicated to the sky. "There's a storm on the way. Be ready to move as soon as I send down the rope. If it's too windy to get you into the chopper, we'll drop you into the ski resort parking lot. Jenna is there with Rowley." He frowned. "I'm assuming you've done this before?"

"Too many times." Raven took the harnesses. "This is like the old days without the gunfire."

Tapping his mic, Kane gave Raven a nod. He put his arm around Emily. "Okay, Shane, haul us up."

"Wait! Wait!" Emily's heart thundered against Kane's chest. "I can't do this."

"Yes, you can." Raven moved close to her. "You trust Dave, don't you? You trust me?"

"Yeah." Emily bit her bottom lip as they lifted from the ground. "I guess."

114   D.K. HOOD

They rose higher and Kane wrapped his legs around her as they reached the tree line. "Look, you can see the falls and the rivers. Soon you'll be able to see the town."

A gust of wind made the chopper sway and they went into a wide arc swinging across the treetops. On one side they swung so close to the rock face Kane dropped his legs to propel them away. Against him, Emily screamed and buried her face in his chest. The wind whistled around them, tearing at their clothes. He wrapped his legs around her again and raised his voice to be heard. "It's okay, just the wind. Carter has everything under control. Not far to go now. You've been on a swing as a kid, right? Talk to me, Em."

Lightning cracked and Emily gasped. Her trembling had become shudders and Kane glanced up. The chopper was still some distance above them. Carter had risen higher to keep them away from the rock face. "Emily, open your eyes. Look at the scenery. We're almost there. Isn't it a lovely view from up here?"

"You can stick your view where the sun don't shine." Emily screwed her eyes shut. "I'm never getting into a harness like this ever again."

Kane laughed. "Now that's the Em I know. I've seen you face serial killers and this little ride scares you? Come on now. As an ME, you'll be expected to do this all the time."

"I might change my mind about being a ME, after all." She lifted her chin to look at him and scowled. "No one told me I needed to be swinging over a ravine to become a medical examiner."

Glad he had her talking, Kane shrugged. "Your dad has dropped into crime scenes many times, or dropped me. After this, you'll be able to do anything. This is a rough ride. It's not always so bad. Next time, maybe you can try alone."

"No way." Emily shot him a look of horror. "You wouldn't expect me to do this alone, would you?"

"Not for a while, no. I'll teach you, or Raven will, to learn to

GOOD GIRLS DON'T CRY   115

rappel from a chopper. You start from a short distance and then work up to it. It's fun. You'll enjoy it once you start trusting your team." The noise from the chopper's engine made it hard to hear her reply, but in his ear Wolfe came through loud and clear.

"I see this wasn't easy. I know that look." Wolfe chuckled. *"We'll get her inside first."*

Kane unlocked his legs. "Turn around, your dad is right there. Grab his hands and I'll push you inside the chopper." He unclipped her and she slid away from him.

Her words carried away on the wind, but Kane grabbed her and thrust her inside the chopper. Wolfe had her harness clipped to the D ring in seconds and gave him the thumbs-up. Kane pulled himself inside and clipped on before unhitching his harness from the fast rope and sending it back down for Raven.

Thunder rolled and lightning cracked across the darkening sky. The wind had increased and Carter was fighting the sudden updrafts. Kane dropped into a seat beside him and tapped his com. "You won't get Raven and the dog up before the storm hits. I suggest you lift him to the ski resort parking lot, where Jenna is with Rowley. I've told him we might do that and he's cool with it. He's military."

"Yeah, so I hear." Carter took the chopper around in a circle. *"Okay, let's try and get lower and do the pickup. This darn wind is pushing me into the mountainside. It's gonna be a rough ride."* He glanced at the sky. *"I figure we have ten minutes max and then we need to get out of Dodge."*

"Everything is ready." Wolfe came through Kane's com. *"I'm lowering the fast rope now."*

Behind him Emily, still sheet white, was gripping the back of his seat. He stood to assist Wolfe and patted her on the shoulder. "Not long now and we'll be home."

116   D.K. HOOD

"I hope so." Emily's voice squeaked through his earpiece. Poor kid had screamed herself hoarse.

Impressed by the speed in which Raven had clipped Ben and himself onto the rope, Kane indicated with a twirling hand signal for Wolfe to winch them up. Through his com, Carter's voice for once sounded anxious.

"I'm taking too much drift. We'll need to go to plan B." He turned the chopper and headed toward one of the ski slopes, lifting Raven and Ben above the treetops and then lowering them.

Moments later they hovered above the parking lot, and with care, Wolfe lowered them to the ground. The window of the Beast buzzed down and Jenna waved to Kane. He waved back and then they waited for Raven and Ben to climb into the Beast before heading back to the ME's roof. As they rose into the sky, the storm hit like a hurricane, tossing them around. The chopper dipped and rose again as Carter fought the controls. Lightning cracked so close the hairs on his arms rose and Emily let out a frightened cry. Rain came in a curtain, blocking out visibility and hitting the windshield of the chopper like buckshot. As the wipers fought against the deluge, everyone fell silent. Kane flicked a glance at Carter, whose face was a mask of concentration as they rode the wind gusts on a roller-coaster ride into Black Rock Falls. The rooftop of the ME's office was barely visible in the torrential rain and Kane breathed a sigh of relief as Carter finally dropped the chopper onto the pad. He jumped out with Wolfe to secure the rails. By the time they dashed into the building everyone was soaked through to the skin. As they walked along the passageway, Kane shook rain from his hair and grinned at Carter. "That was a fun ride."

"Yeah." Carter gave him a lopsided smile, pushed a lock of dripping hair from his face, and punched him in the arm. "Maybe we'll do it again some time."

TWENTY-FOUR

Annoyed, Jenna pushed her phone against her ear. She could never understand why the mayor always needed convincing when she required something immediately. "Deputy Raven's vehicle is covered by insurance and there is absolutely no reason why they shouldn't replace it with a new truck immediately. I have all the paperwork for the insurance including photographs ready and I need a new truck today. I've three active deputies and myself and three vehicles. Deputy Kane has been driving his own vehicle since he arrived here. During this time, we've never claimed for one cent in expenses."

"Very well, if the dealership in town has a new truck that is suitable, you can go ahead and purchase it. Tell them to send the invoice to my office and address it to me personally so I can deal with it right away." The mayor cleared his throat, and in the background she could hear him typing on his computer. "What about lights and sirens and the decals?"

Considering the sheriff's logo would be of little consequence when she needed to move her deputies around during a murder case, Jenna huffed out a sigh. "I can order magnets. They make them up in any decal required and they just attach

118   D.K. HOOD

to the side of the vehicle. It's the quickest and easiest way to get things done in a hurry. I'll make sure it has all the specified decals." She glanced at Rowley. "My deputies are quite capable of fitting lights and sirens to a truck. My husband fitted his and it only took him a short while. We could probably get them delivered overnight, but in the meantime, I would be able to move my deputies around during this murder case. You do realize that we have someone running around Black Rock Falls who has murdered at least seven teenagers?"

"Yes, I'm aware. Get whatever you need and send the bill to me." The mayor disconnected.

Blowing out a relieved breath, Jenna stared at her screen for a few seconds and then turned to Rowley. "Stop at the dealership in town. We need to get a new truck today. Let's hope they have something ready to go."

She took very little time in the dealership. On the lot they had a brand-new Ford Expedition SSV. She took Rowley and Raven's advice that the vehicle was perfect for their needs. She signed all the necessary paperwork, and the manager insisted he could have the SUV ready to drive away by five that afternoon. She glanced at Raven when they climbed back into the Beast. "Speak to Dave when you get a chance. He'll know where to get the lights and sirens. We'll have you ready to go ASAP. Any gear you left in the vehicle, you can grab from our storage at the office. Just take whatever you need and give a list to Maggie so she can restock."

"I've never seen anyone get things done as fast as you do, Jenna." Raven grinned at her from the back seat.

Shrugging, Jenna turned to look at him. "Material things are easy. It's suspects I need right now. I hope Rio has come up with a list of possibles while we've been busy."

"He was working on it when I left." Rowley pulled the Beast to a halt outside the back door to the morgue.

Inside Wolfe's office, she found Kane, Carter, Wolfe, and

GOOD GIRLS DON'T CRY 119

Emily sitting around the desk wearing scrubs. At the counter, Norrell was handing out cups of coffee and smiled at her when she arrived. The room smelled of shampoo and Kane's hair had a seal-black sheen as if he'd just stepped from the shower and Carter looked like a drowned rat. "How did you all get so wet?"

"We needed to anchor the chopper to the roof." Kane shrugged and took a cup of coffee from Norrell. "The weather was kinda crazy up there." He stood, handed Jenna his cup, and offered her his seat before grabbing another chair and sliding it beside her.

"Sorry about the crazy ride." Carter looked at Raven and held out his knuckles to Ben. "The wind was doing its best to smash us into the rock face, so I had no option but to go up the ski slope to keep you out of danger."

"I enjoyed it and so did Ben. He doesn't get upset easily unless I order him to attack." Raven took a chair from a stack in the corner and handed one to Rowley before taking another for himself.

"I'm glad you're here, Jenna." Norrell continued to hand coffee to everyone in the room and then dropped a glass container filled with homemade cookies on the desk. "I can bring you up to date with what I've been doing, since the bodies of the young men were brought into the morgue."

Relieved that someone was working on the case in her absence, Jenna smiled at her. "I would appreciate any information you can give us. We're flying blind at the moment."

"Okay, I can give you a basic rundown of what I discovered and I will upload all the files onto the server once they're complete." Norrell picked up her tablet from the counter and then looked at Jenna. "Oh, and another thing, I've asked Rio to contact the next of kin and arrange for them to come in to identify the male bodies. I've photo-matched each victim, and we can take it from there. If there's any doubt, we'll take DNA swabs, but as the victims were found reasonably early, they sustained no damage to their faces. I'm sure the parents will be able to give positive IDs. I'm starting the identifications later this afternoon. Emily has offered to assist."

A pang of regret gripped Jenna. The parents must be going through misery right now. She squeezed Norrell's arm. "That's good to know. Thank you, I appreciate it."

"Okay, moving right along, apart from the victim with the gunshot wound, which Wolfe will be working on later this afternoon, I've examined the remaining victims and observed the same findings on each of them." Norrell scanned her tablet. "They all exhibited pulmonary edema, which in layman's terms is fluid in the lungs. They had water in the sinuses and stomach, which indicates they were submerged while alive, and I found fluid in the pleural cavity around the lungs. I've taken samples of the fluid and we can match that to the river water. Wolfe took a sample from the river on scene. There is absolutely no doubt, in my opinion, that the boys were hogtied before being submerged in the vehicle and, in layman's terms, drowned. Homicide by asphyxiation in water by person or persons unknown will be my finding."

"I've looked over Norrell's findings and I agree." Wolfe sipped his coffee and sighed. "This is a heinous crime. I did do a preliminary examination of the gunshot victim, and there is an exit wound, so there's a good chance the bullet is embedded in the vehicle. It might be one piece of evidence you can link to the murder—if it's possible to retrieve it. I'll conduct the autopsy on that young man this afternoon. Most likely after he's been identified."

To Jenna's surprise, Emily stood up. Her face was pale and drawn. She adjusted the blanket draped around her shoulders. "The dissected victim hanging in the tree near the ski resort, I estimate was in her late teens. I collected swabs from inside the mouth, took hair samples, and as many swabs from other areas as I had time for before someone started shooting at us. I do

GOOD GIRLS DON'T CRY   121

have photographs and a video of the scene, so we will have a good chance of identifying the body. There was also a message left on the torso that said, 'not mine.' It is the same message found on the girl discovered with the copper pennies on her eyes, and yet the MO is completely different." She swayed a little and sat down suddenly in the chair. "I'm sorry, I seem to be a little dizzy."

"You're in shock." Wolfe pushed a cup toward her and the cookies. "Keep warm, drink your coffee, and eat a few cookies and you'll start to feel a little better. You've been through a traumatic experience, or should I say traumatic experiences, over the last twenty-four hours or so. Don't worry about the case for now. I have Webber running all your samples and he already collected DNA from the mothers of the missing kids just in case we need to search for a match. I'll drive you home once we're through here so you can get some sleep."

"Okay." Emily turned to Jenna. "I'm sorry. I don't usually fall to pieces, but Raven did body-slam me to the ground when the shooting started. I've probably got a concussion."

"Lucky I did or that bullet would have gone straight through your skull." Raven raised both eyebrows. "It wasn't a body slam or you wouldn't have gotten up. Did you really expect me to just watch you get shot? You had a red spot on you."

"Okay, you two, that's enough." Wolfe nodded to Raven. "I appreciate you protecting her."

"I can take care of myself." Emily's eyes flashed with anger. "I don't need a babysitter, Dad."

"Well, obviously you did." Wolfe returned her glare. "Or we'd have been hauling you out in a body bag."

Needing to defuse the situation, Jenna leaned forward. She'd always admired Emily's strength in any situation. "How you managed to keep it together under so much pressure I have no idea. If a grisly crime scene, rockslides, and someone shooting at you isn't bad enough, then Dave hauled you up to a chopper in high winds with a storm coming. I'm not surprised you're in shock. I figure if that happened to me, I'd be hiding under the bed for the rest of the year." She smiled at her. "I'm so proud to have you on my team, Em." She swung her gaze to Raven, who looked just fine. Nothing seemed to faze him. "Are you okay, Raven? I should have asked earlier, I apologize."

"I was a little upset about losing my truck but that new one is mighty fine." Raven grinned at her. "The other stuff, well, I'm used to it—living in the mountains, things happen. Not crime scenes per se, but I've seen plenty of dead bodies in my lifetime, and once you're under fire in battle, how to survive becomes an instinct." He glanced at Kane. "I'm like Dave when it comes to heights, nothing worries me. I don't scare easy. I actually enjoyed the ride up the mountain, it was crazy good." He rubbed Ben's ears. "Ben liked it too."

Needing to get back on the case, Jenna pushed slowly to her feet. Her back ached and her swollen ankles made her boots too tight. "Okay. Thanks for the updates. I need to get back to the office." She looked at Kane and Carter. "Grab your wet clothes. We'll wash and dry them back at the office. Best investment the mayor ever made was installing a washer and dryer in the locker rooms. How many times have we gotten back to the office soaked through or covered in blood?"

"Too many times." Kane picked up a plastic garbage bag and whistled to Duke, who was asleep in the basket, with Zorro dozing on the carpet beside him.

"I'll ride back with Rowley." Raven smiled at Kane. "It's been a long time since I watched someone rappel down a slide rope so fast. Not since my last mission."

"Practice makes perfect." Kane took Jenna's hand and they headed for the door.

As they reached the Beast, she looked at him and lowered her voice to a whisper. "Do you figure he recognizes you?"

GOOD GIRLS DON'T CRY   123

"Nope." Kane frowned as Carter followed them outside. "Just fishing, is all."

Jenna dragged herself into the passenger seat. Raven had known Kane. They'd spent over a week escaping the enemy after Raven's chopper was shot down during a military mission. That was before Kane had plastic surgery and changed his name. She looked at him. "Would it be a problem if he did, do you think?"

"Nope." Kane slid in behind the wheel. "He's solid. I'd trust him with my life."

Jenna shook her head in dismay. "I hope you're right."

TWENTY-FIVE

Once they arrived at the office, Jenna had everyone meet up in the conference room. She asked Maggie to send out for pizza as it was obvious the cookies hadn't touched the sides of Kane's stomach. She could hear him rumbling like a teddy bear all the way back from Wolfe's office. Inside the conference room, Rio had set up the whiteboard and was making additions. He already had a list of all the male victims they'd recovered from the limo and a second list of the missing girls, with photographs. On the opposite side of the board, he had an image of Samantha Haimes and the crime scene photos of the female victim with the copper pennies on her eyes. It was blatantly obvious who the victim was, and Jenna's stomach dropped at the sight of the poor girl. She could only imagine how difficult it would be for her parents to identify her body later in the afternoon. She smiled at Rio when he turned away from the board and she brought them up to date with all the information that she'd received at Wolfe's office. "I can see you've been busy. What do you have for me?"

"Unfortunately, nothing set in stone." Rio rubbed the back

GOOD GIRLS DON'T CRY   125

of his neck but remained at the whiteboard, pen in hand "With the help of Bobby Kalo, we hunted down some of the most recent men released from jail who might be inclined to do this type of murder. If we had some clue to a time frame, it might help."

"How did you determine who might be inclined to do this type of murder because each one of them so far has had different MOs?" Kane leaned back in his chair. "And we would need to find the murder he claims as his to get any type of time frame."

"We went with what information we had. One difference was that the copycat killer of James Earl Stafford didn't rape his victims. The female victim found in Stanton Forest was raped. So we made a list of anyone released from jail who'd been serving a sentence for any type of sexual assault and released in the last six months. We came up with four names: Ben Holloway, Jasper Montgomery, Silas Thorne, Jim Birch. All these men lived in surrounding counties. They could all live in town now, for all we know. I haven't had the time to check them out yet. I've asked Kalo to do background checks and I'm waiting for him to get back to me."

"So I'm assuming these men committed crimes against adults or we would have been notified of any child sex offender releases." Kane rested his forearms on the table and shook his head. "It's a shame we can't flash their pictures all over the media and ask people if they've seen them, but I guess even sex offenders have rights."

Pushing her hair out of her eyes, Jenna nodded. "Yeah, they've done the time and been released. Maybe they're changed men, for all we know. It seems obvious to me that more than one of our murder victims was killed by this man. I don't know why he's doing this, but he must have been interrupted in his killing spree, got sent to jail on a misdemeanor, and a copycat took his place. This is the problem. This guy is mad at the guy who murdered in his place. Someone else got the thrill of the kill while he was sitting in prison doing time for something else. Take note of what Jo said: Serial killers like to own their kills. They relive every second and take trophies. So we need to look closer to home."

"That's easier said than done." Rio sat down at the table and looked at her. "We must assume he's aiming the messages at either you or Wolfe, so we should concentrate on the homicides involving women over the last seven years that involved both of you."

"That's a ton of cases." Kane whistled. "I figure we take it from the date of the oldest copycat murder of the two so far. There will be more. He's trying to prove a point. I figure he won't stop until he's killed all the hostages."

Unable to allow that to happen, Jenna shook her head. "I'm hoping we'll stop him long before he kills them all. He has our attention and made his point. I figure he'll replicate the last kill that was his and it will reignite his fantasy—we know they all have one special fantasy and none of the others would satisfy him. He'll keep one girl for himself. One special kill to prove his point before he moves on. We need to find him. So far, he isn't killing in the sequence the murders occurred, is he?"

"Not for the last two we know about, no." Rio shook his head. "We can't just sit by and wait for him to kill again, can we? There must be something we can do to stop him."

Jenna turned to a knock on the door, and Maggie came in loaded up with pizza boxes. She waved her inside.

"The manager of the pizzeria, Brian Rhoads, is such a nice man. He dropped them by personally."

Jenna smiled. "He is indeed." She opened the lid of a box. "Want a slice?"

"Oh, no, thank you." Maggie smiled at them. "Pizza gives me indigestion."

GOOD GIRLS DON'T CRY   127

After Maggie left and the deputies demolished the pizza, Jenna thought through what little they had on the murders. She looked at her team. "I know we feel useless at this time, but with luck, Wolfe might find something. He'll have test results by the morning." She looked around the table. "For now, we need to rely on old-fashioned police work. Rowley and Raven, I want you to visit the local bars, motels, and Realtors. See if anyone knows or has seen any of the men on our list. Take the photos of the suspects on your phones and be discreet. In the morning, I'll go with Dave to visit some of the ranches that hire over summer." She looked at Rio. "Maybe call some of the local stores who hire casual help, ask if they have hired anyone recently."

Everyone nodded. Jenna stood slowly. "I'll leave it in your capable hands, Rio. Keep me in the loop if there are any break-throughs. I'll be working from home for the rest of the day." She turned to Kane. "Let's go." She looked at Carter. "You too. I figure you've done enough for one day."

"Well, thank you, ma'am, much obliged." Carter stood and pushed on his damp Stetson. He indicated to Zorro to follow him and headed out of the door.

"Is everything okay, Jenna?" Kane walked with her to her office to collect her things. "It's only five after four."

Jenna nodded. "I'm exhausted. If the baby decided to come now, I wouldn't have the strength to deliver it." She smiled at him. "I can work just as well from home with my feet up and a pillow behind my back."

"I know you can." Kane smiled. "How did Rowley handle the Beast?" He wiggled his fingers for Duke to follow them and the dog stood and shook himself all over before charging out of the door.

With a snort of laughter, Jenna looked at him. "White-knuckled but he did a great job. He has so much respect for you and your truck. I don't figure he'd risk driving like a maniac."

"I wouldn't have trusted him to drive you if I hadn't known that already." He followed her out of the door. "Rowley is as solid as a rock."

TWENTY-SIX

Rain fell sideways as they drove back to the ranch. Heavy rain was all they needed after rockslides on the mountain. The more the excess water flowed, the more rocks it dislodged and washed out the soil holding everything in place. Going into Stanton Forest was becoming dangerous and once the storms had passed the forest wardens would be out inspecting the trails that were recommended for the hikers over summer. As the wipers swished back and forth, Jenna relaxed in her seat. They'd collected Tauri from kindergarten and he sat chatting with Carter, but their conversation went over her head as she sifted through the information Rio had supplied. She needed to know more about these sex offenders. Whatever county they had committed their crimes in must have more information about them. She would like to see their rap sheets and any information that might lead her to the perpetrator of the crimes happening in Black Rock Falls.

One important thing came to mind: No matter what county the crimes were committed in, most of the criminals either spent their time in the local jail or in County. Black Rock Falls had built their maximum security prison during Jenna's first

130   D.K. HOOD

term as sheriff. It took the spillover from the Deer Lodge Prison. All serial killers who had been convicted from Black Rock Falls had been sent to County. She needed to discover if the names on the list of potential suspects had completed their sentences in a local jail or had been sent to County.

Whoever was murdering the young people in her town must have been in contact with one of the serial killers she'd arrested. Knowing how possessive serial killers were of their victims, she would imagine that there would have been some trouble between the real killer and the copycat in prison. Or perhaps the real killer had heard the copycat running his mouth over his crimes, and now that he was out of jail, he wanted to put the record straight. Most criminals would be happy to have gotten away with murder, but psychopathic serial killers were different.

In all the information she'd gained over the last seven years or so bringing down serial killers, the one thing she knew for sure was that they didn't change. Once a serial killer, always a serial killer. They might take breaks between their murderous sprees, but eventually the fantasy becomes reality and they can't stop hunting down the next thrill. She imagined what it could have been like for the original killer, listening while the copycat took the credit for his kills. It must have been driving him crazy having someone else in his fantasy, touching the women he considered his property. She made a mental note to ask if any of the suspects on the list had gotten into fights during their sentences. She stared at the windshield wipers going back and forth, back and forth, the sound almost mesmerizing, and tried to put herself inside the head of the serial killer. They were so smart. Maybe they didn't fight the copycat, after all, because their aim would be to get out of prison as soon as possible so they could put things right.

The second thing she considered was the fact that none of these suspects were criminals she'd prosecuted over the last

GOOD GIRLS DON'T CRY   131

seven years. This meant that the crime happened in another county. Wolfe must have been officiating as the medical examiner and produced evidence against them. As a medical examiner for the entire state, Wolfe had moved around many different counties over the last few years, and as the crimes were out of her jurisdiction, they wouldn't have come to her notice—unless they were serial killers and none of the potential suspects had been convicted of murder. If they had been, they wouldn't be walking the streets.

She ran her past cases through her mind, searching for a time gap between murders. They'd had cases where bodies had been frozen and created a time difference between the kills, but this wouldn't solve her puzzle. It seemed that this killer murdered a few women and then the local cops arrested him on a sexual assault charge. The jail time for this charge varies due to a number of conditions: the age of the victim is crucial—an underage victim carries a longer jail term—and if it's the perpetrator's first or third conviction also makes a difference. If the serial killer they're seeking makes a habit of raping his victims prior to killing them, he might have been interrupted. His victim escaped and went to the cops. If they followed up on the woman's complaint and charged the man with sexual intercourse without consent, this would mean a short jail term likely in a local jail, unless the jail was overcrowded and then they might move some of the more violent offenders to County.

"You look deep in thought." Kane glanced at her as he turned the truck into their driveway. "Thinking about our baby?"

Suddenly aware they were almost home, Jenna smiled at him. "I do all the time, but I was going over what information we have for this case. I really need to get to work on finding this animal. I'm pretty sure the message isn't for me. It's for Shane. I believe we convicted a copycat killer, and rightfully so, for the crimes he committed, but one of those crimes belonged to

132   D.K. HOOD

someone else and now that killer wants to put the record straight."

"You'd figure he'd be happy for someone else to take the blame and do the time." Carter blew out a sigh. "You know, I listen to Jo all the time about serial killers and their crazy mixed-up minds, but I still can't get my head around their way of thinking."

"If you did, you'd be one of them." Kane shrugged. "That's the problem, they don't think like we do. They have a completely different outlook on life, when you consider the ones we've interviewed and how many of them really believe that everyone kills people—that it's perfectly normal. They honestly believe they do it as a favor to humanity because someone needs to rid the world of the trash. Go figure that mindset." He pulled up close to the front porch. "Head inside. I'll park in the garage and be in once I've tended the horses."

"I'll come with you." Carter reached for the door and then stopped to unbuckle Tauri. "Wait up. I'll carry Tauri to the porch or he'll get his feet wet."

Jenna unclipped her seatbelt and smiled at him. "Thanks, I appreciate it. I'll put on a pot of coffee and then put my feet up on the sofa." She sighed. "I have a few leads to chase down."

TWENTY-SEVEN

THE MINE

Olivia slid down the slimy damp wall, panting in fear. The man, their disgusting captor, who treated them like pets, had finally left, vowing to return soon. She'd tried to take in as much information as possible about him in case she needed to tell the sheriff. She figured he was taller than her dad and way broader. He had dark eyes, but hidden within the holes of the balaclava, it was difficult to tell if they were brown or dark blue. He walked with confidence, head held high like he owned the place, and spoke to them like he would a dog. His instructions when he decided to give them rations were always the same. "Get on your bed. Sit. Stay." His voice was local, as in Montanan, not from out of state. She figured she could recognize him by his voice and stature.

Since he'd left, she hadn't heard Isabella moving around in her cell. No crying, no rustling of paper. He'd left them supplies and more bottled water, but after abusing her friend, he'd watched her shower, and then dragged her by the hair and tossed her into her cell. Olivia had gaped in horror when he followed Isabella and then spent all afternoon in the cell with her. She didn't know exactly what was happening to her friend, but from the swearing, the monster had a problem with her, but Isabella hadn't screamed like the others—and she suspected that had made him mad. Terrified she might hear him murdering her best friend, Olivia had covered her ears and prayed, but she could still hear him taunting her.

"Scream and let me know you're still alive."

Isabella didn't scream.

Olivia wanted so much to help her friend, but what could she do? From the sounds coming from the cell, she didn't even know if Isabella was alive. She'd waited until footsteps echoed into the distance and then climbed slowly to her feet. She closed her fingers around the bars of her small window in the door and peeked out into the dimly lit vestibule. The sharp musky smell of unwashed male still lingered in the air. Olivia might not have seen her captor's face but she figured she would also know him by his stink. She pressed her face to the bars. "Isabella, can you hear me?"

A rustling sound and then a long groan came from Isabella's cell. Moments later, one hand closed around the bars to the window and then Isabella's face appeared. Olivia had expected to see her friend beaten and bruised, but apart from her wide-eyed horrified expression, her face was untouched. "What did he do to you?"

"I don't want to talk about it." Isabella's eyes filled with tears that streamed down her cheeks. "He said he didn't want to touch my face because he needed me to look good when I went into town." She let out a long moan. "I figure my ribs are broken. He wouldn't stop hitting me, but I couldn't let him win. If I so much as moaned, it got worse. He feeds off pain."

Disgusted, Olivia shook her head. "I figured he was beating you."

"Yeah, he did." Isabella wiped away the tears with the back

of her arm. "He fell asleep for a time, but I couldn't escape. He had me tied to a ring above the mattress. I'm guessing we've all got one just in case he needs to restrain us. I tried everything to get that zip tie undone. I was almost willing to bite off my own hand." She looked at Olivia and her bottom lip trembled. "He wanted me to scream and fight him, but I refused to give him that satisfaction. I've seen the same look in my stepfather's eyes when he used to beat me when I was little. I never cried then either."

"Wasn't he the one who was killed in the truck wreck about six years ago?" Chloe waved a hand through the bars. "That's not the guy your mom is married to now, is it?"

"No, thank goodness." Isabella shook her head and then groaned. "I'm hurting all over and he hasn't finished with me yet. He said he'd be back when it gets dark and then he's taking me into town. If I don't make a fuss and call out to get attention, he said he'll leave me on a bench outside the old library and I can walk to the roadhouse when he's gone." She stared at Olivia. "I'll go straight to the sheriff and tell her what's been happening. I know what his van looks like and I'll try and get the license plate. He's not going to get away with hurting us." She covered her face with her hands and wailed. Tears ran through her fingers. "No one will ever want me when they discover what happened to me here. I'll be an outcast. I'll ask my mom to take us far away. My life is over."

Unsure of what to do, Olivia raised her voice. "You don't need to tell them everything that happened. Just tell them he beat you. We won't tell will we, Chloe?"

"No, we won't say anything." Chloe cleared her throat. "He murdered our boyfriends and kidnapped us, and that will get him life in prison. No one needs to know the rest unless you want to tell your mom. We'll keep your secret. Just get help so we can all get out of here."

Olivia leaned back against the wall. No one had come yet to save them and two of her friends had been released, or so the man had told them. She didn't believe him. He was a monster and she'd never see her friends again. *I just know I'm never getting out of this place alive—none of us are.*

TWENTY-EIGHT

Monday

Rowley sipped at his to-go cup of coffee as he drove along Stanton toward the office. As he'd completed his chores early this morning, the air had been crisp and the ground still held the moisture from the storm, but the sun had risen into a clear blue sky. He didn't mind the rain or the fresh green grass growing all over his ranch and supplying his horses and the new cattle with fresh feed for the summer. It never ceased to amaze him how the seasons changed dramatically each year. Last year had been dry and everyone was fearing the brushfires in the forest. This year had been the complete opposite, with major rain since the melt, floods, mudslides, and rockfalls.

When Rio's voice came over the radio asking for his position, he figured something was wrong. Rio never contacted him before they got to the office. "Copy, I'm on Stanton heading toward town, a mile or so from the Triple Z."

"I received a 911 call about a body on the bench outside the old library not far from your position. Two women are on scene,

138   D.K. HOOD

*Ginger Phipps and Mo Helm. I'm five minutes away. I'll take a
look before I call Jenna."*

Rowley grimaced and his ham and eggs breakfast formed
into a solid ball in his gut. "A body, huh? I'm coming up to them
now. I'll go and take a look."

He pulled his truck up behind the women's vehicle and
twirled his fingers to indicate them to wind down their window.
"You called in about a body? What's your name?" He pointed to
the driver.

"I'm Ginger Phipps and this is my friend Mo Helm." The
woman's voice rose a little and her hands shook on the steering
wheel. "I called 911. The body is over there on the bench. It
was there when we drove past a couple of hours ago and it's still
there now. At first, we figured it was just someone taking a rest,
but when we took a closer look, we can see that she's dead. It
looks like she has something tied around her neck."

"Do you figure she's been murdered?" Mo Helm's eyes grew
wide. "We need to get out of here. It's not safe."

At that moment, Rio pulled up and climbed from his truck.
Rowley looked at the women. "You'll be safe with me and my
partner here. Give him your details and I'll go and take a look at
the body." He walked up to Rio. "Do you want me to go and
secure the scene?"

"Yeah, thanks." Rio took out his notebook and pen. "I'll get
the details and then give Jenna a call."

Rowley stared across the road to the woman sitting on the
bench. He swallowed hard. Even from a distance, he could
make out the blueish hue to her skin and the cord wrapped
around her neck. Already vehicles were slowing down to gawk
and he waved them on as he moved across the blacktop. He'd
walked about ten yards toward the body before the smell hit
him. He stopped, took out his phone, and captured the scene,
moving his phone in a one-hundred-eighty-degree sweep. He
checked the ground searching for footprints, but even after the

rain, the rock-packed ground was as hard as concrete. He circled around a wide distance away and took a few shots of the body from every angle, zooming in. It was the procedure that Jenna had taught him many years ago to avoid contamination of the scene.

As he approached the ruins of the old library, he tripped over a wire a few inches from the ground. As he bent to untangle it from his boots, a flash of light blinded him. The next second a massive explosion erupted from the old building sending a cloud of red dust into the air. He staggered back as a rush of heat overwhelmed him. He needed to get out of there, but before he could take a breath, the shock wave blasted him backward and then lifted him into the air. Heart pounding, he didn't have time to think. Everything was moving so fast. Dust and debris swirled around him as if he'd become part of a tornado.

Disoriented, he tumbled, helpless to do anything. The force of the explosion pushed the breath out of his lungs. He couldn't breathe and his ears buzzed so loud the spinning world had gone silent. As he twirled, grit filled his eyes and crawled up his nose. He flew through the air on his back, colliding with small rocks and glass fragments that glittered around him in the sun, making rainbows. The next moment, the wind vanished and he dropped. His mind went to Sandy and the twins—would he ever see them again? Bracing himself for the crash to earth, he fell back-first and spread his arms for the impact. The ground came up fast and he slammed into the debris-covered dirt. Pain shot through his body as bricks and glass showered down around him, covering his face and chest. Stunned, he tried to move and then a gush of blood ran into his eyes. He looked up as a massive chunk of concrete came hurtling toward him. *Shit!*

TWENTY-NINE

Jenna picked up the call from Rio at five after eight. By mutual agreement, he'd taken the 911 calls overnight so she could get her rest. The call had come in from two women driving into Black Rock Falls from Louan earlier that morning. They'd noticed a woman sitting on the park bench outside the ruins of the old library not far from the Triple Z Roadhouse. On their return trip after picking up feed from the local produce store, the woman had still been sitting there. It seemed strange that someone would be sitting alone on the side of the road for a little over two hours as no buses stopped in that area, and they decided to pull over and check to see if she needed a ride. From Rio's account, the women were close to being hysterical and he had ordered them into their truck to wait for him to arrive. He'd called Rowley as they were both en route to the office to meet him there. Jenna drummed her fingers on the desk. "Did they go and talk to the woman or establish if she was actually dead?"

"*Nope.*" The engine of Rio's truck roared as he raced along the road. "*They said they didn't need to go close, as they could plainly see she was dead. The body has blue lips. One of the*

GOOD GIRLS DON'T CRY   141

*women believes she has something tied around her neck. We'll
check her out when we arrive. Rowley is on scene."*

Taking a pen from the mug on her desk, Jenna raised her
eyebrows at Kane, working at his desk. She turned her attention
back to Rio. "Who are these women? Have you got their details?
If this is a homicide, we'll come down and take a look. If it
doesn't look suspicious, call Wolfe to come and collect the
body."

*"Copy that. The women's names are Ginger Phipps and Mo
Helm."* He gave Jenna their contact details. *"I'm coming up to
the old library now and Rowley's truck is here. I'll keep you on
speaker."*

Jenna listened to the conversation between Rio and Rowley
and looked at Kane. "Rowley will be able to tell without conta-
minating the crime scene. He hates dead bodies."

"I'm having a déjà-vu moment here." Kane stood and went
to sit in front of Jenna's desk. "Do you recall the body we found
on that same bench?"

Leaning back in her chair, Jenna nodded. "Vividly, I figure
we still have the aches and pains from the explosion." Her
stomach dropped. "You don't think—"

An almighty explosion came through the phone and Kane
jumped to his feet. "Jesus, they've hit a tripwire." He headed for
the door. "Come on, Duke."

Getting to her feet slowly—it was her only speed right now
—Jenna grabbed her things and followed Kane through the
door. She moved as swiftly as humanly possible down the stairs.
As she passed Maggie on the front counter, she waved her over.
"Call Wolfe. There's been an explosion at the old library, same
place where someone tried to kill us once before. Carter's with
him. Tell him to bring him and Zorro to check the scene for
explosives."

"I'm on it, Sheriff." Maggie picked up the phone.

Concerned, Jenna kept her phone pressed to her ear as she climbed into the Beast. "Rio, is everything okay? Rio?"

Nothing.

"Dammit, I should have warned Rio about possible explosives." Kane dashed a hand through his hair. "We should have known it was another copycat."

They took off, lights and sirens. Bewildered, Jenna looked at Kane. "How does this killer know so much about our cases?"

"How does he know?" He turned to glance at her before returning his gaze to the highway. "It really doesn't take a genius. Everyone knows about the true crime series written about our cases. They're bestsellers and they bring thousands of tourists here. He'd only need to pick up a copy and everything apart from the details we withheld are there. If he is one of our suspects, he could have borrowed it from the prison library. Serial killers love reading about their crimes."

Jenna stared ahead as the Beast ate up the highway. "I hope Rowley's okay."

As they rounded the bend and hit the straightaway, a cloud of red dust stained the air and Jenna tried Rio again but got no response. She could hear noise in the background. The phone had survived and she imagined it was inside Rio's pocket. "Rio, can you hear me?"

Nothing.

Panic gripped her as they raced past the Triple Z Roadhouse at high speed and then Kane slowed at the sight of Rio in the middle of the highway moving traffic. Jenna stared at the debris-strewn highway and searched for Rowley, but she couldn't find him. Worried for his well-being, her stomach clenched. Had he been injured? Had anyone called the paramedics? She stared at the faces of the people anxious to get through the gridlock of sightseers as Kane took the Beast off-road to get to the crime scene. "Rio's fine and there's Rowley's truck."

GOOD GIRLS DON'T CRY 143

"I see it." Kane weaved around bricks and other debris strewn across the ground. "I believe I can see him inside. I'll pull up alongside."

The moment the Beast stopped, Jenna climbed out and headed straight toward Rowley with Kane close behind. She reeled back in shock at the sight of his blood-soaked face and shirt. She turned to Kane. "I can help him. Can you go and assist Rio? We need to get the road cleared and get these people on their way. I've noticed a few of the locals in the line of traffic. They'll probably help out if you ask them."

"Sure." Kane frowned at the sight of Rowley. "You'll be fine, Jake." He gripped his shoulder. "Do you know what happened?"

"Yeah, after everything you taught me, I tripped over a wire. It was green and I didn't see it." Rowley wiped at his blood-soaked eyes. "It tangled around my feet and when I bent down to free it, there was a flash of bright light and then everything went to hell." He frowned. "A huge lump of concrete missed me by an inch. I rolled away just in time."

"That's why they call them tripwires. Even trained soldiers miss them. Don't be so hard on yourself." Kane looked back at Jenna. "I'll leave Duke in the truck. There's glass everywhere." He headed toward Rio.

Concerned, Jenna examined Rowley. He looked awful and was having trouble opening his eyes. No wonder with all the blood. "Hang in there, Jake. I'll grab a few things from my truck."

Jenna went back to the Beast and grabbed the first aid kit and then hurried back to Rowley. He was sitting in the driver's seat of his truck with his legs hanging out of the door, pressing a bunch of tissues to his head. She opened the back door and rested the first aid kit on the seat and pulled out some wads of cotton. She handed them to him. "How are you doing?"

"I wasn't knocked out." Rowley dropped the tissues into an

evidence bag at his feet and then pushed the wads of cotton onto a gash on his forehead. "It happened so fast. I was taking photos and tripped. I bent down and, whoosh, what was left of the old library exploded. It threw me into the air, tossed me around some, and then dropped me."

Having experienced explosions more than once, Jenna understood. "Are you badly hurt anywhere else?"

"No, bruised is all." Rowley tried to smile, his teeth looking bright in his blood-soaked face. "And I'll be coughing up brick dust for the next year."

Pulling on examination gloves, Jenna unwrapped bandages from the first aid kit. The cut on his head needed sutures but for now all she could do was to try and stop the bleeding. Wolfe would be along soon, and he carried everything he needed for emergencies. "I'll wrap a bandage around your head and clean you up. Wolfe is on his way."

"I don't need the paramedics." Rowley wiped at blood-soaked eyes. "I didn't even feel what hit me. I figure it must have been glass that cut me."

Jenna lifted his chin. "Let me take a look." The cut poured blood and Jenna pressed a thick pad on it. "Put pressure on the cut. It needs a few stitches."

Once she had bandaged his head, she went about cleaning the blood from his face. She used saline solution to wash the blood from his eyes and opened a packet of wipes for his hands. "There, now you look a little more presentable. How is your eyesight? Can you see everything clearly?"

"My eyes are fine now you've cleaned out the blood, but my ears are ringing something awful." Rowley checked his pockets. "I've lost my phone. I took photos and a video of the scene. The explosion picked me up and threw me over there." He pointed north of the body. "I figure whoever set the explosion wanted to take us out."

Maybe not. The killer hadn't set the explosion near the

GOOD GIRLS DON'T CRY 145

body. It was another attention-getter and Rowley had walked right into it. He was lucky to be alive. Jenna patted him on the shoulder. "I believe it's another copycat. You'll recall when Dave and I found a body here, there was a tripwire and we were blown sky-high? Don't worry about your phone. They can withstand shocks. I'll call it as soon as Dave and Rio have cleared the spectators. We'll hear it for sure." She handed him a bottle of water. "Wash out your mouth and sit tight. Carter is on his way with Zorro, and they'll clear the area for us and then we can take a look at the body. I see the explosion didn't touch it."

"It knocked it sideways. She was sitting upright. The bomb was set in the building behind. They used just enough explosives to throw a few broken bricks and glass around. Those left from the last time, I guess." Rowley sipped water and spat and then sipped again. "It's just as well. If anything bigger had hit me, I wouldn't be talking to you now."

THIRTY

The one thing Kane loved about living in Black Rock Falls was the townsfolk. The moment he started moving rocks, vehicles pulled over onto the grass and people climbed out to help him. Two gardeners had wide brooms and were industriously sweeping glass from the blacktop and collecting it in garbage cans. He glanced over at Jenna to see her speaking with the two witnesses and turned around as Wolfe arrived with Carter driving Jenna's sheriff's department vehicle close behind. Wolfe had positioned his medical examiner's van to obscure the view of the body from the road. As usual, Carter was all business. Dressed in a Kevlar vest and a riot helmet, he opened the door for his dog, Zorro. The dog also wore a protective coat and on Carter's instruction headed toward the explosion site.

Kane deposited a few large rocks onto the side of the road and then headed toward Carter. As he watched Zorro go through his paces, Wolfe came up beside him. He kept his attention on the dog as it moved back and forth, covering the ground between the bench and the damaged building.

"This looks a little too familiar for my liking." Wolfe cleared his throat. "It's another copycat, isn't it?"

GOOD GIRLS DON'T CRY   147

Nodding, Kane flicked him a glance. "So far, they all are. If this one has the same message, we've become involved in some type of morbid game."

"Jo believes he's trying to make a point." Wolfe rubbed his chin. "So far, all of these cases are mine. I produced the evidence needed to convict. I stood up in court to deliver my evidence to the best of my ability, but what if I'd gotten one wrong? I find it hard to believe as I check and recheck every result."

Unable to believe his ears, Kane snorted. "I've never known you to make a mistake in all the time we've been together." He sighed. "The thing is, Shane, many of the cases that we have solved had very little or no positive evidence. Those killers we caught in the act. I'm starting to believe this may be one of those cases. Maybe this person was arrested for a minor charge during his killing spree. This would mean he couldn't murder anyone over the period of time he was in jail. Most of our cases are all over the media, and it's possible the coverage triggered another psychopath, and he took on the fantasy of killer number one. The second killer decided to copycat him and could have moved in seamlessly. We would have never known as all the evidence pointed to the second killer."

"You mean it would have just been a coincidence that the guy who was doing the killing was arrested around the same time as the copycat took over?" Wolfe shook his head. "That's a little far-fetched. Most of the cases we're involved in, the psychopaths kill over a period of a week or two before we catch them." He sighed. "I believe you're mistaken. Mainly because I don't make a habit of making errors when it comes to convicting killers. Well, I have spoken to Jo a number of times about this, and her only explanation is that the copycat is using historical kills as his template. If you look back on some of our cases, they have involved cold case files. In those cases, most of the evidence has been destroyed or is nonexistent. I honestly believe that this is what the copycat did to annoy this psychopath, and he is willing to risk everything to put the record straight."

Understanding exactly what Wolfe was saying, he nodded. "Yeah, well, Jo is the expert. I just hope we figure out who this guy is before he kills anyone else. He must make a mistake soon. When he does, we'll catch him. I pray it's soon, before any more young girls pay with their lives for his vanity."

"All clear." Carter waved at them and removed his helmet. "It really stinks over here. I suggest you mask up."

"Okay." Wolfe indicated to his assistant, Webber. "Let's get this show on the road."

Kane handed Carter a mask from his pocket and they followed Wolfe to the body. As Webber took photographs, he gazed at the body of a girl maybe sixteen to eighteen. She fit the description of a girl on the list missing from the limo. The victim had long black hair. Her face was blue and eyes bulging. Her blackened tongue poked out from between her lips. She was wearing a thin summer dress and slippers a couple of sizes too big. Her hands were zip-tied in front of her.

"That's interesting." Wolfe moved around her and then picked up her hair. "She has stun gun burns on the back of her neck. He stunned her and then strangled her."

A name shot into Kane's mind. "That's the work of Dallas Strauss, but this guy didn't have the knowledge to tamper with a regular stun gun. His one didn't kill outright. That's why he strangled her. Yet he left her here on the bench and added an explosion. It's like he combined two different cases."

"Maybe he muddled them up." Carter scratched his cheek. "He's crazy. We can't expect anything logical from him, can we?"

Kane shrugged. "I guess not."

"Dallas Strauss didn't leave the bodies on park benches. He broke into the victims' houses or was invited and left them sitting in front of the TV." Wolfe stretched the body along the bench, slit open the front of the dress to take the liver temperature of the victim. He indicated to the abdomen and shook his head slowly. "Massive bruising. She was beaten and we have the same message: 'not mine.' From the blood loss, he did this before he killed her. I hope she was stunned at the time." Wolfe made a small incision on the upper right-hand side of the abdomen and inserted the thermometer. He removed it after a minute or so and read the reading to Webber. "It's the same as the air temperature. I'll make a determination about time of death back at the lab, but from the rigor, I'd say she's been here overnight. I'm surprised nobody noticed her before now."

"I figure not many people would risk stopping after dark along this stretch of highway." Carter peered at Kane over the top of his face mask. "Placing a girl here could easily be a trap and in Serial Killer Central, most folks would accelerate and not look back."

Walking around the body, Kane examined the soles of the slippers. "Her footwear is dirty. My guess is she walked here." He indicated to the length of the cord around her neck. "I figure he used this like a leash. It's long enough to prevent her from running away." He shot a glance at Wolfe. "Her thighs are bruised, so she could have been assaulted. Can you confirm that?"

"I'll conduct an autopsy as soon as we get her into the morgue. If you want to observe, give me an hour or so to prepare. I'll need to do a preliminary examination, so say two hours, okay?" Wolfe narrowed his gaze. "None of the victims were raped in any of the cases he is portraying. You need to talk to Jo about why he's doing this. It might be significant."

Kane rubbed the back of his neck and turned as Jenna made her way slowly toward them. "Yeah, I'll call her later." He turned to Jenna and kept his body between her and the victim. She'd already seen enough, going on her pale face and wide-

150   D.K. HOOD

eyed expression. He gave her a rundown. "Wolfe's done here. He'll do the autopsy in about two hours." He placed a hand on her arm. "It's nasty, isn't it?"

"The poor girl. I'm not sure her parents should see her like that. Maybe we'll ask for DNA samples instead of a viewing, but that's not why I came over. I need Shane to examine Rowley before he goes anywhere." Jenna turned as Wolfe came to her side, his eyebrows raised in question. Jenna indicated to Rowley's truck. "I'm guessing no one mentioned that Rowley was in the explosion and has a nasty gash on his head. I've tried to stop the bleeding. Can you take a look at him or would you rather I call the paramedics?"

"No one told me. I'm sorry. I'll look at him right away, but I need to change my PPE before I touch him. It won't take long." Wolfe frowned. "If he's mobile, can you ask him to sit in the bed of the Beast? It will give me more room to work." He turned to Webber. "Kane will help you get the body into the van."

"He seems okay, but he's lost a ton of blood." Jenna turned and picked her way slowly through the debris and back to Rowley's truck.

Hating not to be with her in case she tripped and fell, Kane kept one eye on her as he helped to load the body bag into the ME's van. In that time, Wolfe had changed, washed his arms in alcohol, and pulled on clean scrubs and examination gloves. They walked together to the back of the Beast. Blood-soaked but sitting upright in the bed of the truck, with his legs dangling over the tailgate, Rowley gave him a wave. Kane gripped his shoulder and Jenna hovered close by as Wolfe examined Rowley and inserted seven stitches into the wound on his forehead. "Is he okay?"

"Yeah, no concussion, but that might come later." Wolfe peeled off his gloves and looked at Rowley. "I'm sending you home for forty-eight hours. Sandy will need to keep you under observation for the rest of the day. You know the deal: she'll

GOOD GIRLS DON'T CRY   151

need to check you every two hours overnight. Can she do that?"

"Yeah, she'll make sure I'm okay." Rowley blinked and looked away. "For a moment there just before I hit the ground, I wasn't sure if I'd see them again."

"Yeah, that's happened to me many a time. It's not a good feeling but don't dwell on it. You're okay. If there's any change, Sandy has my number." Wolfe turned to Jenna. "He can't drive. Webber can drive his truck if someone gives him a ride back to town."

"He'll need to wear scrubs. My truck has blood all over." Rowley frowned.

"Then he can take it into town to get it cleaned. We'll pay for it." Jenna smiled at him. "We'll drive it back to you when it's done." She waved Rio over. "Can you give Jake a ride home? You'll need to grab his rifle and collect his gear from his truck."

"Okay." Rio shook his head and pulled a face at the sight of Rowley. "Sandy is going to be upset when she sees you. Maybe you should call her before we arrive."

"I've lost my phone." Rowley rubbed the back of his neck. "And my hat."

"Ah, then this belongs to you, Jake." Carter waved a phone in an evidence bag. "Zorro found it." He waved a hat at him. "I found your hat too."

"Thank goodness." Rowley took it from the bag and the screen lit up. "Great, it works. I'll call Sandy and then send all the images of the scene prior to the explosion to the server."

"Thanks, Jake, but take care of yourself, okay? Send the images but rest up. We'll manage." Jenna looked at Kane. "I've sent the witnesses on their way. They didn't actually see anything. No one hanging around and no vehicles parked in the vicinity."

Kane nodded slowly. "Somehow, I figured you'd say that. We done here?"

152   D.K. HOOD

"Yeah, we have everyone sorted. We'll head back to the office and hunt down suspects, but I want to be at the autopsy. I need to see what murder this links to. It's obviously a copycat. We need to pull up files and check out the details." She sighed. "Rio had Kalo hunting down the whereabouts of the suspects and if they're anywhere near town, I'll need to call him before we head off to the morgue."

Kane opened the door to the truck and helped Jenna inside. "Yeah, and I need to talk to Jo. This case has taken a twist and she might have a better idea of who we're dealing with." He blew out a sigh. "That poor girl was tortured before he murdered her. That was no thrill kill. It was cold and calculated. This is a new breed of monster."

THIRTY-ONE

THE MINE

Refusing to give up the fight to survive, Olivia washed her face and hands and dried them on her tattered dress. Convinced that their captor had a day job close by, going on the almost regular times he dropped by to bring them food and bottled water, he wouldn't be back soon. So far, he'd check on them at least twice a day, and each visit had been harrowing. He enjoyed intimidating them and taunting them. One time he sat at the desk in the vestibule and ate a burger and fries knowing they were starving. Sometimes he spent his time choosing which one of them to give all his disgusting attention to. It was as if he enjoyed making the others witness her humiliation and then he'd put her back in her cell and leave. She'd hoped that was the end of it, but it never was. He was a creature of habit and would return to spirit away his brutalized captive at night—never to return.

It surprised her that he'd allowed her to keep the pendant hanging around her neck. He hadn't checked it. Inside held a watch—it had been a gift from her grandma for her sixteenth birthday—and she could gauge when he'd return. She could almost set her watch to the time he came and went. If he dropped by early in the morning, it was before five and he stayed for only a very short while to give them water and military supplies before dashing out. This meant he worked for a boss and was expected to arrive at a certain time each day.

She assumed they were still in Black Rock Falls because it was miles to the next town. As their journey had been in the dark, she hadn't seen any landmarks, but they hadn't gone up the mountain. She believed they'd headed into the lowlands and she tried to recall any places where there were mines. The only old mineshafts she could recall were out of town on the south side of the industrial area between Black Rock Falls and Blackwater. She remembered a lesson at school about mining in the area, and many years ago some of the old mines produced millions of dollars in gold.

Being locked in a small cell for so long, boredom had made her examine her surroundings closely. She understood how the cell had been made. It was very old, and from the marks on the walls, the cell had been hewn out of solid rock using hand tools. She recalled that the miners a century ago had made the cells to store their tools. They'd probably kept their gold locked up in one of the cells as well. When she'd arrived, she'd noticed the tunnels went away in different directions, but this one went only to the small vestibule with the office area, shower, and cells. The entrance had two strong metal gates, so it made sense that he was keeping them in part of an ancient gold mine. She recalled that at some time in Black Rock Falls history a mineshaft with similar cells had been used as a makeshift prison during the gold rush.

Olivia blew out a long sigh. Knowing their location wouldn't help them unless she could escape and that wasn't happening anytime soon. The monster would be back in the next few minutes and she wondered if it would be her turn to suffer the humiliation and abuse before being dragged off in the darkness to an unknown future. The isolation was getting to

GOOD GIRLS DON'T CRY   155

her, and her imagination was taking control, feeding her mind with unspeakable images. Trying hard to keep it together, she sat on the mattress and leaned against the damp wall, not caring if the cold seeped through her thin dress. Nothing she could do would stop the monster. She'd tried to talk to Chloe but her friend had been hysterical all day. This morning, the monster had stood staring at her through the bars of her cell for a long time before he left as if he was considering what terrible things to do to her. The sounds of vomiting in between sobbing in terror had echoed through the caves all day and nothing Olivia could say would get her to talk to her.

The footsteps came slow and deliberate as usual, but this time the monster whistled an old country tune. He must be in a good mood tonight. Olivia stood and went to peer through the bars and the strong smell of takeout wafted toward her. Her stomach rumbled at the aroma, but if he planned to torment them by eating in front of them again, she'd ignore him. Hunger gnawed at her belly and right now she'd be happy with the Army rations. They were way past their best-by date and disgusting, but it was better than starving to death. She blinked as he came into view. He looked different tonight. Instead of the coveralls, he'd chosen a dark blue hoodie with matching sweatpants. The balaclava was different too. She could see his thin lips through an opening over the mouth and noticed when he smiled at her that one of his front teeth was crooked. Her stomach dropped. *Why is he smiling at me?*

THIRTY-TWO

BLACK ROCK FALLS

As Jenna reached the Beast she turned to Kane. "You mentioned that the victim walked to the park bench. Do you believe that Duke will be able to follow her trail? I know there's glass there, but Zorro managed to get through it okay without hurting himself. Do you figure it's worth taking the risk to find out where she came from?"

"I guess so." Kane rubbed his chin. "Duke isn't stupid and I'm sure he knows not to walk on broken glass." He lifted the dog from the back of the truck and attached a long leash to his harness. "We need to get to Wolfe before he leaves and grab something that belongs to the victim so that Duke can use it for a scent." He handed her the leash. "You head on toward the bench and I'll run and catch up with Wolfe. Don't trip over the broken bricks and tell Duke to heel. I don't want him pulling you over when he gets excited."

Jenna sometimes wondered if Kane figured she had a brain at all. She rolled her eyes and shook her head. "I'll be fine." She gave him a shushing gesture with her hand and led Duke, who was being extremely quiet, beside her toward the bench.

Moments later, Kane came back carrying something

contained inside an evidence bag. On closer inspection it turned out to be one of the victim's slippers. Jenna handed the leash to Kane as he opened the bag. She gagged as the stink of death wafted out and she turned away as he held the bag in front of Duke's nose and gave him the order to seek. Duke wandered around for a few minutes sniffing the ground going back and forth in front of the bench and then took off in a northerly direction. They followed a line of trees alongside the road opposite the forest for some ways before crossing the road and heading along a narrow trail. Jenna recognized the trail as one that many off-road vehicles used to gain access to the many fire roads running through Stanton Forest. A little out of breath, she stopped walking and turned to look at Kane. "The killer must live locally to know these trails through the forest. Remind me to ask Kalo if any of the suspects were raised in Black Rock Falls."

"Do you need to take a break?" Kane pulled Duke to a halt.

Waving away his concern, Jenna shook her head. "I'm fine. I just get a little out of breath when we're walking fast."

The trail opened up onto the fire road and Duke wandered around and then sat down in the middle of the road. Jenna walked up and down searching the hard-packed gravel road for any signs of tire marks or footprints but found nothing. "Absolutely nothing, no signs of her even coming this way."

"I believe I have something." Kane pulled an examination glove out of his pocket and stretched it over his large hand. He plucked a few strands of long hair hanging from a branch of a pine tree and held it up to show her. "This must belong to the victim. I figure it shows the direction that the vehicle went. So not toward the mountains. This guy is either in town or farther afield, maybe in Blackwater."

Jenna pulled out a small evidence bag from her backpack and opened it for him. "It certainly looks the same color. I'll take any evidence right now, even if it means a directional one." She straightened, pressing her fists into the small of her back. "I'm sure looking forward to not carrying this extra weight around." She smiled at him. "At least I'll be able to carry it in one arm or another."

"Looking at the size of your bump, I figure you're going to need two hands." Kane gave her a wide smile. "I'm not sure whether I should be sorry or pleased."

Jenna snorted. "There's absolutely nothing wrong with a big healthy baby." She slipped her arm through his and stared through the forest. In the summer it was glorious, with many shades of green and the fragrance of pine mixed with the wild-flowers scattered in patchwork colors all across the ground. "It is a lovely afternoon for a stroll through the forest. It's such a shame that this beautiful place is the choice for many murderers. It should be a place where people can come and be happy and not looking over their shoulder all the time for someone determined to end their lives."

"People are happy here, Jenna." Kane strolled along beside her. "We're happy here, aren't we? I figure you can't let a few people spoil your life. Whatever the tragedies that occur here, we should rise above them and still enjoy the beauty of this place. I'm grateful every time I wake up and look out of the window. Almost every day the landscape is different. The changing colors of the sky, the trees, and mountains are all so amazing. I've lived in many places throughout my life, and I'll admit I love the beach. Walking along wide stretches of golden sand with the sea lapping against your toes is relaxing, but this place has a peace about it. I figure we're here to protect it and the people from the monsters who want to destroy everything beautiful in our lives."

Leaning her head against his shoulder as they walked, Jenna blew out a long sigh. "I have no idea who sent me here. It wasn't a choice I made myself and I'm sure it wasn't for you either, but whoever did obviously knew something that we didn't. I figure

GOOD GIRLS DON'T CRY   159

that Black Rock Falls has a very dark past that's been hidden for a long time. We know from the lack of documentation that criminal behavior wasn't recorded and many of the cases never investigated. I know many people came back from wars over the years, disturbed and likely suffering from PTSD. We know many of them lived off the grid in the forest. I figure local law enforcement turned a blind eye to what they did." She waved a hand in dismissal. "I'm not saying that all these people turned out to be serial killers, but maybe years ago it became common knowledge that Stanton Forest was a good place to hide. Being so vast, with many old mining cottages throughout, plenty of available water, and good hunting, it's a perfect place to live off the grid whether you're somebody wanting to be away from people because of the wars or because you intend to kill people." She looked up at him. "Maybe during the time that we're at home on parental leave we should take the time to look through some of the old newspapers that are now online that go way back to the first broadsheets that were published in the area and see what we can find. I figure in the ten or fifteen years prior to my taking office, murders were happening all over, and the local sheriffs were putting them down to animal attacks. It will be interesting to see how many we discover."

"Yeah, I'd like to know." Kane walked backward along the trail and then turned back around to walk beside her. "It makes sense. I don't believe all this just started happening when we arrived. I figure we were the first cops to enforce the law, is all."

When they reached the Beast, Stanton was empty apart from the odd vehicle passing by. Every member of her team had departed. Wearily, she climbed into the passenger side and fastened her seatbelt. She tapped her bottom lip, thinking. "We're going to be one man short for a while and I believe the next couple of days are going to be crucial to finding this killer. I'm going to call in Johnny Raven again. He is a great help and has a good investigating mind, plus he is a little intimidating

160   D.K. HOOD

when it comes to questioning suspects." She shot Kane a grin. "Much like you, huh?"

"I figure the dog helps." Kane slid behind the wheel after putting Duke in the back seat. "A K-9 is good to have beside you when you're interviewing a suspect. It often keeps their attention on what you're saying. Although the dog can just sit there as placid as anything, everyone knows it only takes a hand gesture and they'll attack."

Jenna took out her phone and made the call. "Hey, Raven, how are the dogs going?"

"I have a couple of rescues coming along for personal protection at the moment and they're doing just fine." She could hear strange little snuffling sounds in the background. *"I'm at Blackhawk's ranch on the res. We are looking at a new batch of puppies especially bred for the K-9 program. There are eight in the litter and they are all even in size. With luck they'll all be good enough to train, but you never know until the time comes if they have the right temperament to be a K-9."*

Jenna cleared her throat. "They sound wonderful. I wish I could see them. The reason I called is that Rowley has been injured in the line of duty and will be laid up for at least forty-eight hours, maybe more. We're in the middle of a murder investigation and I really need your assistance if you can come into the office tomorrow."

The agreement Jenna had with Raven was that he would be on call when she needed him, and in the meantime, he could carry on his profession of training dogs as well as being the local doctor in the forest community. He'd completed all his necessary training to be a deputy in her department and was very good at his job. He'd even taken a recent refresher course and renewed his chopper license. She considered them very lucky to have him on the team.

"Yeah, sure, I'll be in at eight o'clock. Do you have any files available to get me up to speed? I can look over them tonight."

GOOD GIRLS DON'T CRY   161

Glad that she had someone else to rely on, Jenna smiled. "I'm heading back to the office now from a crime scene, and Wolfe will be conducting the autopsy in a couple of hours. I'll have everything uploaded to the server ASAP. There are already files available from the previous two murders. The first one involved the limo with ten high school students inside on their way to the prom. You'll recall we found it at the bottom of the river but only the male students were inside? We discovered that four of the males had been restrained but the girls are missing and we've been finding them murdered. Three so far and there's still two missing and we don't have a clue who's doing this. Rio has a couple of suspects, which we are hunting down. This is why we need your assistance. Another set of eyes on the evidence or lack of it will be very helpful."

"Okay, as soon as I get home, I'll get onto it. I'll see you in the morning." Raven disconnected.

"You might as well call Kalo as well. If he's come up with anything, we may be able to talk to someone this afternoon." Kane drove into the Triple Z Roadhouse and pulled up at the pumps. "I need some gas. Do you want to stop at Aunt Betty's for lunch before we get back to the office?" He checked his watch. "Unless you'd rather eat after the autopsy?"

Jenna shook her head. "Not really. I'll call Kalo, and yeah, I'd like to stop at Aunt Betty's for lunch. We'll have at least an hour for our food to settle before we head into Wolfe's office. From what I saw at the crime scene, I won't feel much like eating afterward."

As Kane pumped the gas, she called Kalo. "Hi, Bobby. I believe Rio contacted you earlier with a list of suspects. Do you have any information on them?"

"Yeah, I found two of them." Kalo tapped away on his keyboard, *"I found Jim Birch and Silas Thorne close by. Birch lives in the back room of the livery stable in Black Rock Falls and, as far as I can ascertain, works there with the horses. He also*

repairs saddles in the workshop. It's his trade. The other one is Silas Thorne. He is a ranch hand over at the Silver Buckle, I believe that place is situated on the outskirts of Black Rock Falls and Blackwater. He is looking for accommodation and is apparently staying at the shelter in town. I was able to hunt him down at the shelter via Father Derry." Kalo sighed. *"I'm still trying to locate the other two. It seems to me when prisoners get out of jail they vanish into the smoke. None of these men were on probation. They had completed their sentences and were released. So finding them is going to prove difficult unless they open a bank account or obtain a legal document. If necessary, I could try facial recognition, but most of the images I was able to obtain are old and I would imagine they have changed their appearance since, but we can try if push comes to shove."*

Grateful for any help, Jenna made a few quick notes in her book. "It's the start we need in this investigation. So far, we have zip. These men are not probable suspects. They are only possibles. All were released from jail in the last few months for sexual assault. We have absolutely no idea who is doing this as there are no clues and every single crime scene is different."

She went on to tell him about the various murders and Carter's involvement with the explosion. "It was good we had Carter here with Zorro to clear the scene for us. It would have taken us a few days to get the bomb squad in from Helena." She paused for a beat. "Could you possibly update Jo on everything I've told you and ask her if she could please look over the files I'll be uploading this afternoon? Dave would like to pick her mind about the murderer. This man is very different from anyone else who we've had to deal with and he seems to have an ax to grind with a copycat killer. The problem is we don't know which copycat killer he's talking about."

"Yeah, I figure someone who cuts messages into the corpses is a new breed of psychopath." Kalo whistled. *"I'm sure glad I'm not living in Black Rock Falls right now, but if you need me, I'm*

right here on the end of the phone. I'll be in touch as soon as I can discover information on Ben Holloway and Jasper Montgomery." He disconnected.

A shiver ran down Jenna's back as she stared out of the window and into the forest. Girls were dying and there wasn't a thing she could do about it. *I wonder who's going to be next?*

THIRTY-THREE

Black Rock Falls appeared almost sleepy as they glided through town. Jenna turned to Kane. "The livery stable is at the next crossroads. Why don't we drop by now before we have lunch and at least we'll have one interview out of the way?"

"That sounds like a plan as long as you're okay." Kane gave her a long look. "You've been going nonstop since we left this morning. You must be exhausted."

Exhausted didn't come close to Jenna's energy level, but the opportunity to interview a suspect was more important right now. She shrugged and glanced at him. "It's normal to be a little tired but it's not something I can't deal with. I'll be sure to tell you when I need to take a break. I must admit though that sitting down in Aunt Betty's Café and eating a nice lunch is something I'm looking forward to."

Behind her, Duke gave a short bark. She turned to look at him and rubbed his silky head. "It seems that Duke agrees with me. We haven't been into Aunt Betty's Café for almost a week and I figure he's getting withdrawal symptoms. He's probably been dreaming about all the leftovers he hasn't eaten."

As Kane pulled the Beast into the parking lot outside the

GOOD GIRLS DON'T CRY 165

livery stable, Jenna glanced at her notes. "The man we're looking for is Jim Birch. From what Kalo told me, he lives in the back room of the stables and works with the horses and repairs saddles." She scrolled through the notes on her tablet. "This guy was arrested for indecent handling of a girl under the age of eleven. He has just finished serving a three-year term. Somehow, he hasn't shown up on the sex offender registry in this county. There's something dreadfully wrong with the system if people like this can slip into town without our knowledge. I've checked all the men on the list that Rio compiled and none of them have been registered as sexual offenders in Black Rock Falls."

"This might be something we need to do manually." Kane turned off the engine and looked at her. "It's not difficult to sort through the released prisoners who might cause a problem if they happen to wander into our town. The way AI is moving so fast at the moment, I reckon Kalo could create a program that can do this for us." He smiled at her. "That's something you could ask him about. Anything that would make life easier would benefit us."

Nodding, Jenna narrowed her gaze as she peered into the darkened stables. "This gives us a reason for being here and for interviewing any of the others who happen to wander into town. Offenders are required by law to register with local law enforcement agencies in their jurisdiction where they're living. I found none of these men on the sex or violent offender registry, so knowing they're living here, we have every right to question them."

"Okay, let's do this. I'm starving and Aunt Betty's Café is calling my name." Kane climbed out of the truck and waited for her.

The smell of warm horses, leather, and hay wafted out through the doors of the stables as they approached. The mingled aromas had a soothing effect on Jenna. The stables on her ranch were a place she liked to go just to sit and look at the horses. She pulled her mind back into the now as their boots clattered across the cobblestones. Inside was a child sex offender and maybe even a serial killer of the worst kind. She would need to bring her A game when dealing with him. She glanced at Kane as they approached the open doors. Moving from bright sunlight into a dim interior was dangerous. She nodded to Kane, who placed his back against the wall before turkey-peeking inside the stables. Heart pounding in her chest like a military tattoo, she waited until he'd slipped inside to clear the area before she followed.

The stables were larger than Jenna imagined. Rows of stalls faced each other over a center line of concrete flooring. Horses' heads hung over doors watching them with interest as they walked toward them. A few of them snickered a greeting, and then a man came out of a small room on one side. This obviously wasn't Jim Birch. His description was six-three and two-seventy pounds with dirty-blond hair and brown eyes. Birch also had a tattoo of a snake running around his neck. The man who came out to greet them was in his sixties, with rugged skin tanned like creased leather from years of working outside.

"Sheriff Alton, what brings you here?" The man came toward her, pushing his cowboy hat up at the front. "Are you looking for a mount?"

Keeping alert for any movement, Jenna shook her head. "No, thank you. I'm looking for Jim Birch. I was given reason to believe he works here."

"I hope there isn't a problem because I often employ men who've done their time." The man rubbed the nose of a horse close by and looked at her with piercing black eyes. "Jim is a good worker and I needed an experienced saddler. Most people who stable their mounts here often need a quick tack repair and having someone on site makes it cheaper and easier for my clients."

GOOD GIRLS DON'T CRY   167

Wondering why he was giving her a rundown of his business, when all she needed was to speak to Jim Birch, surprised Jenna. It was as if he was making excuses for him already. She nodded, hoping to appear agreeable and no threat. "I'm not here to question the reason why you employed Jim Birch. I need a quiet word with him if he is available to speak with us. Is he here?"

"Yeah, I'm here." A man wearing a plaid shirt, blue jeans, cowboy boots, and an old black Stetson stepped out from the room, wiping his hands on a rag. He gave Jenna the once-up-and-down look as if appraising her, and then his gaze fixed on Kane briefly before looking away. "What is it you need to speak to me about?" He indicated to the man beside him. "We can talk in front of Mr. Cotton. He knows everything about me. I've done my time and want to move forward with my life. Having you come here to question me makes it look as if I've been breaking the law again."

"That's because you have broken the law, Mr. Birch." Kane rested the palm of his hand on the butt of his pistol. "You are a sexual offender and it's required by law for you to report to us when entering our town. It came to our attention that you have not been put on the list."

"I haven't had time to go to the office." Birch shrugged nonchalantly. "It's been pretty hectic since I arrived, being a tourist season and all. We have horses going in and out all day."

Not having time to listen to his excuses, Jenna took out her notebook and pen. "Well then, I suggest we take down some details so that I can enter you on the list, but first I need to know when you arrived in town and exactly what you've been doing. So start off with the day you arrived and I want details of everything between then and now."

"That is absolute nonsense." Cotton's fists balled on his waist. "This is a free man; you're not permitted to hassle him in this manner."

Slightly annoyed, Jenna met his gaze. "I could have sent my deputies to pick him up and bring him down to the office, but I chose to come by and see him personally. I can leave now and send them to arrest him for breaking the law, which will probably send him back to jail. He knows full well that he is required to make his presence known to law enforcement when arriving in town." She looked directly at Birch. "The choice is yours, Mr. Birch. Answer my questions or we'll take a ride down to my office."

"I'll make it easy for you." Kane moved closer to her side. "When did you arrive in town?"

"A week ago Friday last." Birch shuffled his feet. "I saw a flyer in the diner in Blackwater looking for a saddler. I called Mr. Cotton and he offered me the job and a room out back." He pulled a face. "You don't understand, I was framed. The woman I was living with became jealous of a waitress at the saloon. I was getting sick of her accusations and decided to leave. The next thing I knew I had the cops on my doorstep accusing me of touching her eleven-year-old daughter. Trust me, I didn't lay one hand on her, but one of my ex's friends testified they saw the kid sitting on my lap watching TV. That was enough to make me do time."

"I would arrest you too if I'd seen you with an eleven-year-old on your lap." Kane's mouth turned down. "Isn't appropriate behavior for a man of your age." He drew himself up to his full height. "The sheriff has more questions for you. I suggest you answer them so we can be on our way."

Jenna lifted her chin and stared at him. "Let's start with last Friday night. What were you doing between the hours of seven and ten?"

"I went to Aunt Betty's Café for supper and after that I walked around town checking out the local saloons. There isn't too many to choose from in this town, is there?" Birch removed his hat and scratched his head. "I came back here and went to

GOOD GIRLS DON'T CRY   169

sleep—unfortunately alone." He sighed. "Don't ask me for people's names to give me an alibi. I don't know anyone in town by name, apart from Mr. Cotton here."

After making a few notes, Jenna looked at him again. "Do you recall seeing a white limo driving through town on Friday night during those hours we mentioned?"

"I can't say that I do." Birch smoothed his hair and replaced his Stetson.

"Were you in the vicinity of the Glacial Heights Ski Resort on Saturday?" Kane's gaze hadn't moved from Birch's face.

"During the rockslides?" Birch barked a laugh. "I'm not that stupid."

Noting that he knew exactly where the rockslides were located, Jenna lifted her gaze to him. "Did you happen to be anywhere in Stanton Forest between Friday and today?"

"Nope." Birch shifted his feet again and cast a glance at his boss.

"And what about this morning? Where were you?" Kane let out a long sigh. "Anywhere near the old library on Stanton?"

"You mean during the explosion?" Birch shook his head. "Do I look as if I've been in an explosion?"

"You appear to know the area. Have you lived in Black Rock Falls before?" Kane met his gaze.

"I spent some time here with my pa as a kid." Birch shrugged. "I lived in Butte for about seven years."

Jenna thought for a beat. "Have you ever owned a bow or a crossbow?"

"Yeah, I used one for hunting some years ago." Birch sighed. "Apart from my vehicle, I lost all my things when I went to jail. Everything I owned was at the house where I was living with the woman who accused me of touching her daughter. I've never returned there to collect anything. My truck was outside the bar in Blackwater. The sheriff towed it to an impound yard and lucky for me it was still there when I got out. It was still legally in my name and so I was able to claim it for the price of storage. It took me a time to get it running again."

"What else do you drive?" Kane swung his gaze to Mr. Cotton. "Does he have access to vehicles on the premises?"

"Yeah, we have a flatbed and a van, plus a couple of horse trailers." Cotton wiped a hand down his face, clearly annoyed with the interrogation. "Look, Sheriff, I have no problems with Jim. He comes to work on time and does his job well. Why can't you just leave him alone to live his life? He ain't hurting anyone."

Folding her notebook, Jenna put it slowly back inside her pocket with her pen and turned to Birch. "That's all for today. I want you to make time to come into the sheriff's office before the end of the week to officially enter your name on the sex offender registry. Folks in Black Rock Falls have the right to know who they're dealing with. If you don't show, I'll be back personally to arrest you." She gave Kane a nod and walked out of the stables.

Inside the Beast she turned to him. "I find it very strange that a guy who's just arrived in town knows about the rockslides in the Glacial Heights Ski Resort and about the explosion. He seems a little too slick for me. I don't trust him."

"We will talk to Susie and Wendy at Aunt Betty's Café and see if they recall him." Kane started the engine and backed out of the parking lot. "He would blend into the local population but the snake tattoo on his neck would be something noticeable." He sighed and headed along Main. "I agree, things don't add up with him as a stranger. He knows too much about the town. I don't believe he got all his information from spending some time here with his pa. When he was a kid the ski resort didn't exist, and the rockslides are all over not just in that area. The problem is, we need a little more than gut instinct to stop this guy."

THIRTY-FOUR

Over lunch Jenna spoke to Susie Hartwig, the manager of Aunt Betty's Café, and Wendy, the assistant manager, about seeing Birch in town. Both of them recalled seeing him drop by for meals occasionally but couldn't recall exactly what days he was in and what time. Susie had offered them copies of the CCTV footage over the last forty-eight hours. It was something Jenna could consider if she required an alibi for him, but right now, she needed to know if he'd been seen in any of the places where they'd found the murder victims.

Time flashed by and they needed to be at the medical examiner's office for the autopsy, so they decided to forgo visiting the ranch to speak to Silas Thorne until later. In normal circumstances Jenna would have sent Rio and Rowley to interview Thorne but was hesitant to send Rio alone into a possible serial killer situation. The problem being that most psychopathic serial killers gave the impression of being safe and nice. They could easily lure people into a false sense of security. Not that she believed Rio would fall for such a ruse, but over the years she'd learned to err on the side of caution. If she couldn't make

172   D.K. HOOD

it with Kane later this afternoon, she'd send Rio with Raven first thing in the morning.

Right now, her priority was to collect evidence to build a case and the only evidence available would be on the victims. As she headed into the morgue, the acrid smells of antiseptic and decaying remains greeted her. Ignoring her roiling stomach, she chewed on her bottom lip. It was crucial that Wolfe discovered something of value during the autopsy. Like a boat without a rudder, the overwhelming feeling of inadequacy surrounded her. It was as if every turn she made brought her up against a brick wall. The vicious killer had left no clues, nothing, and girls were dying. Serial killers and criminals now had access to instant information about DNA and trace evidence and made sure they left none behind. Each case was getting harder to solve and more and more she relied on instinct to guide her in the right direction. She gripped her hands so tightly her fingernails bit into her palms. *I must stop this monster, but I don't know where to look.* She closed her eyes for a second. *Please, God, help me.*

"Jenna." Kane's arm came around her shoulder. "I figure we need to look closer into the men convicted of the crimes this guy is copycatting. There may be a connection. Did any of our suspects come into contact with the convicted killers during their time in prison?"

Jenna removed her jacket and pulled on scrubs and PPE gear from the alcove outside the examination rooms. "I'm sure Rio asked Kalo to hunt that down for us." She sighed. "I'll need to ask him. It might point us at least in the right direction." She looked at him. "Although, I'm not visiting any serial killers in prison. Not when I'm this close to giving birth. Can you imagine being stuck there and telling our kid when they grow up that they were born in a prison?" She shook her head. "No way."

"Oh, there y'all are." The door to the examination room

GOOD GIRLS DON'T CRY 173

whooshed open and Wolfe beckoned them inside. "I've completed the preliminary examination. We know which girls are missing from the limo. Norrell was able to obtain dental records and mitochondrial DNA samples from the mothers. Although I do have a positive ID from the parents of the victim found in Stanton Forest. The one with the copper pennies on her eyes? There is no doubt she is Samantha Haimes." He frowned over the top of his face mask. "All the victims that we found in the limo have been identified. I'll give you a complete rundown of the autopsies that Norrell completed in my absence. As we assumed, four died from asphyxiation due to drowning and one to a gunshot wound to the heart. I have released the bodies of the male victims to the parents for burial."

Jenna leaned against the counter and folded her arms across her chest as Wolfe removed the sheet from the victim found on the bench outside the old library on Stanton. She had no desire to remain while he cracked the victim's chest and checked the organs. Her main concern was the cause of death, when it occurred, and if he'd discovered any trace evidence they could use against the killer. "There is one thing that seems to link these victims together that wasn't in the original crimes. This killer sexually assaults his victims. I figure there's a reason for this and we'll be talking to Jo later, in the hope that she can shed some light on why he is doing this."

"The two victims that I've examined have both been raped." Wolfe's eyes showed deep concern. "The killer didn't take any chances, using not only spermicides but also condoms during the attack. They've showered and washed their hair prior to death, which leaves very little evidence to go on. However, the last victim has traces of vegetation under her nails. I've examined these very closely under a high-powered microscope. I believe the samples could be of moss. The exact species and where it can be located is unknown but I've sent the samples and all the information I have available to a colleague of mine who specializes in species of flora from Montana. I'm hoping we'll be able to narrow down an area where it came from. It might tell us where the killer is keeping the girls."

"Do we have an ID on this last victim?" Kane moved closer to the body and examined the face.

"No, not a positive ID at this time but I am assuming this is Isabella Coleman, going by the photographs supplied by the parents. I'm arranging for them to come by for a formal ID at four this afternoon." Wolfe raised an eyebrow. "Why? Is there something I've missed?"

"No, I just find it strange that the faces of the victims haven't been touched." Kane glanced at Jenna. "It's obvious he used his fists on this victim's torso. He made her suffer and then walk to her death." He shook his head, his eyes flashing with anger. "This reminds me of the men who beat their wives but don't touch their faces to hide it from the neighbors." His gaze returned to Wolfe. "We assume he didn't know these girls, so this violence toward them must be part of his fantasy."

"It's a violent crime and very personal." Wolfe nodded. "I agree. Usually a man will attack a woman's face during the assault. They know deep down that a woman values her looks, so messing them up makes them feel good. In the back of their minds, it's not about sex; it's about punishing them. They'll often strangle them or put a hand across their mouth. All these aspects are missing in these cases, which makes me believe that raping them meant something completely different to this guy." He pointed at the pattern of bruising. "Look at that. It's almost methodical, as if he did this to get a reaction from his victim. A frenzied attack where the victim is fighting back would appear different."

Shivers ran up and down Jenna's spine. She couldn't believe what they were saying. "You're saying she didn't fight back when he was beating her? That's hard to believe unless she was unconscious at the time."

"She wasn't unconscious. The killer wouldn't have gotten pleasure from punching an unconscious woman. I figure she refused to give him what he wanted. As in screaming and fighting back. She might have encountered brutality in her life previously and these women turn off and just take the beating."

Horrified, Jenna nodded. As an undercover agent, she'd faced abuse and taken it to survive. "Is there any other proof of this?"

"If y'all look here, see, there are no defensive wounds." Wolfe lifted the victim's arms. "During a beating like this, I would normally see bruising to the forearms. She might have had them up to protect her face." He indicated toward the refrigerated wall where he kept the bodies. "Samantha Haimes' case is different. She fought back but not with her arms; she has bruising on her knees and legs. In my opinion, he restrained her hands above her head during the assault. There are ligature marks on both wrists."

Swallowing hard, Jenna considered the evidence and then shot a glance at Kane. "I need to know if any of the victims have studied serial killers or had an interest in them. Look at what we're seeing here. This is exactly what I would do. Screaming and pleading is what they love, right? They tend to lose interest if the victim is passive. If the victims knew not to try and reason with a psychopath and not to feed his fantasy, they might be spoiling his kills. The beating is to get a reaction—he needs the fear to make it perfect."

"That makes sense on what I'm seeing here." Wolfe leaned against the counter. "He's not angry. This is controlled violence."

"If it wasn't anger, maybe it's some type of twisted sexual gratification?" Kane nodded slowly. "Doing this is significant to this killer. It separates his victims from the originals. I'd just like to know his reason. There must be a reason."

"One other thing." Wolfe went to the screen on the wall and scrolled through his notes. "The stomach contents of Samantha Haimes indicated that she'd been living on Army rations. If you recall the case where the killer kept his victims in an old mineshaft, he fed them on Army rations."

It was as if a light came on in Jenna's head. "Yeah, vividly. So if we can discover an area where that moss is growing and if it is found deep underground, we'll know he is keeping the girls in caves or an old mine."

"The problem with that is there are thousands of them all over Stanton Forest." Kane blew out a sigh. "We'd never get to them before this killer proves his point."

THIRTY-FIVE

Armed with Thermoses of fresh coffee from Wolfe's machine, Jenna and Dave headed toward Blackwater. It hadn't taken Jenna more than a few minutes to discover the location of the Silver Buckle Ranch, a cattle and horse ranch set out on the lowlands between Black Rock Falls and Blackwater. As Kane accelerated along the highway, Jenna called Rio to bring him up to date with the autopsy findings. "The parents of Isabella Coleman are attending a viewing at the medical examiner's office this afternoon at four. I need you to be there. Due to some inconsistencies in the attacks on the victims, we are considering the victims might have some knowledge of psychopathic behavior. I'm not sure if this is something that they would study in high school, but one of the girls might have a special interest in it. Maybe they've read Jo's books or perhaps they enjoy watching crime programs on TV." She took a breath. "Would you please ask the parents and the previous victims' parents as well?"

"Yeah, I'll have time to go and speak to Samantha Haimes' parents before the viewing." Rio's chair scraped as he stood and his boots could be heard clattering over the tiled floor. *"I'm on*

my way now. I'll call you when I've spoken to them." He disconnected.

"What information do we have on Silas Thorne?" Kane lifted his to-go cup of coffee from the center console and took a sip. "I've read his rap sheet and he did time for sexual abuse of a child. The rape charge against him was dropped due to the victim refusing to testify at the last minute. Seems he gets his kicks out of following young girls and touching them in a crowd. He was caught on CCTV in a line outside a bakery in Louan with his hand up a girl's dress."

Pulling her tablet out of her backpack, Jenna scrolled through her files. "Born and raised in Louan, he spent a year at Black Rock Falls High School. That was apparently due to some repairs being made on the one in Louan. So he would be familiar with the local area." She cast her gaze through the information that Rio had uploaded to the files. "The ranch hand job was organized by the social worker at the prison. Apparently, the Silver Buckle often takes criminals straight out of jail for their summer season. They normally have bunkhouse accommodation available, but after a recent fire, they are short on beds at the moment. From Rio's notes, Thorne is staying at the shelter in town." She looked at Kane. "Father Derry always believes in giving people a second chance, but we should give him a heads-up if we believe this man is capable of killing people."

"I figure you should call him now." Kane frowned at her. "He might be able to give you a rundown on the character of the guy. You know Father Derry is very astute when it comes to assessing a person's character."

Jenna made the call and listened with interest as Father Derry explained the situation around Silas Thorne. After disconnecting she turned to look at Kane. "He said he hasn't seen very much of him since he arrived. He leaves for work early in the morning and doesn't come back until late at night.

His first impression was that he was quite charismatic. He also mentioned that Thorne had no family support. His parents died when he was in prison, leaving debts that resulted in losing the family home. All the family's belongings, including any keepsakes he might have had as a child, were all given to Goodwill or destroyed when the home was sold."

"So if Thorne is a serial killer, we can assume that any trophies he gathered during his last killing spree were hidden at the house somewhere." Kane tipped back his Stetson. "I wonder how someone like that would deal with losing something so precious."

Jenna thought for a beat. "Then to discover that someone else had been taking credit for your kills—that would be enough to push him over the edge, wouldn't it?"

"Maybe we could discover his feelings about losing the house?" Kane accelerated and pulled out to pass two eighteen-wheelers. "And his parents dying and leaving him alone wouldn't have been nice, although most serial killers have no empathy for anyone, not even their parents."

The information Jo Wells had given her was never far from Jenna's mind every time they faced a possible serial killer. "Perhaps his parents were psychopaths as well, or at least one of them. There's always a reason for triggering a violent episode and it's usually a close family member."

THIRTY-SIX

Deep in thought, Jenna stared out of the window over the majestic lowlands. Miles of golden wheatgrass moved in the wind like waves on a giant lake. In the distance, a herd of bison made its way up a small hill. Outlined against the sky, the lead bull waited for the herd to catch up. She lifted her phone and took a picture. The sight was the essence of Black Rock Falls. The timeless scene was as if she had captured one second in a century of unspoiled landscape. She peered at the image and smiled at Kane. "This is perfect. I'm going to enlarge and print it. It will look great in our office at home."

They found the Silver Buckle Ranch without difficulty and drove along the winding driveway to find a bustling cattle business. Large buildings and holding yards surrounded a huge ranch house. Men were walking around moving horses from one place to another. Others were setting out in trucks loaded with fencing materials. They pulled up outside the main ranch house where a sign that said OFFICE sat above an open door. Exhausted from a long day on her feet, Jenna got slowly out of the Beast and followed Kane up the steps to the office door.

GOOD GIRLS DON'T CRY   181

Raised voices came from inside, and when Kane went through the door she waited just outside.

"Oh and now the sheriff is here." A sweaty-faced irritated man dabbed a bunch of tissues over his wet brow and glared at them. "What now? Who has done something wrong, this time?" He shook his head. "I give these guys a break and all the thanks I get is that they vanish leaving a mess to clean up behind them."

"I have no idea what you're talking about." Kane went to stand in front of the desk, ignoring the two men on either side picking up papers from the floor. "What seems to be the trouble? Is there anything we can do to help?"

"No. It's too late." The man behind the desk got to his feet and held out his hand. "Art Bligh, I own the Silver Buckle." He shook Kane's hand and then waved absently toward the door. "I hired these two ex-crims to rebuild the bunkhouse that burned down and they vanished overnight taking all the tools with them, including my truck. I called it in just before and spoke to Chief Deputy Rio, who said he would put out a BOLO. As no one has seen the two men for the last twenty-four hours, I figure the chances of finding them are remote. I guess I'll just have to cut my losses and hire someone else."

Jenna wondered why this man seemed to hire only ex-crims, unless it was his way of getting cheap labor. Men desperate for a job so that they could leave prison would work long hours for practically nothing. People in desperate situations did desperate things and not every ex-crim was a lost case. She moved slowly into the room. "We're looking for Silas Thorne. He isn't in any trouble, but we need to ask him a few questions."

"Silas Thorne? Let me see. That name rings a bell." Bligh walked over to a whiteboard attached to the wall and stood there for a few moments scanning the contents. "He's one of the general hands, so could be anywhere on the ranch at this time of the day. Right now, they're bringing in some of the horses from the paddocks. He might be in that bunch." He turned to a man stacking papers on his desk. "Do you know Silas Thorne, one of the new guys?"

"Yeah." The man nodded to Jenna. "I saw him in the west wing stables not long ago. I'll take you there."

"Doesn't he have a phone?" Kane removed his black Stetson, smoothed his hair, and replaced it.

"All phones are switched off when the men are on duty." Bligh shook his head. "I'd walk around my ranch and all I'd see is men staring at their darn phones. They're either messaging their friends or playing games. I don't pay my workers to play games. They can do that on their own time."

Jenna held up a hand. She needed to speak to Bligh before they left. "What is the deal here with the employees? Some of them stay on the ranch in the bunkhouses. What about meals? Are they supplied as well?"

"Yeah, we supply meals." Bligh blew out a sigh as if his patience was wearing thin. "I prefer they remain on the ranch twenty-four/seven, then I don't have to hunt them down when it's time for work. Since the bunkhouse burned down, we have six men staying at the Triple Z Motel on their own dime. There are three others staying in town in various places. Since the B and Bs have become popular since the tourist influx, I'm guessing they're staying there. It's not something I ask about. It's their business. If they want to arrive in time for breakfast, it's included with the job."

Taking in the information, it was obvious any worker going back and forth on a regular basis would be noticed by the others. Jenna turned her attention on the man who had offered to take them to Thorne. "We know that Thorne lives in town at the moment, so he would be one of the men who comes and goes during the day. Is he usually here for breakfast or does he stay back for dinner?"

"Yeah, I do believe he arrives here before breakfast each

morning." The man pushed back his cowboy hat and gave her a long look. "In fact, he's here for most meals as far as I recall, although I do remember him mentioning that he wanted to have a meal at Aunt Betty's Café. I offered to lend him a few bucks, but he said he had money in the bank from prior to going to jail."

Jenna motioned him out of the door and they followed him slowly down the steps and toward a large stable with sliding doors out front. "What is the food like here? Being as it's a beef cattle ranch, is steak on the menu?"

"Yeah, the food is great and plenty of it." The man rubbed his belly appreciatively. "Bligh might be a hard-ass, but he looks after his workers. He raises pigs and chickens as well. The bread is made on the ranch."

"So there'd be no reason for Thorne to go to Aunt Betty's Café for a meal?" Kane scratched his chin. "Does he have a sweetheart in town?"

"He hasn't said as much, but I figure maybe he has because he never shows here unshaven." He waved a hand toward the other workers. "It's a ranch. Most guys can't be bothered to shave and grow a beard. We're usually too tuckered out to do much after work. It's a hard twelve-hour day here."

They reached the stable and Jenna stood for a few seconds to allow her eyes to become accustomed to the dim light before looking around. She could see a tall broad man using a pitchfork to toss straw into empty stalls. "Is that him?" She turned to the man accompanying them. When he nodded, she cleared her throat. "We can take it from here, thanks."

They walked up to Thorne and he ignored them and kept on breaking up the bale of straw and tossing it onto the floor of each stall. When Jenna called out his name, he turned and gave her a slow smile. "Mr. Thorne, we'd like to ask you a few questions."

"I wondered how long it would take you to get to me."

184   D.K. HOOD

Thorne leaned on the pitchfork and eyed them both with amusement. "It's all over the news about the kids going missing, so the first people who you come and see are the ex-crims." He waved a hand as if encompassing the entire ranch. "I hope you've got plenty of time. There must be at least thirty of us here. What made you single me out today?"

"We're starting with the men who were released from jail recently and then working our way back." Kane took out his notepad and pencil. "I'm sure you won't mind answering a few questions."

"I do, but there's not anything I can do about it, is there?" Thorne shook his head. "If I don't comply, you'll put me in the back of your cruiser and take me to the sheriff's office for interrogation, even though I've been here all the time minding my own business. I've paid for my mistakes and you guys are gonna hound me for the rest of my life, aren't you?"

Tiredness weighed heavy on Jenna and the last thing she needed was attitude from this guy. "Once you've answered the questions, we'll probably leave you alone."

"Ask away." Thorne continued to pitch the straw into the stalls.

Kane went about asking him the exact same questions as they had Jim Birch. To Jenna's surprise, Thorne dropped the smart-ass remarks when Kane mentioned about finding a limo with the bodies of five young men inside. This fact hadn't been released to the media and it was obvious that Kane was using the information to see what reaction Thorne had to the news.

"So you were in town on Friday night?" Kane straightened and his pen hovered over his notebook. "Where did you go and what did you do?"

"I walked mostly." Thorne wiped a hand down his face. "After being locked up for a time, walking under the stars is a luxury. I like to walk every night before I go to bed, no matter how tired I am. It's very relaxing." He stared into space for a

GOOD GIRLS DON'T CRY   185

few seconds and then shook his head. "Darn shame about those young guys. I do recall seeing them. I was walking past Antlers. It must have been around six-thirty. It's unusual to see a long white limo driving through town anywhere in this part of the country. Those boys had the windows open and were hanging out waving and making a noise. It's a shame they didn't make it to the prom."

As that was the only useful information that Thorne had given them, Jenna thanked him and led the way back to the Beast. Inside she looked at Kane. "What do you think about him?'

"At first, his arrogance caused me some concern." Kane started the engine. "Most guys who have just done time are a little more careful around law enforcement. To be honest, we really don't need much of an excuse to pick them up for questioning, do we?"

Jenna nodded. "That's true, but he does move around and no one checks his movements. All the murders could have been committed by him within the time frame of him arriving here. Father Derry doesn't keep his eyes on every man staying at the shelter. Thorne is arrogant, but then if he hasn't done anything wrong, why would seeing us worry him?"

"True." Kane left the driveway and headed back along the highway. "Call Rio. I'm taking you home. It will be past five before we get into town. He can lock up tonight. We'll start fresh in the morning."

Blowing out a sigh of relief, Jenna made the call. "Can you follow up with Kalo on any of the ex-crims' association with the copycat murders?"

"*Yeah, sure. Carter wants a word.*" He passed the phone to Carter.

"*I'm hunting down the suspects who have knowledge of explosives or have searched for information online. When I'm done here, I'll head back to the ranch.*" Carter sighed. "*I've checked out all the bomb fragments I collected at the scene. Wolfe has run a few tests on the residue as well. Everything is easily purchased. Any miner could get their hands on explosives. This bomb was pretty basic."*

Jenna shot a glance at Kane. "Ah, good idea, and did you discover anything useful?"

"Yeah, it was a basic pipe bomb." His chair squeaked as he stood. *"I might be clutching at straws, hunting down if any of them had experience with explosives, but no stone left unturned, right?"*

Jenna nodded. "Yeah. When we have nothing, that one small clue might just be enough to crack the case wide open. We'll see you at home." She disconnected and turned to Kane. "This morning we had nothing and now slowly things are coming together. I hope we can identify him before he needs to kill again."

THIRTY-SEVEN

Tuesday

Kane piled scrambled eggs onto plates and followed that with a stack of bacon. Beside him, Carter was spreading liberal amounts of butter on toast. He looked at him and smiled. "We'll domesticate you yet."

"I've always been domesticated." Carter flashed him a white grin. "I need to be to feed myself and keep my house clean. One thing I know about women is that they appreciate a man who keeps his house clean and can put a good meal on the table."

"That wasn't my first priority." Jenna looked at Kane and smiled. "But if Kane didn't cook, we'd be living on a diet of burned toast and frozen microwaved meals." She shrugged. "I can clean but I don't have the cooking gene. I've tried but nothing apart from choc-chip cookies turns out edible. *That* recipe my grandma taught me when I was about seven."

"Oh, I love your cookies." Carter smiled. "You'll need to teach me how to bake them one day when we're not chasing down criminals."

"I will." Jenna laughed. "It's like watching a miracle—but I need to stay close by the oven just in case I forget and burn them."

Kane ruffled Tauri's hair and then slid a plate in front of his son. He indicated to a drawing of trees and a cabin stuck on the refrigerator. "That's a fine picture you drew for me yesterday at kindergarten."

"It's Uncle Ty's cabin in the woods." Tauri nibbled on a strip of bacon. He looked at Carter. "Why don't you stay there when you're in town?"

"It's just a fishing cabin I use from time to time when I want to get away from people." Carter moved the coffee pot onto the table and sat down. "Your mom and dad need me close by right now, so I stay in the cottage."

"I like when you stay in the cottage." Tauri licked his fingers. "I like it when Aunty Jo comes as well and brings Jaime. She's funny. I like her."

"I like her too." Carter added fixings to his coffee.

"Has anyone contacted you since last night?" Jenna looked up from her plate. "I figure there's a ban on calling me. It's so annoying."

"Yeah, I did get a call from Kalo." Carter stirred his coffee and placed the spoon gently on the saucer. "None of the suspects who we're interviewing has any connection to explosives." He shrugged. "That's not a definitive answer to say that they have no knowledge of explosives. We have no idea what paths their lives have taken or what experience they've gained. Like I mentioned before, some of the simplest yet deadliest explosions are made from readily available materials."

"So nothing more from Wolfe at all?" Jenna pushed a forkful of eggs into her mouth.

"No." Carter frowned. "His workload is astronomical. It's all hands on deck there at the moment. Norrell has her entire team working in the examination rooms to get all the tests completed."

GOOD GIRLS DON'T CRY   189

"It's the moss I'm more interested in than anything." Jenna sipped her coffee and sighed. "It might give us a clue to where to find the girls."

"He did mention that he'd sent the sample to a very experienced person in the field." Carter bit into a slice of toast, chewed, and swallowed. "I figure it comes down to if the person he sent it to drops everything to examine the sample or it gets put in a line of work. I'm sure that Wolfe would have asked it to be a priority as lives are at stake."

When everyone was done eating, Kane cleared the table and Jenna got Tauri ready for kindergarten. When she disappeared through the door to Nanny Raya's apartment, he turned to Carter. "Do you figure that Jo has had time to profile the killer? I have some ideas myself, but we really need her expert view on this guy."

"We should get her on a video call this morning and see how things are going." Carter stacked dishes into the dishwasher. "Kalo mentioned he had a few leads on the other suspects to hunt down and was still searching through prison records to discover if any of our suspects have been in contact with the original serial killers. Personally, I figure this would be remote because everyone that you've sent to prison is in County and not in the general population. There's no way they'd allow a crossover. It's too dangerous."

Nodding, Kane wiped the table and straightened. "What's dangerous is Jenna being involved with catching this psychopath. I know she's struggling to keep going every day. The baby is very close and I figure she should be resting up and she completely refuses to take it easy."

"You need to see things from her side." Carter leaned against the bench. "She feels responsible for everyone under her care. There's a threat out there and she intends to stop it. I know you're concerned. All you can do is support her the best you can and we'll all try to keep her out of harm's way." He blew out a

190   D.K. HOOD

long sigh. "That's all we can do. For all the years I've known her, she makes her own decisions. She's strong and I figure she'll know when it's time to stop working."

Not convinced, Kane rubbed his chin. "I sure hope you're right."

* * *

They arrived at the office a little before eight, and Kane found Rio and Raven waiting for Jenna to give them instructions for the day. As they headed for Jenna's office, his phone buzzed. It was Kalo. "Hi, Bobby, what have you got for me?"

"I found the location of Ben Holloway. He's living out at Blackwater but is working at the meat processing plant in Black Rock Falls. I've uploaded the details to the server. I've also searched through prison records going back five years and found no connection whatsoever between any of the suspects and the original murderers."

Kane nodded and followed Jenna into her office. "Thanks. I appreciate it." He disconnected.

"So I'm being kept out of the loop again, am I?" Jenna gave him an eye roll as she sat down at her desk. "Can you bring me up to speed, please?"

Kane smiled at her. "I'm sorry. It wasn't intentional. I was just taking some of the weight, is all."

After giving her the details of Kalo's call, he placed his tablet on her desk and sat down. Carter sat beside him, and Raven and Rio stood with their backs against the wall waiting for instructions.

"I called Rowley before and he's doing fine." Jenna looked at Rio. "I'm guessing his head hurts more than he's saying, so I've told him to come back after he's had the stitches removed."

Kane smiled. "Did he argue?"

"Nope." Jenna frowned. "Why?"

GOOD GIRLS DON'T CRY   191

Rubbing the back of his neck, Kane looked at her. "He won't admit he's hurting but he must be if he didn't insist on returning to work. I'm glad you made him stay home. Head injuries have a habit of sneaking up on you."

"I'm aware. Okay." Jenna made a few notes on a piece of paper and then handed it to Rio. "This is where you'll find Ben Holloway. Head out and interview him about his whereabouts over the last few days and ask him why he hasn't reported to the office as he is a sex offender. That's your reason for speaking to him today. Use it as an excuse to find out what he's been doing since at least Friday. Ask his employer if he arrives on time and if he's had any days off work." She lifted her head and stared at him. "You know the cases. Ask the questions."

"Got it." Rio stared at the note.

"Another thing." Jenna turned her attention to Raven. "Maggie received a call this morning to say that your vehicle is ready to be collected at the dealership. It's unmarked at the moment but we are in the process of getting the decals printed. You can collect it on the way back from the interview. Everything is ready. You can just drive away. They're expecting you."

"Thanks, I appreciate it." Raven pushed his hat on his head and grinned. "That was fast."

"Just lucky, is all." Jenna smiled. "They had one on the floor." She waved them away. "Get at it. We need to find this killer."

Kane waited for them to close the door. He stood to adjust the screen on Jenna's computer. "Let's see what Jo has to say about our killer."

The screen opened and in moments Jo was smiling at them with Bobby Kalo sitting beside her. "Morning, Jo. Have you had time to look over the files on our killer?"

"Yeah." Her forehead puckered into a frown. "Each action he takes gives me more of an insight into his disturbed mind. I figure we should take it one case at a time and see where it leads us."

"That works for me." Jenna leaned back in her chair. "I'd love to know how he managed to get into the limo in the first place. He must have hijacked the driver the moment he left home. Nobody saw him in the vehicle and the parents all agreed that everything went like clockwork." She sighed. "I wonder why the driver didn't alert the parents."

"You know the killer was carrying a weapon." Jo peered at them through the screen. "We don't know what hold he had over the driver. Maybe he threatened to kill his wife and kids. More likely he held the gun on him or gave him some story about it being a prank on the kids in the limo. Whatever, we'll likely never know the answer, but it shows just how cunning this killer is and how he can manipulate people."

Wanting Jo to move to the profiling, Kane leaned forward, his forearms resting on the desk. "It was well planned and executed. I figure the killer knew about the kids' plans to hire a limo. It was all over their social media and mentioned in the local newspaper."

"Yes, so I see." Jo cleared her throat. "We must consider the drownings. It was a very callous act and shows no empathy toward the victims whatsoever. To him, they were just disposable. He didn't need them and the quickest way of handling two problems at the same time would be to drown them inside the vehicle." She looked at her notes. "The young man he shot in the chest proves there was a certain amount of rebellion. All of the males were hogtied prior to drowning. The killer couldn't possibly achieve this alone and hold a weapon on ten teenagers, so it's obvious he ordered them to tie up each other. When one of them complained, he shot him to prove a point. The others would then have complied, not knowing what was in store for them."

"Do you really believe that the girls just stood around and

GOOD GIRLS DON'T CRY 193

allowed him to drive that vehicle into the river?" Jenna shook her head. "I really can't see that happening."

"From Wolfe's notes, all the victims have ligature marks on their wrists." Jo glanced at the screen. "I would imagine he tied the girl's hands behind their backs and moved them to a secure place, perhaps a vehicle of some type, before going back and disposing of the males. He could easily have locked the girls inside a vehicle, a bus or maybe a van. I would imagine he went back to the limo, started the engine, and just let it roll into the lake."

Having come to the same conclusion, Kane nodded. "Yeah, I agree, and the girls would have been terrified by this stage. They would be expecting him to kill them. If he was holding a gun on them, they would more than likely comply believing that they may be able to escape later."

"Okay, moving on to the first victim." Jo added the images that Emily had taken to the screen. "The actual method of murder is irrelevant across all the victims because we know he is copying past murders. The message on the bodies is relevant because it tells us he is angry that someone else has taken the kudos for killing these women. Like I told Wolfe, serial killers believe their kills are like possessions. They take pride in each one. They don't care about the victims, but the fact they've murdered them is important to them, even though they might not remember their names."

"Do you believe he is saying he's better than the other killers, or what?" Jenna raised both eyebrows.

"No, I don't believe so." Jo pushed a lock of hair behind one ear and leaned back in the chair. "I figure he could have murdered a girl and left a note saying the others with the same MO were his from the get-go, but that wouldn't be any fun for him, would it? The thrill of the kill, and avoiding being caught, is something that feeds their ego. You—and I'm including everyone on the team—are included in the game he's playing.

He's leaving you clues and at the moment, because he believes he's outsmarting you, he would be enjoying it immensely." She stared into the camera. "Think on his level for a minute. He has planned this out to the last second and didn't want to risk being seen pulling victims off the street. Instead, he kidnapped a whole bunch of them to use to prove his point."

"I see." Jenna chewed on her bottom lip. "So why is he raping them and brutalizing them? I'm sure you noticed the bruising on the last victim. He didn't touch her face. That in itself is unusual, isn't it?"

"I believe he wants them to look as close to the original crime scene photos as possible." Jo clasped her hands on the table. "None of them were beaten around the head. It shows me that he is trying to get a reaction. Maybe the girls aren't begging and screaming, so he beats them. He needs their fear. It's what feeds his fantasy."

"And the sexual assault?" Jenna shook her head. "Is that to make them scream as well?"

"Very likely, but there's another more valid reason. The sexual assault makes it personal to him. He's saying, 'These murders might not be mine, but this one is.' In this way, he's claiming the girl as his property." Jo drummed her fingers on the desk. "He would also be using it as showing his domination over his captives. We must assume he has them together somewhere, so subjecting one at a time to his depravity would keep them under control." She looked directly into the camera. "I'm assuming this man is in his thirties, single, and lives alone, and from the marks on the victim's bodies, he has large hands. As no trace evidence has been discovered on the victims, we can assume he has short hair and no beard. It's very likely he has completely shaved his body to eliminate any evidence. We see this often in cases of multiple sexual assault."

Kane exchanged a meaningful look with Jenna. "What

happens when he runs out of victims? Do you figure he'll start taking girls off the street?"

"Yeah, unfortunately I do." Jo blew out a long breath. "I figure he's been planning this for years. All he needed to do was get out of jail and then find a suitable group of women he could kidnap. Summer is the perfect time. With groups of people going hiking and camping all through the forest, it wouldn't be too difficult for him to just come across a group and take who he needs. This is a very dangerous killer. He doesn't have anything to lose and has everything to gain by receiving the notoriety he seeks. In his mind, he believes he earned it. He won't stop until the story hits the media and gives him the accreditation he believes he deserves." She stared into the camera. "He has two girls left and he wants to settle this, move on, and start killing somewhere else. I believe he'll reveal his true victim very soon."

THIRTY-EIGHT

Raven found Rio a little standoffish. He couldn't determine whether the guy had a problem with him for some reason or another. He had gotten along with everyone in the office. They had accepted him and understood he had a few quirks from living alone in the forest for a number of years. Rio however was different. When they were together, he was over-the-top professional and didn't engage in the normal conversations most people working together enjoyed. He wondered if it was because of Rio's retentive memory. Maybe the man had so much in his head he'd rather not take on any more information. He glanced at him as they headed along the highway out of town toward the industrial area. "Do you know where the meat processing plant is, or do you want me to enter the coordinates into the GPS?"

"I know where it is." Rio gripped the steering wheel noticeably tighter. "The last owner kidnapped people for body parts and converted their remains into fertilizer. It closed down for a year before it was sold again. This owner is legit. Kalo checked him out."

Scratching his cheek, Raven allowed his mind to drift back

to the media reports about the meat processing plant and nodded. "Yeah, now you mention it, I do recall something about that."

"Do you mind if I ask you a personal question?" Rio shot him a glance and a nerve twitched in his cheek.

Wondering what was on his mind, Raven shook his head. "Nope. I'm an open book."

"When did you first meet Emily Wolfe?" Rio's eyes stayed fixed on the road.

Smiling at the memory, Raven raised one eyebrow. "Last winter. Around the time her sister was in the plane wreck. Why?"

"No reason really." Rio headed along an exit ramp and onto a winding road past factories. "We had a thing going and then she suddenly changed her mind. I figured it might have been because she'd met you. Are you seeing her? I mean you were stuck in the mountains with her overnight. You must have gotten close. Near-death experiences do that, right?"

Blindsided for a second, Raven stared at him. So this was it. His interest in Emily was causing a problem. "No, I'm not seeing her. I'd like to, but in the mountains, she found me over-protective, and as you know she is a very independent woman." He smiled. "If it's on your mind that I tried to steal your girl then you're way off base. I don't move in on women who are seeing other people. It's not my style. I prefer to avoid complications. I'm old-school... maybe too old-school for Emily."

"Nah, she likes you." Rio turned into a parking lot and the odor of blood and meat drifted into the truck. "Rowley told me and he heard it from his wife. But you're right, she's independent. Her priority is becoming an ME and working with Wolfe. I took second fiddle to that for a couple of years. The moment I told her I might try and get a sheriff's position in the future, she dropped me like a hot stone."

Not believing his explanation, Raven grunted. He'd come to

see both sides of Emily during their time together. She might be independent, but Dave Kane was a hero figure to her. She admired him and how he cared for Jenna. He figured if he wanted to attract Emily, he'd need to be her best friend, someone she could depend on—and trust. He'd made great headway so far in their friendship, but he wasn't planning on rushing in and spoiling things. Some things were worth waiting for and he'd wait a lifetime for someone like her.

He could feel Rio staring at him and cleared his throat. "That's too bad but it's better you found out now than live a lie until a messy divorce." He shrugged. "I'm working two jobs right now, so romance is the last thing on my list. I figure, love comes along when you least expect it and sweeps you off your feet. I'm looking for forever. The rest is just a waste of time."

"That's a good attitude to have. I might try that myself." Rio pushed on his hat. "Now let's go see what Ben Holloway has to say for himself."

Raven glanced at the entrance and all the prohibited notices. "I'll leave Ben in the truck. Can you buzz down the windows?"

"Sure." Rio glanced at Ben. "He's the quietest dog I've ever met."

Laughing, Raven reached for the door handle. "Yeah, he is until you make him angry."

They strolled into the meat processing plant and came to a front counter. Notices all around prohibited visitors from entering the premises. Raven stood to one side as Rio made inquiries at the desk. From time to time, men walked past wearing white coveralls and rubber boots, pushing large containers from one area to another. The men were streaked with blood. A bad smell hung in the air like a miasma of various stinks, including blood, offal, cow manure, fear, and antiseptic. The woman at the desk made a few phone calls and then sent them to a lunchroom along one of the passageways.

"We apparently wait here and someone will go and get him from the kill floor." Rio wandered around the room staring at the posters giving information about various diseases in livestock and how washing your hands before eating is imperative. "I hadn't realized there were so many diseases in livestock in this state."

Shrugging, Raven removed his hat, smoothed his hair, and replaced it. "It's all over unfortunately."

They'd waited for at least fifteen minutes before squelching footsteps came down the passageway. Raven had seen an image of Holloway, but this man looked completely different. His face was rugged, with a large nose, and he wore a hairnet obscuring the color of his hair. He figured he must be at least six-two and his calloused hands showed recent hard labor. He wouldn't be doing that on the kill floor at a meat processing plant. The work there was gruesome and it took someone with a strong stomach to manage the death, blood, and smells without puking.

"Mr. Holloway." Rio took out his notebook and pen and stared at the man. "We've dropped by to ask you why you haven't reported to the sheriff's office in Black Rock Falls to inform us that you are working in our county and on the sex offender registry. It's required by law."

"I'm not living in Black Rock Falls." Holloway's brow creased into a deep frown. "I'm registered in Blackwater, which if you had taken the time to call them, you would have known instead of wasting your time coming here to interrupt me at work."

Anger rolled off the man and Raven moved closer to the door to prevent him from running away. He wasn't sure if Rio's approach to this man was warranted under the circumstances. Boots and all sometimes had the opposite effect on people you needed to cooperate. He flicked a glance at Rio who gave him a slight nod. "I'm sorry that you've been misinformed. Anyplace you work you'll need to report in.

Being a sex offender is something the people of Montana have a right to know. Women working here need to be aware that you're here as well so that they can protect themselves if necessary."

"Protect themselves from me?" Holloway's smile was more of a grimace. "I spent four years in jail for something I didn't do. Why is it they raise us to respect women, when they're the first people to put in the boot when you're down?"

Shifting his weight from one foot to the other, Raven tried to get a take on this guy. One thing was for sure—he hated women. "I don't believe that's true, but we're not here to discuss your case with you. Just for the record, could you tell us when you started working here?"

"Yeah, three weeks ago." Holloway crossed his arms across his chest, displaying strong forearms. "It was the only work I could get. I wanted a forestry job. I'm qualified. I used my time in jail to make myself a better man. Seems that killing cows isn't everyone's choice of a career, but I hunt, so blood and guts don't worry me."

"Thanks, can you give me a rundown of where you were between Friday last and today?" Rio stood feet apart and back straight. "We need a timeline of your activity for our log."

"You must be joking?" Holloway looked from one to the other and snorted in derision. "I don't have to tell you jack shit. You've informed me of my negligence, and I'll remedy it right now. My name is Ben Holloway and I'm a sex offender. Please make sure I'm on your sex offender registry." He glared at Rio. "Got that?" He indicated to Raven. "He is my witness. Need me to sign anything?"

"Nope." Rio folded his notebook and put it slowly back inside his pocket. "FYI, Black Rock Falls has CCTV cameras all over. If we run a facial recognition program and we discover you've been involved in any criminal activity, we'll be back." He poked a finger into the lunch table. "This is my jurisdiction. Just remember that." He pushed past Holloway and headed for the front door.

Raven stared after him and then looked at Holloway. He didn't like the guy and his aggression was a problem. He obviously had no fear of law enforcement and most people were a little intimidated during questioning. This guy was very confident. "Thank you for your time. Don't worry about any repercussions from your boss. We told the woman at the counter we had recovered stolen property belonging to you. Have a nice day." He left Holloway staring after him.

Outside in the parking lot, he found Rio leaning against the hood of his truck. "Was that good cop, bad cop? I've never done that before. Maybe a heads-up next time?"

"Nope. He's hiding something." Rio waved a hand toward town. "We're going back to report nothing. It makes us look incompetent."

Frowning, Raven turned to him. "I don't agree. That guy is volatile, hates being locked up at work. He's on the edge of needing to get away and could easily be the killer. He has no respect for cops and he's a smart-ass. Give that information to Jenna. She'll find good use for it."

"Well." Rio stared at him. "Kane said you were good. Maybe I've underestimated you."

Raven chuckled and pulled open the door to the truck. "It's called life experience. If you'd served in the military, you'd understand."

"One thing is for darn sure, that's never gonna happen." Rio started the engine. "Let's get out of this place. It gives me the creeps." He pointed to a bone-crushing machine. "See that thing there. They use it to crush all the leftover bones and other stuff to make into fertilizer or dog food. Some crazy psychopath tried to stuff Rowley into it." He shuddered. "That week I gave up tending my garden."

Raven tried not to laugh. "That's nasty but it's a shame

about your garden. Not that I have one. Mine is the forest, wild and untamed."

"Oh, now don't start me on the forest." Rio gave him a sideways glance. "I'm a towny, born and bred. I like places where you can see what's coming for you and there's not something big enough to eat you around every tree." He turned out onto the highway. "Let's change the subject. Do you like football…?"

THIRTY-NINE

THE MINE

Chloe backed away as the man stepped inside her cell. His early morning visit had been degrading and she'd hoped his time with her was over. When he returned, Olivia had told her it was five after six at night. She'd watched with morbid curiosity when he led Olivia out of her cell and allowed her to take a long hot shower. He'd insisted she wash her hair and had given her fresh clothes to wear before moving her into another cell that was set apart from the others. As far as she knew, he hadn't touched her—yet. A shiver went down her spine knowing what this man was capable of. Knowing that Olivia would not cry out, just like Isabella, frightened her even more. After seeing the bruises on Isabella's battered body, she'd come to the conclusion that keeping quiet during the abuse made it worse. The moment he'd walked into her cell she'd started screaming. He'd smiled at her and when he left an hour later, he'd told her she was perfect. Perfect for what?

Trembling all over when the door opened slowly, Chloe stood just looking at him. He said nothing but tossed her a pile of clothes. She pulled on a skirt and top that resembled something her grandma would wear and slipped on shoes a size too small. Her skin crawled as he watched her dress, but she pushed it aside and just looked at him. Her heart pounded when he twirled his fingers to make her turn around.

"Hands behind you." He attached zip ties to her wrists and pulled them so tight they cut deep into her flesh.

Dizzy with fear as he spun her around to face the door, she stood to attention awaiting his next command. She gasped as the cold metal muzzle of a gun pressed into the back of her neck.

"Be a good girl." His moist breath washed over her ear, smelling of onions. "It's your turn to leave. I'm taking you to a friend's place. You can take a nice hot shower and wait there. Once I've left, you can call your parents to come get you."

Could it possibly be true? Was he letting her go at last? She stumbled forward into the darkness of the tunnels, the only light coming from the bouncing flashlight he held in his hands. As they went through the final gate and he locked it behind him, Chloe took in deep breaths of fresh air. She stared into a sky filled with stars, but the moon was only a small sliver in the dark sky.

The entrance to the mineshaft had changed since the last time she was here. A large camouflage tarpaulin held up by a frame concealed the white van parked beneath. She didn't have a chance to see a license plate as he slid open the side door and pushed her roughly inside. The door slammed shut behind her. Nothing had changed and it was still as dirty as before. Dust covered the bubbling tint on the windows and the takeout wrappers still littered the floor. The van had sped off before she had the chance to sit down, and without the use of her hands each time he turned a corner, she rolled around the floor trying to get her balance. Finally, as they hit a straightaway along a highway, she managed to crawl on her knees to the back of the van and place her back against the wall.

Chloe made out headlights along the highway but couldn't

GOOD GIRLS DON'T CRY   205

recognize any landmarks. She couldn't make out any street-lights, and at this time of night Main would be busy. Aunt Betty's Café, the restaurants, and pizzeria would be open and brightly lit. The van turned right, leaving the highway, and headed along a bumpy dirt road or perhaps a driveway. She peered out of the window at a ranch house with light streaming from the front window. It lit a large sign of a Realtor's smiling face, with the name Barb Furlich and proclaiming the house was for sale. Chloe swallowed hard. Who would she be meeting inside the house? The man drove around back and climbed out, but he didn't go to the back door. He went to a set of sliding glass doors on the back porch. After a few minutes, he slid open the doors and pushed back the drapes.

Very afraid and shivering although it wasn't cold, Chloe waited for him to open the van. She tried to avoid eye contact as she scrambled out. The gun was there again, this time pressing hard into her ribs. She staggered up the steps to the porch and went inside the house. He urged her through the kitchen and to the stairs. He said nothing as he guided her to the top and into the master bedroom with a bathroom attached. The room was spotlessly clean, the huge bed had military-style tight corners but the floor was covered with plastic sheeting. Terrified, she turned to look at him over one shoulder. "What do you want me to do?"

"Undress on the sheet. Fold up your clothes and put them inside my backpack." He dropped his pack on the floor and pulled a knife. He smiled when she flinched as he sliced through the zip ties and then gave her a push. "Then wait for me in the bathroom."

Unease slid over her as she reluctantly removed her clothes. It was too late to run and, from the remote location of the house, no one would hear her if she screamed. Past being embarrassed, she pushed her clothes into the backpack. The plastic crackled underfoot as she walked to the bathroom. It was modern, recently renovated, and spotlessly clean with the faint aroma of cleaning products. A large mirror hung over the two-sink vanity. The clawfoot bath was deep and the shower large enough for two. She folded her arms across her chest and stared at the door. If he meant what he'd said, she'd take a shower and then he'd leave. Goosebumps ran over her cooling flesh when he appeared in the doorway naked. Frightened, she backed away. Why had he allowed her to see his face?

Panic had her by the throat and she couldn't think straight when he handed her a lipstick. She just stared at it in her hand not knowing what to do.

"I want you to write a message on the mirror." He waved his gun at her. "Write: This one is mine."

Hand trembling, she wrote the message and then handed him back the lipstick. What did the message mean? What was going to happen to her? Hot tears streamed down her cheeks as he ushered her into the shower.

"Take a hot shower and wash your hair." He leaned against the counter watching her. "Shut the shower door."

She complied with his wishes, closing the shower cubicle behind her. With the steam billowing all around her she couldn't see him through the glass. She washed her hair with the fragrant shampoo and matching conditioner. The soap was wrapped in paper and she removed it and sniffed at the lily of the valley fragrance. Everything suddenly seemed surreal, as if living in a nightmare that changed every few seconds. She finished and slid open the door to a wall of steam and she stepped out, seeking one of the big white fluffy towels piled on a shelf beside the shower, to dry herself.

The man came at her in a naked blur. Something thumped hard into her chest in a painful rush of heat. Uncomprehending she stared at him. The silver blade of a knife flashed and she grasped her chest, horrified to see blood spurting from between her fingers. Why was he doing this to her? She tried to cry out as the room spun around her. Dizzy, she couldn't catch her breath as the bathroom grew fuzzy at the corners of her vision. Her knees folded under her and she crumpled to the cold floor. Blood spread out around her, spoiling the pristine white tile. Confused, she blinked to bring his smiling blood-spattered face into focus.

"Goodbye, Chloe. The pleasure was all mine."

FORTY

Wednesday

Details of the murder cases ran around Jenna's mind all night. She hadn't slept well and no matter how she tried, she couldn't get a grip on who'd murdered the students in the limo. The wait for Wolfe's associate to send results on the sample of moss taken from the last victim was driving her crazy. She'd reviewed the suspects' interviews and tried to match them against what Jo had told her, but she couldn't make a case for either of them so far. She'd read a brief report from Rio about the interview with Ben Holloway, but would chase that up after she'd spoken to her deputies this morning.

It was fortunate that Carter had decided to stay around, he didn't have any cases to work in Snakeskin Gully and his superior officer had given him the green light to stay for as long as necessary. With her team in the office all seated in front of her desk, Jenna leaned against the pillow supporting her back and placed her feet on the footstool under the desk. Resting her hands on her belly, she glanced at all of them. "First of all, I'd like to inform you that I will be remaining in

GOOD GIRLS DON'T CRY 209

my office for the next few days at least. If we have any breaks in the case, you can do a live feed to me via video call, if it is safe to do so. I need to consider the risk to my baby. I hope you understand."

"We'll handle things just fine." Rio met her gaze. "Do you want me to update the whiteboard now?"

Seeing the understanding in Rio's eyes, Jenna smiled. "I would like your personal opinion of Ben Holloway." She looked from him to Raven. "How did he seem to you?"

"Angry and he hates women." Raven rested one hand on Ben's head. "He has an attitude. Well, I guess you might call it a chip on his shoulder. What I didn't see in him was the usual charismatic personality we see in serial killers, but as you know, they're very smart and that could have been an act."

"I agree." Rio ran his fingers around the rim of the hat on his lap. "He took offense at us being there and refused to answer questions about his whereabouts. I guess when we ask questions it's up to the people we're interviewing to agree to give us information. Remaining silent is their right. So this man comes into the same category as the other two, in that he is a possible but there's no proof."

"It's a shame we couldn't get a bullet from the kid who was shot." Kane sighed. "It was a through-and-through wound. I guess I could put on diving gear and go down and see if I can find a bullet in the wreck."

Jenna nodded. "If we need a bullet to prove who killed him, you can go by all means, but I recall Wolfe saying that he'd searched the inside of the limo for bullet holes and found nothing other than a small hole in one of the windows. He was unable to determine whether the hole was from a bullet or had been there previously or had happened when the limo was driven into the river."

"It's deep and very dark down there." Carter peered at her as he chewed around a toothpick. "The current is exceptionally

210   D.K. HOOD

dangerous. There's no way Kane should go alone. If you need a second diver, I'm available."

Jenna shook her head. "I'll consider all the other evidence before I put you both at risk. It's likely long gone."

"One more piece of information we need to discuss." Rio stood and went to the whiteboard. "Kalo called early this morning. He has located Jasper Montgomery. We can take him off our list. He's been held in remand at County awaiting a court hearing since Wednesday last, so it can't possibly be him."

Twirling a pen in her fingers, Jenna watched as Rio added notes to the whiteboard. "The short list of suspects. This case is becoming a nightmare."

The phone on her desk rang and she picked it up. "Sheriff Alton."

"I figure someone has been murdered, Sheriff. There's so much blood. We all ran out and jumped in my car and drove away. I've left the house open."

Writing notes, Jenna quickly put the phone on speaker so the others could listen. "Okay, you're safe at the moment. Take a few deep breaths. What is your name and what exactly happened?"

"My name is Barb Furlich, I'm a Realtor. I was showing a house in Bison Ridge. I was there only yesterday making sure it was perfect for the showing this morning. I had two clients with me, Monique Webby and Donna Tesman Bihn. We looked at the ground floor first and then went upstairs. When we went into the master bedroom, it smelled terrible and I'd cleaned it only the day before. You see, the owners are living in another state."

Casting a glance at Kane, who stood and pulled on his jacket, she held up one finger. "Okay, what did you see?"

"Blood everywhere, massive amounts of blood." Barb sucked in a shuddering breath. *"I didn't go all the way inside, but I couldn't see anyone. There's a message on the mirror. It says: This one is mine."*

GOOD GIRLS DON'T CRY   211

Jenna remembered the case and her stomach clenched as a wave of fear rushed over her. No one was safe. Writing frantically, Jenna cleared her throat. "Okay, I'll need the address of the house and I'd like you to bring the other two women to my office immediately. You can give a statement at the front counter. I'll need all of you to give us details of exactly what you saw."

"We're on our way." Barb disconnected.

Jenna scribbled the address on two pieces of paper and handed them to her deputies. "Okay, Carter, you're with Kane. Rio and Raven, you too. It's a very secluded area, so watch your backs." She pushed a hand through her hair. "If this is the same as the Freya Richardson murder, don't waste any time, grab the trail bikes, and head out to the grave site we discovered at Halloween. If the old graves we found belonged to this killer, it's likely he'll take the body back there." She looked from one to the other. "Video the crime scene and upload it so I can see what's happening. I'll call Wolfe to meet you there. Go!"

Jenna wanted to go with them so much, but common sense prevailed. She had faith in her team. She called Maggie on the front counter and asked her to take the statements of the women who discovered the crime scene. "When they're done, send them up here and I'll talk to them. Thanks." She hung up.

She looked down at Duke, who never left her side now and scratched his silken head. "I'll pull up the files on the Freya Richardson case."

It had been a strange case. They'd discovered old graves and then new ones appeared at Halloween. All seemed to be murdered by the same man. She perused the files and scanned the reports that Norrell had uploaded about the previous victims. The bodies had been there for some time, as long as seven years and as the MO was exactly the same, they had naturally presumed that the killer had been restricted from killing between the old and recent murders. One main thing that

212 D.K. HOOD

linked the murders together was the old phones left in each grave site. Each phone had the previous murder recorded on it. She scratched her head. How did the copycat know about the phones? One of the graves had been empty and they assumed that the original killer had been disturbed. His last kill never eventuated. But what if that grave had contained a victim after all, and the copycat killer removed the body and the phone from the grave to use in his first victim's burial? It was possible but not something they had considered because at that time they didn't know a copycat killer had been involved.

Her phone chimed. It was Kane. "Is there a body?"

"*Nope.*" Kane's face appeared on the screen. "*Rio has videoed the entire scene and taken still shots, but I'll walk you through.*" He turned the phone around to capture the blood-soaked bathroom and the message. "*It's identical. Although the message is in lipstick and there's not one here. He must have taken it with him.*" He turned the phone back around. "*We're done here and have collected everything we need. Wolfe has just arrived with his team. He's armed and so is Webber. We'll come by and grab the trail bikes and head into the forest.*"

The horrific scene looked surreal on a phone screen. She had tried to take in all the details. "Okay. The blood looks fresh, so you might be close behind him. Make the guys wear their Kevlar vests just in case the killer is still hanging around."

"*I'm on it.*" Kane disconnected.

On a hunch, Jenna called Kalo. "Bobby, can you go back seven years and see if any of our suspects were in jail?"

"*I've checked them all out. Apart from the time they've done in Montana, they're clean.*"

Pushing hair behind her ears, she thought for a beat. "Okay, then can you do a search across the US and see if any crimes match the Freya Richardson case going back, say, fourteen years?"

"*I can but it will take time, and I know you don't have time.*"

GOOD GIRLS DON'T CRY 213

Kalo's chair squeaked as he moved from one computer to another on his desk. *"I'll set it up and see what comes up. I'll broaden the parameters as well, just in case the bodies were never found."*

Jenna smiled. She admired Kalo's expertise. "Thank you so much."

It took some time before the crime scene files appeared on the server. Jenna watched the video and then scrolled through the photos. She had the previous crime scene images open and ran them parallel to the new ones. She swallowed hard. Who had died here? Chloe Bennett or Olivia Cooper? The attack in the bathroom, the lack of footprints apart from the victims, the imprint of where a towel had lay over the blood. It was identical. They'd assumed the killer had entered the house when the victim was in the shower, stripped off to murder them, and then showered away any evidence. He used a bunch of towels to prevent any footprints and wiping up any others he might have left during the stabbing. The towels were never found. The bodies wrapped and taken away to be buried in the forest. The worst thing was that he recorded the murders but didn't bury them with the victim—no, he buried the recording of the previous victim's death with the body. Copies of the audio files were discovered at the killer's home—but now they knew the new killings were copycats.

A knock on the door announced Maggie. She walked inside with three women and introduced them. She handed Jenna their statements. "Thanks, Maggie." She looked at the three ashen-faced women. "Please take a seat. Can I get you anything? Coffee? Water?"

All three shook their heads. Jenna glanced over the statements. As usual, Maggie had been thorough. Each one stated the time of the incident and the exact movements up to discovering the blood-spattered bathroom. They'd even included the weather. She looked up at the women. "Okay. Just a few ques-

214   D.K. HOOD

tions." She directed her first questions to the Realtor. "Ms. Furlich, how many people knew the house was open for inspection this morning?"

"Any amount. It's on our website, but we ask for anyone interested to call me first so I can give them a guided tour." Barb frowned. "I didn't want a rush of people arriving and not being able to supervise them properly."

Jenna moved her attention to the other women. "As passengers in Ms. Furlich's vehicle, I would assume you took in the surrounding scenery on the way to the property. Did either of you see anyone or a vehicle coming from the property?"

They all shook their heads. "When you went into the bedroom where you found the blood, did any of you touch anything? A door handle? Did you peek into the closet?"

"No, we didn't touch anything upstairs." Barb frowned. "I did notice the glass doors leading out back were open. I assumed I'd left them open the previous day. It's not something I do. I check everything but I was running late. I needed to meet another client at a property in town, so I could have forgotten to close the door."

Sorting through the statements, Jenna handed one to Barb Furlich. "If you can add that to your statement and sign it. We'll make sure to check the door. Did you close it before you left the premises?"

"Yes, I did," Barb looked mortified. "I closed it when we arrived." She made the changes. "I didn't know, I'm sorry."

After taking the statements and scanning them into the system, Jenna handed a copy back to each woman. "It's okay, but we'll need your fingerprints and a sample of DNA to use for elimination purposes. When you go back downstairs, Maggie will do it. The DNA swab is just from inside your mouth. It's painless and simple." She looked from one to the other. "You've all had a nasty shock. If you suffer any nightmares or flashbacks,

GOOD GIRLS DON'T CRY   215

please consult a medical professional. Thank you for your time today."

The women stood and left the room. Jenna called Maggie and told her what she needed. She checked her watch. Kane should be at the gravesite by now. She leaned back in her chair, chewing on her bottom lip. Not being in the thick of the action was torture, as was waiting for information. Patience, in her case, wasn't a virtue she enjoyed.

FORTY-ONE

THE MINE

Not knowing what was going to happen next was getting to Olivia. Early this morning the man had arrived carrying a plate of fresh hot pancakes drenched in butter and maple syrup. He'd made her stand against the wall and placed two cups of to-go coffee with the fixings on the small table in her cell, backed out without saying a word, and left. After hearing his footsteps die away in the distance, Olivia had fallen onto the food, eating it with relish. After wrapping the second to-go cup in her socks to keep it hot, she'd spent a long time sipping the coffee and licking every small trace of syrup and butter from the plate. Why was he being nice to her?

After he'd ordered her to take a shower the previous day he'd placed her in this cell. It was different from the others. It had a bed with clean sheets, a table and chair, and snack food on shelves. Although the walls were the same hewn rock, no damp dribbled down them and they were void of moss. After Chloe had left with him, she had lain awake most of the night waiting for him to return, not knowing what he had planned for her— but he hadn't returned.

Her mind had been conjuring up what could be happening

GOOD GIRLS DON'T CRY 217

with Chloe. Where was she? Had he hurt her? Chloe had been so scared when she left, and her look of pure terror as he dragged her away chilled her to the bone. She didn't believe she could ever get the image of her terrified face out of her mind. Being the last person locked inside this terrible place and having no one to talk to would drive her insane.

The other thing she had now was light in the form of a small battery-operated lantern. Shivering, she pulled a blanket around her shoulders and sat at the table sipping her coffee. She stared at her nails. She'd always had nice nails but now she'd bitten them down to the quick. She looked at the bloody stumps, regretting biting them as they were her only weapon. The past few days kept circling around in her mind. She had witnessed things so horrific no amount of counseling would ever remove them from her memory. That's if she ever survived this place. No matter what the man told her, she wouldn't believe him because if he'd released the others as he'd promised, one of them would have alerted the sheriff.

She scrubbed her hands down her face, and her heart pounded with the implications. There could be no escaping the truth. He'd killed them all and she'd be next.

FORTY-TWO
STANTON FOREST

The ride along narrow trails through Stanton Forest would have been a respite from the murder case in different circumstances. The forest was glorious in summer. The scent, now a familiar friend of pine and fresh alpine air, brushed Kane's face. The trees and all around created an abundance of nature's glory. He wished he could stop and enjoy it. Using GPS coordinates, he led the way in a direct route to the gravesite they discovered last Halloween. There was an easy way through by following the fire roads if they needed to travel by truck, but as time was of the essence, using the trail bikes and taking the game trails made more sense.

He glimpsed deer and elk as they roared along the deer paths. Clouds of birds flew into the air, angry at them for disturbing their paradise. They drove through crystal-clear mountain streams, with the sun glistening like diamonds across the water, and along trails crisscrossed with zebra stripes, and all the while high above them the mountain watched, its peaks still carrying a cloak of snow with the reminder that, even in summer, winter was only a short time away.

As Kane reached the fire road adjacent to the trail leading

GOOD GIRLS DON'T CRY 219

to the gravesite, Carter drove up beside him. "It's just through there. I figured I'd stop here for a moment and see if I could find any tire tracks or evidence of anyone being here recently."

"Ask Rio to do it and we'll head on through the trees, just in case we catch him in the act." Carter grinned around his toothpick. "Although I figured the trail bikes would have given us away some."

Pressing his mic, Kane spoke to Rio. "Check along this fire road for any signs of recent tire tracks. The last time the killer brought the victims here he stopped on this road and carried them through the forest."

"Copy that."

Scanning the area for any sign of movement, Kane revved up his trail bike and headed for the gravesites. As the clearing came into view, he slowed abruptly and held up one hand. Ahead of him a neatly dug grave, with the soil still damp, sat in a patch of sunlight. He pressed his mic again. "I have a visual on a grave. I'll contact Wolfe. Be vigilant. He could still be in the area."

Pulling his phone out of his jacket, Kane removed his helmet and made the call. "The soil looks fresh, maybe a little bit dried around the edges, but most of it is still damp."

"Is Raven with you?"

Kane looked down the trail, he could hear the other trail bikes. "Yeah, he's here."

"He's not trained in forensics, but being a doctor I'm sure he will be able to uncover a small portion of the grave to see if there's a body in there. I want you to take very detailed images and a video of the entire scene all around and every portion of the grave. Look for footprints. I want you to leave the camera rolling as he removes a small portion of the soil." Wolfe blew out a long sigh. *"We'll finish up here, and if you find a body, we'll head out right away. Send me the coordinates."*

Looking at Carter, Kane nodded. "Okay." He sent the coordinates and disconnected. He tapped his mic and explained the situation to the others. "We need to do this now."

Rio and Raven arrived in a roar of engines. Kane pulled his forensics kit out of his backpack, gave Raven gloves and a face mask. He pulled on gloves, covered his face with a mask and waved Raven toward the grave. "I'll help. Rio, you do the filming; Carter, you've got our backs."

"Not a problem." Carter pulled his weapon and scanned the area.

They waited for Rio to take images and a video of the grave and then set about carefully removing the soil. Kane could think of nothing worse than finding a buried body of a young woman. He recalled standing and watching as Norrell carefully removed the topsoil to find the body wrapped in a sheet, a phone tucked in neatly beside them and wrapped in a plastic waterproof bag. It was as if the killer had intended to keep the phone in good condition for someone to find in the future. Beside him Raven worked methodically, his brow furrowed in a deep frown. When the edge of a white sheet appeared, Kane sat back on his heels. "This looks exactly the same as the last grave we uncovered here. The victim was wrapped in a bedsheet taken from the bedroom of the house. I saw that the bed had been disturbed but I didn't really take any notice."

"Okay, I'll just remove a little of the soil, to make sure it's actually a body. I'm sure killers have been known to bury other things as a decoy." Raven moved more soil and tufts of hair appeared, sticking from the sheet. "Yeah, it's a body. We'll leave the exhumation to Wolfe. I might destroy valuable evidence."

Kane made the call. "We'll wait here until you arrive. We don't want any wildlife disturbing the body."

"I'm on my way." Wolfe sounded tired. *"That makes nine this animal has murdered. We need to take him down."*

Nodding, Kane cleared his throat. "Don't worry. We will."

He called Jenna and explained the situation. "Rio is

GOOD GIRLS DON'T CRY   221

uploading the video and photos to the server now. We're waiting for Wolfe to arrive. He will be coming the long way around, so it might be a time."

"Just stay alert. This man is dangerous." Jenna cleared her throat. *"I've been scanning old case files since you left. I'm trying to work out his next move. If this is his kill as he stated on the mirror, what is he planning on doing with Olivia? He's proved his point."*

Kane turned slowly, scanning the forest. "Maybe it's the end of that cycle of killing. He wanted recognition but since then he's created another fantasy. Being locked away, all he'd be thinking about is his next kill. His mind would be creating millions of scenarios. Maybe he plans Olivia to be the first. He has her, no need to kidnap another victim. All he needs to do is to create the fear in her. I figure by now the poor kid is terrified, if she's still alive."

"We can only hope she is." Jenna yawned. *"Oh, heavens, that sounds like I'm bored. I'm just tired. When we've caught this guy, maybe I'll get a good night's sleep. It's been playing on my mind constantly. I just can't figure him out."* She sighed. *"It's because it all seems aimed at us. He's shifting the blame onto us by saying we made a mistake and now he needs to kill all these poor girls to make it right."*

Giving Rio a wave, Kane walked back along the trail to the fire road to wait for Wolfe. "That's a typical serial killer, isn't it? They never take the blame themselves, do they? It's always the victim made them do it, a dog barking, or a voice. This is just his way of validating another fantasy. He must have planned this in his head for years." Kane leaned against a tree, his gaze never leaving the forest. "After getting out of prison, he just waited for a group of girls to go out together. He'd have seen the story in the newspaper or on social media about the limo in town and the group of kids using it to go to the prom. The new service for weddings and all that made the news. He

222   D.K. HOOD

just bided his time until he had a nice group of kids he could use."

"That makes sense, but how did he get into the limo and take out the driver?" Jenna stirred a cup of coffee and tapped the spoon on the rim of her cup.

Shrugging, Kane pressed the phone to his ear. "I've given this a lot of thought. We don't know when he climbed into the limo. It most likely was at the last house. It's surrounded by trees. He'd likely followed it and waited for an opportunity. I figure he has two vehicles. One to transport the victims and another, likely a motorcycle. Something he could leave in the trees and come back later to collect it. The second vehicle is a van or a small bus."

"Yeah, that makes sense." Jenna sipped her coffee. *"I feel guilty drinking coffee while you're stuck out there in the forest."*

Kane chuckled. "Don't be. I have a backpack filled with energy bars and plenty of water. I'll do for a time." He looked up as a white van came into sight. "Wolfe's here. It shouldn't be too long now. See you soon." He disconnected.

It didn't take long for Wolfe to examine the grave and uncover the blood-soaked sheet covering the slight form of Chloe Bennett. Four of them lifted her out and placed her on a body bag before Wolfe unwrapped her. Kane winced at the number of injuries the poor girl had sustained, but it was the neat bundle of phones that caught his attention. "There's a phone or maybe more."

"Four phones?" Wolfe changed his gloves and opened the bag. "They all have charge." He opened the sound files and they all listened.

"Oh, my God." Rio ran a hand down his face. "He's recorded all the murders."

FORTY-THREE

Thursday

Jenna stood at the window in her office staring at the mountains. Set against a clear blue sky, they stood majestically like sentries protecting their town. The forest spread out in dense green foliage. The tall trees, their trunks straight, marched up the mountainside in a seemingly endless battalion. It was so vast that people could walk in and vanish without a trace. She'd spent the entire morning searching through all the files of previous cases trying to get her head around what was inside the killer's mind. "Where are you, and where are you keeping Olivia?"

Her voice caused Duke to yawn, stand up from his basket, and walk toward her. He'd recently returned from a long walk with Kane, which had obviously included a few snacks from Aunt Betty's Café, and he'd been sleeping in his basket. Jenna rubbed his ears and smiled at him. "Sorry to disturb you. I was just talking to myself." She shook her head and went to sit at her desk. "Now I'm holding conversations with a dog. Is that a sign of madness?"

224   D.K. HOOD

It was strange being in the office alone, but Kane, Raven, and Rio had insisted on attending the autopsy of Chloe Bennett. All hoped that Wolfe would discover something to pin the murder on one of their suspects. The error that placed all the murders on the one serial killer was yet to be determined, but Wolfe had explained to her earlier that they'd worked the opposite way around. The more recent murders matched the MO of the cold cases, and as the killer hadn't denied murdering the cold case victims, they were attributed to him. Not that adding another two murders to his body count would have made any difference to his prison sentence.

Her phone buzzed but it wasn't Wolfe calling about his autopsy results. It was Emily. Surprised, as Emily worked long shifts at the hospital, Jenna's first instinct was that something was wrong. "Hi, Em, is everything okay?"

"Yeah, sure. Everyone is fine." Emily was wearing her squeaky rubber-soled shoes that made strange noises when she walked on tile. "Dad mentioned that you required the results from the moss examination ASAP. They just came through and Dad is still conducting the autopsy on the poor girl who was murdered yesterday, so I figured I'd give you a call."

Relieved, Jenna took a pen from the cup on her table and pulled her notepad in front of her. "Shoot. You can upload the details to the server so I can show the team."

"Okay. Well, the moss is *Seligeria campylopoda*, a moss that grows in dark places, so caves or similar, but they also found soil in the sample. Let me see." Emily paused as she read the results. "They believe it's tailings, and the residue would suggest it came from an old gold mine. Does that help?"

Head spinning, Jenna stared into space. "I need to look at something to make certain, but I figure I know where the killer is hiding Olivia. When Dave comes out, ask him to call me. If I'm correct, we'll need to move on it right away."

GOOD GIRLS DON'T CRY 225

"Okay. I'll go inside now and see him. I hope you find her." Emily disconnected.

Scanning through the murder case files, Jenna found the one involving a killer who used an old mineshaft that had been converted into cells for prisoners during the gold rush. As this murderer was apparently following the crimes depicted in the true crime series written about Black Rock Falls, he'd know the location. It was isolated and the last time she'd seen, it had heavy chains and padlocks on the gates. None of which couldn't be broken with a heavy set of bolt cutters. Her stomach twisted at the thought of sending her team down the dark mineshaft. She looked at Duke. "Here I go again stressing out again like a mother hen. I have three highly trained deputies, Kane, and a Navy SEAL. They could take down a serial killer trapped in a mineshaft with one hand tied behind their backs."

Duke whined and the top of one eye lifted to look at her before he turned around three times and flopped down in his basket. Jenna tapped her pen on the desk thinking. That's if the killer was in the mineshaft, but what if he wasn't? What if Olivia was alone? If so, they'd get her to safety first and then lay a trap for the killer.

They wouldn't be able to drive to the mineshaft. She recalled the area and from the foothills to the road lay miles of open lowlands covered with wheatgrass. They'd be seen and heard from a mile away. Unable to contain her excitement, she stood and went to the supply closet and checked the combat gear. They'd need camouflage, their Kevlar vests, and weapons. She nodded, seeing the stacks of clothes, all neatly piled on the shelves behind signs depicting the sizes. She turned and walked to the gun safe. Everything inside she'd stripped down with Kane and cleaned just days ago. The ammunition boxes were full. Everything was good to go. She stared at her phone. Had Emily told Kane yet?

As if on cue, her phone buzzed. She sighed with relief

seeing Kane's name on the caller ID. She explained her theory. "I remember Wolfe dropped us there by chopper, but we'll need Carter for the takedown. This guy is dangerous."

"Yeah, I've just watched an autopsy. He must be stopped." Kane's boots clattered on the tile in the morgue. *"We could do what we did last time. Wolfe can pilot the chopper, and he has everything we need to rappel down some ways away from the mine and come in with stealth. The only problem is that if the killer's read the book about the case, he'll be expecting us to do that. So we'll need to be sneaky. I'll bring everyone up to speed and we'll head back to the office. I have a plan."*

Jenna stared at the clock. "If Olivia is there, there's a chance this guy is still at work. It would be better to get her clear before he arrives."

"Yeah, that's a given, but we'll play the cards we're dealt. This is still a hunch, right?" Undaunted, Jenna shook her head. "No, I'm convinced. It fits. Olivia is there. I'm sure of it."

"Okay, we're on our way." Kane disconnected.

FORTY-FOUR

In the conference room, Jenna stared at the map of the lowlands displayed on the screen. It never ceased to amaze her how military men organized a mission. Kane naturally took charge, pointing out the areas where they'd be most exposed and mapping out a plan to get into the mine without being seen. She waited until he'd stopped talking and looked at him. "So exactly how do you plan on getting to the mine without him seeing you? We don't know if he's there or he could be anywhere close by."

"I already have that organized." Kane pulled on a Kevlar vest before checking his weapon. "I commandeered a lineman's truck, and they also supplied me with a jacket. Rio has volunteered to climb up the pole and make like he's working. He'll act as our lookout and if anyone sees him, he'll pass as being perfectly normal as they're always working on the lines in that area, so I'm told."

"Rio will drive close to the hillside." Carter moved a toothpick across his lips as he indicated to the map. "The rocky outcrops are just uneven enough to prevent a line of view from the mine's entrance and give us cover. He'll drop us there as he's

228   D.K. HOOD

turning the truck around and we'll head back to the mine undetected."

Seeing many unforeseen dangers recalling the last time they were down that mineshaft, Jenna frowned. "This guy is an unknown quantity. We already know he uses explosives. What if he has the mineshaft booby-trapped?"

"That's why we're taking Zorro with us." Carter stepped back from the screen and filled his pockets with ammunition from a stack on the table. He looked at Jenna and held up a small shoulder bag, which he slung across his chest. "If we find anything, I can disarm it. We'd already considered possible IEDs."

"I'll be leaving Ben with you." Raven geared up and smiled at her. "We won't fit him in the truck and he likes Duke." He patted a first aid kit slung over one shoulder. "I'll be taking care of Olivia."

Time was ticking down and the team had moved at warp speed to get ready. Jenna looked from one to the other. "Your first priority is getting Olivia to safety. If she's there, we've found his lair and we can set up a stakeout to take him down the moment he shows. Rio, you take Olivia and bring her here." She looked at Kane. "Anything else?"

"Yeah, if we get her out when he's not there, Rio should go and take Raven with him. They can bring Olivia to you and then drop the truck back and pick up their vehicles." Kane scratched his cheek. "If they can wait somewhere close by, maybe in the industrial area, they can come in when we have the killer restrained or need backup. We'll need the vehicles to bring the killer here. We'll all be communicating by coms. The phone service out there is sketchy." He slid a water flask into his belt. "We need to move out."

Stomach clenching like it always did when they were ready to face down a killer, Jenna exchanged a look with Kane that said everything she needed to say. She wouldn't be by his side

GOOD GIRLS DON'T CRY   229

this time watching his back. The next moment, he slid from loving husband and father into combat mode in a split second. If she hadn't known him for so long, it would be frightening. "Save the girl and do what's necessary to take that monster down."

"Copy that." Carter grinned around his toothpick. "We'll be home in time for dinner."

As the team headed out of the door, boots clattering on the tile, Jenna went back to her office and leaned both hands on her desk. Her heart pounded and her stomach twisted as the problems and dangers of dealing with a complete unknown rushed through her mind. They'd dealt with many vicious murderers in their time, but they'd always had an idea of their limitations based on their crimes. This one was different, an unknown quantity, a multiskilled killer looking for his next thrill. She stared up at the ceiling. "Keep them safe."

FORTY-FIVE

Olivia pressed against the wall as footsteps came along the passageway. The flashlight bobbed up and down and soon her captor came into view. He ignored her and went to the desk. Under one arm, he carried a laptop and spent a few minutes setting it up and attaching cables. She couldn't make out what he was watching but then recognized the logo for the local news channel. The picture-in-picture second screen showed what must be outside, so a CCTV he'd set up maybe. Olivia stood on tiptoes to see what was happening.

The man sat stroking a long lock of hair. The screen flickered, making his masked features look grotesque in the dim light. Who did the hair belong to? A shudder went through Olivia and her mouth went dry. Was that Chloe's hair? She couldn't see what was on the news but whatever it was it made the man groan and sniff the hair. The sight of him was almost pathetic, but then something caught his attention and he stood abruptly, sending his chair tumbling backward.

"What is a lineman's truck doing here?" He picked up his chair and sat down at the desk. His fingers flew over the keyboard. "There is no scheduled maintenance in this area and

GOOD GIRLS DON'T CRY 231

the power is working just fine." He stood, grasped the hair, and twisted it in his fingers. "This is a setup." He paced around the small area, staring at his feet. "This isn't in the book. It says they came by chopper. I need time to get away." He dug a finger into the screen. "This wasn't the plan. Now I'm going to make life difficult for you." He tossed the hair on the desk.

Heart pounding, Olivia fixed her attention on him. What was he going to do? Who was coming? She strained her eyes to see the small screen, but could only make out a waving field of wheatgrass. A loud scraping sound came from close by and the man pushed a trunk into the middle of the passageway. When he flipped it open, Olivia caught her breath. A ton of wires and what she believed to be metal pipes. The man took a device out and she could see his smile through the open mouth of the balaclava. He suddenly turned and looked at her as if suddenly remembering he had company.

"See this, Olivia?" He waved the device around, its wires trembling. "This is a surprise for the cops who think they're going to sneak up on me."

Swallowing her fear, she turned her gaze on him. "What are you going to do to them?"

"Blow them sky high." He chuckled. "Then we can leave. There's more than one way out of this mine. Some old-timer told me to follow the old railroad tracks and we'll come out some ways along the hillside. While they're inside looking for us, we'll be long gone." He waved the explosive device at her. "That's if any of them are alive."

When he dived into the trunk, grabbed something, and headed toward her cell, Olivia shrank back against the back wall, terrified at having him so close, crowding her. Would he try and kill her?

"Stand very still." His dark eyes stared right through to her soul. "You're my ticket out of here." He touched the knife in his belt. "I will kill you or cut you up and leave you to bleed to death slowly if you don't do as I say."

Horrified, Olivia sucked in a deep breath, tasting his sweat on her tongue. He moved closer and pushed her arms into a vest with wire running through it. Was he planning on electrocuting her? She gasped for air as he tightened the straps. "What is this for?"

"One scream or warning and you'll find out." He smiled at her. "Be good and I'll make you famous." He walked out of the cell, slamming the door behind him, and stared at the computer screen. "Showtime!"

FORTY-SIX

The sun had dropped in the sky, leaving a line of shadows along the perimeter of the hillside. Kane kept close to the rocky outcrop until they came to a deep fissure that would conceal the team from view. He tapped his com. "What do you see, Rio?"

"There's a white van concealed beneath a large camouflage tarpaulin outside the mine entrance. The metal gate appears to be intact." Rio paused for a beat. *"I'm seeing what could be a CCTV camera above the entrance to the mineshaft. I wouldn't have noticed it, but it must have a sweeping motion because the lens caught the light just before."*

Beside Kane, Carter was miming shooting a rifle. He nodded. "You sure you're not seeing the scope on a rifle?"

"Yeah, I'm sure. There's no place to conceal a shooter above the front of the mine. All I see is straight rock with hardly any cover." Rio grunted and his breath caught. *"These darn lines are live. I can't appear to be working on them. If I touch the wrong thing, I'll be toast... literally."*

Kane moved his attention to Rio's position. "Change of plan. Climb down and head back to where we left the vehicles.

234   D.K. HOOD

We'll need you back here pronto with a transport vehicle when we catch this guy."

"*Copy that.*"

Waving the team forward, Kane edged through the shadows toward the mine entrance. He scanned the area where Rio had spotted the camera and noted that it was set high and well above the entrance. He tapped his mic. "The CCTV camera is covering the road. I don't figure it covers the entrance, so as long as we keep down, we should be able to get in without him seeing us."

Duck-walking to the mine entrance Kane ran his fingers over the chain hanging free on one side of the large metal gate. On one end hung an open shiny new padlock. In the dirt at his feet sat a rusty discarded lock. He kicked it with his toe, noting the cut where a bolt cutter had sheared it from the chain. He eased the gate open slowly hoping it wouldn't creak, and waved Carter and Zorro inside. Having an explosives sniffer dog and a bomb disposal expert with him was an advantage, especially when hunting down a perpetrator known to use explosives. He switched on his bodycam to record the takedown and ducked in behind Carter with Raven close on his heels.

Kane had been in many unusual situations during his time in the military, and small claustrophobic spaces didn't worry him—although he'd admit pitch-black root cellars gave him the creeps. Both members of his team were ex-military and would have endured the same type of training as he had. He trusted they wouldn't freak out in the oppressively dark environment. Unable to use flashlights, Kane moved along behind Carter, feeling his way in the dim light with one hand on the damp moss-covered walls. Stale air around them coated his tongue and tasted like the inside of a mausoleum, as if a thousand corpses had been buried close by.

As they moved deeper inside the tunnel, the outside light slowly vanished. Once they turned a corner, the way ahead would be pitch black and each step would be into unknown danger. Ahead, Carter held Zorro's leash, trusting his canine friend to keep him safe. It never ceased to amaze him how Carter worked with Zorro. The dog understood the need to be silent and communicated with Carter using body language. When he stopped abruptly, Carter turned and pressed a hand on Kane's chest. Something was directly in front of them.

Kane recalled the layout of the mine, many passages branched off from the main one, but they needed to turn a corner before anyone would see them. They could risk a penlight without being detected. He took one from his pocket and played the beam across the floor. A fine wire glistened in the light. Moving closer he followed the tripwire to an explosive device. The idiot had set a device that could bring down the roof. Heart pounding, he held the flashlight steady as Carter went to work. Although he'd seen Carter work previously, and trusted him, it didn't stop the trickle of nervous sweat running down between his shoulder blades. Beside him, a ripple went through Zorro. The dog understood explosions and he'd never seen him back away from some of the most dangerous devices. Behind him, he could hear Raven breathing hard. As Carter worked, he could have cut the tension inside the tunnel with a knife.

The threat neutralized, they moved forward. Small rocks dislodged as they continued downward, each tiny pebble sounding loud in the silence. Ahead, the tunnel broke into many dark endless maws, and Kane counted six possible places for the killer to be hiding. He recalled the layout of the main area. The last time he'd been down here, an underground office and storage area lay directly ahead. They had assumed if Olivia was here, her kidnapper would be holding her in one of the cells. As they moved forward, Carter suddenly flattened himself against the wall, one arm flaying behind him to stop Kane. Kane pressed his com. Even in the caves the coms would work, and

236   D.K. HOOD

with Carter, no language was necessary. He tapped a message to him and received the reply:

"Don't move. Someone's in the passageway on the left."

Without hesitation, Kane pulled his weapon, stepped past Carter, and keeping his back to the wall, aimed his penlight into the darkness. The sight chilled him to the core. He waved the others forward and moved the penlight beam slowly across a macabre scarecrow dressed in a tattered sheriff's uniform. Obviously female, the head, made from a roughly sewn burlap sack, had large haunting eyes and an open mouth drawn with bright red lipstick. The outstretched arms were attached to a crossbeam and the legs hung to the floor. Kane's attention moved to the necklace, made from a piece of yellow twine with a dozen locks of hair attached. Bile curled his gut at the sight of the killer's trophies, proudly displayed. An involuntary shudder went through him as he moved the light lower. A long kitchen knife protruded from the swollen belly. Now this had gotten personal.

He indicated for Carter to move forward. The passageway widened, and ahead, he made out a small flickering light. The next second, voices came from every direction, women's voices, pleading, crying, and begging. Kane tapped his com. "He's playing the recordings of the murders, the sick freak. He's trying to psych us out. Fat chance of that. Spread out. Carter, take the left; I'll take the right. Raven, this is going to get nasty. Hang back and watch our backs. We're going in."

At a signal, Zorro moved forward and then stopped and sat down. Kane looked at Carter when the dog turned around and moved back to Carter's side.

"He smells explosives, a cache likely C4 or Semtex. If it were an IED, he gives a different signal."

Kane nodded. Carter's voice had come through his earpiece at just above a whisper but he could hear it just fine. He indi-

GOOD GIRLS DON'T CRY 237

cated to keep going. Ahead was an unknown quantity who liked to play mind games.

As screams echoed around them, Kane dropped deeper into the zone and embraced the cold unemotional state. Nothing would stop him taking down this killer. He moved forward keeping his back to the wall, behind him Raven retraced his steps. As they moved through one open metal gate and then another, the single bulb hanging from the roof illuminated a young girl tied to a chair wearing an explosive vest. The girl's eyes looked hopeful at the sight of him but she shook her head and tipped it sightly toward the right. He stopped midstride and glanced at Carter before scanning the small space. It hadn't changed since the last time he was here, an office type space, a shower, and cells. The mind-altering screaming of tortured souls finally stopped and a man's voice replaced it.

"There you all are, ready to take me down." The man chuckled. "I didn't figure you'd make it past the tripwire. The last deputy didn't."

Unfazed, Kane indicated toward one of the open cell doors and then looked at the girl, who gave him a slight nod. "Sheriff's department, why don't you come out and we can discuss this? No one needs to die today. So far, we have you only on kidnapping Olivia. If she's okay, then it won't be so bad. I'll put in a good word with the judge if you cooperate."

"You won't need to, Deputy Kane, because I'm walking right out of here, but first you need to hear my story." The man walked out of the cell, dressed in black and wearing a balaclava. In one hand he held a device, and his other rested on a Glock pushed into his belt.

"Why would we care?" Carter was aiming his weapon at the man's head. "You put down that detonator and we'll talk."

"No way." The man shook his head. "This is my guarantee of freedom."

238   D.K. HOOD

Keeping his M18 pistol leveled on the man's chest, Kane stared into eyes like empty sockets. "So you wanna deal?"

"I want the truth, is all." The man waved the detonator. "Didn't you understand my notes? All those murders and people you put in prison, but you got it wrong one time. I'm putting the record straight and then I'm out of here."

"How did you know the details of the murders you copied?" Raven moved closer.

"Easy. I read the true crime series about the murders in Black Rock Falls." He shrugged. "The author went into great detail, which made them a breeze to copy, but I mixed up a few to make life difficult for you." His posture suddenly changed. "No more talking. Put down your weapons. I'm walking out of here."

Kane didn't move an inch. "That's not gonna happen. I don't make deals in caves. Come down to the sheriff's office, we'll get you a lawyer, and then we'll talk." He read him his rights.

"You're wasting your breath." The supremely confident man's mouth curled into a smile. "I win. You'll never risk Olivia's life." He chuckled. "I know how you think. If I didn't, why do you figure I kept Olivia alive? Look at her, she's perfect and I want to kill her so bad, but then I'd lose my bargaining chip."

"So you want to confess your sins?" Carter gave a cynical laugh. "Sorry, we didn't figure we'd need to bring a priest." He looked at Kane. "Remind me to add one to our team the next time we're hunting down scum."

"I'm no fool. I've seen the bodycam. Whatever happens here will be recorded. I'll tell my story and then I'm leaving." The man waved the device. "This detonator has a long range and you'll never figure out how to disarm the vest, so you'll let me go and then maybe hope to catch me later—but don't hold your breath. I've been enjoying myself for a long time and

GOOD GIRLS DON'T CRY   239

nobody's caught me yet. Well, not for murder. You see, I'm in and out before small-town cops like you discover the bodies."

"Why did you try and shoot the woman with me at the crime scene out at Glacial Heights?" Raven stepped closer his weapon drawn. "She hasn't done anything to you."

"You and she were in the way." The man shrugged. "I knew if I took you out, the sheriff would come running." He moved his black eyes to Kane. "I needed to put things right."

Examining the detonator, Kane recognized the improvised type, and the man's thumb hovering above a red button. He flicked his fingers at Carter to stand down. "Okay, we're listening. So the murders in the bathrooms were yours. Is that the message here?"

"Yeah." The man's grin spread under the gap in his balaclava. "I like to kill in threes on Halloween because it leaves a lasting memory. People get scared when they believe I'm coming back, but in truth I move around. I don't kill every so many years. I kill all the time. I just make it three on Halloween in the same town. Not just here but all over the good old USA."

Frowning, Kane stared at the delusional man. "So you're saying we arrested the wrong guy for the Halloween shower murders? If I recall, you were in jail over that time."

"Yeah, I was but I met this crazy guy in jail." The man leaned against the wall as if he had all the time in the world. "He was on remand for killing dogs. We talked about killing. You know, we recognize each other. Psychopaths have a kinship —a respect for each other. I let him run his mouth and the conversation went onto my kills. They'd been all over the media. He didn't know I was the killer, but I told him how neat it would be to record the murders and place them in the graves." He sighed. "He raved on about how much he'd love to become famous like the Halloween Killer. The next thing I know, this guy is copying my shower kills right down to the recordings and burying them in threes." He stabbed a finger in his chest. "The

240   D.K. HOOD

first ones you found were mine. He messed up and got caught. I'm setting the record straight."

"You could have sent us an email." Carter shook his head. "All this is drama queen overkill."

"So you believe, but it seems to me I have the upper hand here." The man waved the detonator. "I'll make it simple for you. I walk out of here and she lives."

The threat was real but this guy was a master manipulator playing out a scene in his deluded mind. Kane rolled his shoulders. "You figure I'm gonna allow you to walk out of here when you've threatened to kill my wife? I'll give you one chance. Place the detonator and the weapon on the ground, put your hands on your head, and you leave here alive."

"I press this button and we all die." The man held up the detonator, his thumb poised over the red button. "I've got nothing to lose."

The deafening sound of a shot came from beside Kane as Carter discharged his weapon. The bullet hit the man in the shoulder, throwing him to the ground. The detonator slid across the floor stopping at Olivia's feet. The girl screamed in terror as Kane dashed forward to disarm the perpetrator. In a split second, the man went for his Glock. On instinct, Kane aimed center mass and fired. The gunshots reverberated through the mineshafts in endless echoes. He stared down at the man, as a patch of blood spread across the massive hole in his chest. It wasn't necessary to check his vital signs, but Kane kicked the Glock from his hand and then bent down. He removed the balaclava and pressed fingers to the man's neck. He shook his head. "This is Silas Thorne. I interviewed him. He was a ranch hand out at the Silver Buckle." He straightened. "You okay, Olivia?"

"Get this vest off of me." Olivia stared at Kane with terrified eyes. "He was going to blow me up. Get me out of here." Her entire body shook and her teeth chattered. "I don't want to die. Please help me!"

GOOD GIRLS DON'T CRY   241

"Calm down." Carter placed a hand on her shoulder. "Keep shaking like that and you'll trigger the bomb and we'll all die. I can get you out, but you must sit still."

"I'll try." Tears spilled down Olivia's cheeks as she looked at Kane. "You killed him." Her eyes widened. "Is he really dead?"

Nodding, Kane squeezed her shoulder. "Yeah, he's dead." He pressed his com to talk to Rio. "The perp is down. Get here ASAP."

"*Copy.*"

Raising an eyebrow, he looked at Carter. "Gutsy call. What made you shoot?"

"I know the device. It's not what most suicide bombers and the like use. They arm their bombs to explode when they *remove* their finger. That type needs two pushes on the button to explode. It's a failsafe." Carter shrugged and went to Olivia. "You're gonna be fine. Just sit still for a little longer and I'll have you out of this in no time." He went to his knees beside Olivia and then glanced up at Kane. "Jenna won't be happy. She wanted him alive."

Kane waved his concerns away. He'd seen Jenna's horrified expression at the autopsies. "It was him or me. I don't figure she'll shed a tear for this guy." He went to stand beside Olivia, keeping his body between her and the corpse. He crouched beside her. "You were very brave. Those signals you gave me saved all our lives. Carter here will free you, but you must try and remain calm. I'll be right here holding your hand, okay?" He indicated to Raven. "This is Dr. Johnny Raven. Once we're out of here, he'll take a look at you and then we'll get you to the hospital."

"No hospital. He didn't hurt me. I just want to go home and see my mom." Olivia searched Kane's face. "My friends? Are they okay? He raped them and beat them. I'm glad he's dead."

Ripping off the Band-Aid was Kane's only choice. He

242 D.K. HOOD

squeezed her hand. "They didn't make it. I'm sorry for your loss."

"Oh, my God." Tears streamed down Olivia's face and she trembled. "You gotta get me out of here." She gasped in air at a frantic pace. "Don't let me die. Please, get the bomb off of me. I can't stand it a second longer." Her lip trembled and she sobbed, her entire body shaking.

"The bomb will trigger if you don't sit still." Carter's face was slick with sweat as he cut wires. "This is a little more complicated than I imagined. It's gonna take time."

"Oh, Jesus." Olivia tore at the vest. "Get this thing off of me."

Kane gripped her hands. "Take deep breaths. Carter can't help you if you shake. If he cuts the wrong wires, we're all toast."

"You can say that again." Carter looked at Raven. "Can you give her something? She needs to relax."

"Olivia, look at me. Now, take some deep breaths." Raven moved closer. "I'm going to give you a tranquilizer." He took a shot from a small case and pushed the needle into her thigh. "You're doing fine. It will all be over real soon." He smiled at her. "Slow breaths... in and out, in and out."

"I need more light." Carter looked at Kane, his face etched in concern. "This set up is like a bowl of spaghetti. It has traps all over."

Kneeling beside him, Kane pulled out his MAGLITE and held it steady. "Take your time. We have all day."

Beside him, Carter's face was tight with tension. His teeth dug deep into his bottom lip as he worked. Minutes ticked by and each time Carter's pliers closed around a wire, everyone held their breath. Intent on the almost impossible task facing Carter, Kane tried to slow his racing heart as his friend made each snip, followed by the long second's wait for an expected explosion.

Sweat ran down his face, and Kane gritted his teeth as he watched each delicate move. Carter's intent gaze moved back and forth, tracing wires and cutting them like a surgeon performing brain surgery. He hardly dared to breathe for the fifteen agonizing minutes it took before Carter lifted the vest from her. He sighed with relief and nodded to him. "Great job." He looked at Olivia. "You're okay now. Put one arm around my neck." He lifted her into his arms. "Let's get you out of here."

FORTY-SEVEN

Jenna met the team as they spilled back into the office. She stared at Kane. "Silas Thorne? He's dead? What happened?"

"See for yourself. Although it was dark down there." Kane removed the bodycam and handed it to her. "He had Olivia wired with explosives and threatened to blow us all sky high. Carter hit him in the shoulder. I went to disarm him and he drew down on me. It was self-defense."

"There is a nice confession on there as well and Dave read him his rights." Carter moved a toothpick across his lips. "We saved the girl. It was a successful mission."

Jenna fingered the bodycam and frowned. "Where is Olivia?"

"In the conference room." Kane indicated behind him with his thumb. "Raven is checking her out. She looks okay, scared to death but no major problems. He didn't hurt her. I guess he was saving her for a special kill. I gave her my phone to call her mom. Her parents will be along soon. They're happy for you to question her and she'll tell you everything that happened the night of the prom and since then. She's seventeen and a credible witness."

GOOD GIRLS DON'T CRY 245

Clearing her throat, Jenna looked from one to the other. "So you walked out and left the body for the rats?"

"Nope." Carter smiled at her. "I called Wolfe, and his team is heading there now."

Kane and Carter were both dirty and their faces streaked with sweat. She waved them out of her office. "Okay, you go and take a shower. I'll order some food from Aunt Betty's. Ask Rio to sit with Olivia, so Raven can do the same. I'll watch the footage and then speak to her." She smiled. "Seems to me, you handled everything without me. Great job." She picked up her phone and placed a delivery for takeout.

As Kane and Carter headed for the locker room, she leaned back in her chair and smiled at Duke. "I do believe it's time for me to go home and wait for my baby to arrive."

She slid the card from the bodycam into her computer and watched the dark footage. She could clearly hear everything that had happened. She swallowed hard at the sight of the scarecrow and chills ran down her spine each time Carter diffused the bombs. The confession was there to a point, but she needed to know what happened on the night of the prom.

Jenna picked up her recorder and headed to the conference room. Olivia was sitting up on the sofa wrapped in a blanket drinking hot chocolate. She looked at Raven. "I need to question her. Is she okay?"

"I'm fine, just a little sleepy." Olivia smiled at her. "Thank you for finding me. I knew you'd come."

Taking a seat opposite, Jenna turned to Raven. "Go and clean up. The takeout will be here soon."

"Thanks." Raven smiled at Olivia. "You're in good hands." He hurried from the room.

Keeping her expression pleasant, Jenna looked at Olivia. "Your parents will be here soon, but your mom said it was okay to talk to you about what happened. I'll record it so you won't need to keep repeating it, but you might have to answer a few

246   D.K. HOOD

questions later. One thing I need to know is how did Silas Thorne get into the limo?"

"I don't know." Olivia gripped the cup with both hands. "We didn't see him until we heard a gunshot and then saw the blood splashed on the window between the driver and us."

Jenna nodded. "Okay, I know it's painful, but what happened next?"

She listened in horror as Olivia described the terrifying moments before she saw the limo drop into the river. Without prompting, she went on giving as much detail as possible. The girl gave a very harrowing description of her time in the caves. Sickened by the vivid descriptions, she thanked Olivia and stood. "Deputy Rio will stay with you until your parents arrive. Please don't hug them. I'm sure the medical examiner will need to take samples from your clothes. Thorne might be dead but there will still be a full investigation. I'll be sending details of his crimes, plus his DNA, across the US. There are many unsolved crimes and he might be responsible for many of them." She squeezed Olivia's hand. "You've been so brave, but please take the help you need to recover. I'll always be here if you need to talk."

"I've proved to myself I'm stronger than I thought." Olivia gave Jenna a determined look. "I'll never forget what happened, but I won't fall apart. I need to live a normal life. I want to remember my friends and tell their stories. I want to make sure this never happens again."

Nodding, Jenna motioned to Rio to come inside. "I'll work hard to make sure men like him are caught and brought to justice. Deputy Rio will wait. I'll send someone down with takeout. I'm sure you must be starving." She patted Olivia on the shoulder and headed for the door.

Exhausted, Jenna walked back to her office. The case was solved, the team still running smoothly and very capable of tying up any loose ends. She'd wait for Kane to shower and eat and then she'd thank everyone and head home. For now, she'd leave law enforcement to her trusted team. She smiled as Kane, Carter, and Raven came into the office carrying a box of takeout. "The takedown went like clockwork." She looked at Kane. "It was a clear case of self-defense and Carter, wow, that was some fancy finger work." She swung her attention to Raven. "You just fit into the team as if you've been here all along. Thank you, for solving the case." She looked at Kane. "When you're done here, take me home. I want to spend the next week or so relaxing." She smiled. "As of this second, Rio is in charge."

"About time." Kane grinned at her. "Let's go."

FORTY-EIGHT

Monday, the Following Week

In his dream, Kane ducked and weaved as four men attacked him somewhere in the middle of a desert. His hand went instinctively for his weapon and came up empty. He never slept unarmed, never, and where the heck was he? He spun and kicked and the other men ran away. Now that never happened. The man on the floor rolled around, groaning and panting. He should leave before someone found him. He tapped his ear. "Gigabyte, do you copy?"

"Dave. Dave, wake up." A familiar voice came close to his ear.

Kane opened his eyes. The bedside lamp was on and Jenna was shaking him. He rolled onto his back, his mind still in combat mode, and forced tight muscles to relax. "I'm awake."

"It's time." Jenna smiled at him. "Contractions are seven minutes apart."

Springing out of bed, Kane pushed his feet into his boots and reached for his jeans. "Okay. Call Nanny Raya."

"I have already. She's in the spare room. I don't need her

GOOD GIRLS DON'T CRY 249

with me." Jenna's face turned red and she moaned and puffed out breaths.

Panic he'd never experienced in his life hit him in the pit of his stomach. "Is it real bad?"

"Not yet." Jenna sucked in a deep breath and smiled. "On the bright side, it's the Fourth of July. Our baby will have fireworks every birthday."

Duke whined and walked in circles before resting his head on the bed beside Jenna.

"I'm okay, Duke." She rubbed his head. "You go and lie down in your basket and watch over Tauri until we get back."

Kane grabbed a pair of jeans from the closet and then stared at his feet, wondering when he'd put on his boots. He glanced at Jenna, who looked at him and raised one eyebrow.

"Maybe it will be easier to take off your boots." Jenna's lips quivered into a smile. "Are you okay?"

Kicking off his boots, he hopped on one foot to pull on jeans. He shook his head in disbelief at waking up without a brain. They'd been over the sequence of events hundreds of times, what to do first, when the time came. He had this. He dressed in record time and ran to the front door to get the Beast from the garage. He left the truck idling and hurried inside for Jenna's hospital bag, sitting packed beside the front door. He tossed it onto the back seat, slid behind the wheel, and was hurtling along the driveway before he realized he'd left Jenna behind. He slammed his hands on the steering wheel and threw the truck into reverse. "Get a grip, you idiot. She needs you right now."

He ran the plan they'd discussed through his mind again. First, make sure Tauri was cared for, check the contractions, call Wolfe, get bag, go to hospital. Too easy. He'd jumped straight to step four. Getting Jenna to the hospital had somehow become his first priority. He drove back to the house and dashed inside. As usual, Jenna was calm and in control. She had Wolfe on the phone and was listening to his instructions. Feeling a little stupid, he sat on the bed beside her as she disconnected. "Is there anything I can do? The Beast is outside and I've got your bag."

"You might want to put on matching boots and your sweater is inside out." Jenna grinned at him. "It's okay. It will probably be hours yet, but Wolfe said to head off between contractions and make sure to place a wad of towels on the seat—just in case my water breaks."

Staring at his reflection in the mirror, Kane chuckled. "Well, that's a first. I was dreaming so vividly. I figure my brain hadn't turned on when you woke me."

"Dave, you're combat-ready in an instant. Please, don't stress." Jenna smiled at him. "I'm okay. We'll look back on this day and laugh ourselves silly."

Changing his sweater for a T-shirt and jacket before sitting down to change his boots, he went to Jenna and took her hand. "I don't want you to worry. I'm going to be with you every second of the way."

"I'm not worried." Jenna squeezed his hand. "I'm excited. The contractions are stronger than I imagined. I'm glad I rested up for a time." Her cheeks pinked. "Oh, this one is five minutes." She panted through it and sipped water. "Time to go." She struggled out of bed and pulled on her gown and slippers. "Hand me that pile of towels." She pointed to the nightstand. "I had them ready."

Without thinking, Kane gave her the towels and then swept her into his arms. He headed for the front door. As they passed the security alarm, he held Jenna so she could set it before they left. He set her down beside the Beast and covered the seat with towels. Soon, he had her safely inside and they were on their way. He drove fast and soon they arrived at the hospital. Nurses dashed out and swept Jenna away, leaving him at the counter to

GOOD GIRLS DON'T CRY   251

give them her details and fill out forms. Once done, he tried to follow her but doors had locked, barring his access.

He went back to the counter and looked at the weary nurse. "I need to be with my wife."

"Take a seat. The doctor will come and get you." The nurse waved him away.

He'd promised to be with her. What the heck was happening? This wasn't in the plan. He paced up and down, his boots sounding loud in the quiet area. He hated hospitals. The smells reminded him of his long stay after the car bombing. Staring at the locked double doors to the inner sanctum, he willed someone to come out. It had been twenty minutes. Jenna needed him. Relief flooded over him when Wolfe walked through the glass doors. He hurried toward him. "They've taken Jenna. I don't know where she is. They went through there and no one will open the door for me."

"I'm sure glad y'all didn't threaten anyone, Dave." Wolfe smiled at him. "It's all good. The nurses are just getting her into a gown and into the birthing suite." He patted Kane on the back. "I figure your baby will be along soon."

Kane shook his head. "She said it will take hours."

"We'll see." Wolfe led him into a room along the corridor and handed him a pair of scrubs. "Fathers come here first to change. You can leave your things in the locker." Wolfe pulled off his jacket and dressed in scrubs. He went to the sink and scrubbed his hands and then pulled on examination gloves.

Kane copied him and they left the room by a backdoor. They walked along corridors and into a large room with bright lights. To his relief, Jenna was sitting up in a bed, face red and puffing. A nurse was holding her hand. He went to her side. "I'm here now. They wouldn't allow me to come in."

"They were waiting for Shane. They won't call in the obstetrician unless something goes wrong. So far, everything is looking good. Contractions are three minutes now." Her face reddened. "Here we go again."

He took her hand and she squeezed it so hard his bones ground together. The classes he'd taken with her fell into place and they worked together. From that moment on, things went so fast he lost track of the time before Jenna started to push. "This is really happening, Jenna. You're on the last mile."

"That's easy for you to say." Jenna gripped his hand. "I'm exhausted."

Sometime later, with Wolfe's encouragement keeping Jenna going, Kane mopped the sweat from her face. She'd worked so hard. "Come on, Jenna. Our baby is almost here."

"One last push, Jenna." Wolfe smiled at them. "Dave, you need to be here."

Kane moved to the end of the bed and stared in wonder as Jackson Daniel Shane Kane, a mop of black hair standing up in all directions and his red face defiantly angry for being so rudely disturbed, screamed his arrival. His hands trembled as Wolfe wrapped the wiggling baby and handed it to him. Once in his arms, Jackson stopped crying and looked up at him with huge blue eyes. Overflowing with love and cheeks wet with tears, Kane grinned at Jenna and laid the bundle in her arms. "We have another son."

EPILOGUE

Although Jenna kept one eye on the office, she enjoyed her time at home. Rio was doing fine and had followed up on the case. The hair trophies were found to be a match to other missing girls in various states. Carter had taken the case to the FBI director and all the details had been shared across the USA. Hopefully, the bodies of the lost girls would be discovered and cold cases closed.

Rowley had made a full recovery and was back at work, the ragged scar on his forehead a testament to how close he'd come to dying. Although Kane had spoken to the deputies about the dangers of hidden explosives, Jenna had arranged for Carter to give them a refresher course. The FBI had been very accommodating and Carter had spent an entire week with them.

Olivia, it seemed, had been approached for a movie deal for her story. The young girl had come through her ordeal better than expected. Her parents were handling everything and had secured an agent to represent their daughter. Jenna hoped it wouldn't bring her team under the spotlight, but the mayor was ecstatic. Tourism would boom in Black Rock Falls once again.

Being a new mother was exhausting. Although Jackson was

a dream, he decided that the feed at two in the morning was playtime. Kane had amazed Jenna on how swiftly he'd slid into the baby's routine. He'd take the night shift, allowing her to go back to sleep after feeding Jackson. They kept the baby in his crib beside their bed. He had a nursery, but right now they wanted to immerse themselves in the bonding process.

It had been wonderful to see Tauri's big smile when they sat him down and gave him the baby to hold. Jenna sat beside him. "This is your brother, Jackson."

"He looks like Daddy." Tauri touched the baby's cheek. "He is so tiny."

Jenna laughed. Jackson had weighed in at a little under ten pounds. He had huge feet and hands, big blue eyes, and a mop of thick black hair. She nodded. "Yes, he does look like Daddy. He has his big feet."

"He'll grow really fast and before you know it he'll be playing with you." Kane ruffled Tauri's hair. "You'll be able to teach him languages."

"I might teach him how to walk first." Tauri grinned. "But he's too small yet. Maybe later."

Friends had arrived in droves to see the baby. The house was soon filled with gifts and flowers. Wolfe dropped by often and always with Norrell. She'd seen the longing on Norrell's face when she'd held Jackson. Her wedding to Wolfe would be at the end of the month. It was wonderful to see such a happy couple.

Later that night, as Jenna fed Jackson, she looked at Kane. "Do you figure Shane and Norrell will have kids?"

"They're young enough." Kane leaned back on the pillows. "I have no idea. It's not something he discusses with me. Shane is a very private person."

Jenna sat Jackson up and patted his back. "You know, I'm glad we decided to take leave and spend time with Jackson. Later, I'll only go into work when necessary, so he gets used to me coming and going. He'll have Nanny Raya as a constant and I'll make sure she's involved from the get-go so he won't fuss if we need to go to work."

"You can oversee the office from home." Kane yawned. "If necessary, you can even visit crime scenes via video calls. It will all work out fine. Our team will manage. If another serial killer comes along, you can always call in the FBI to assist the team." He took Jackson from her and rested him on his shoulder. "This is our time with our baby. Life and crime will go on without us. Trust me, there will be a ton of cases coming along for us to solve when we return to work full-time. There's no need to rush. Right now, both our boys need us at home." He stood and walked from the room, singing softly to his son.

Surrounded by the warm love that feeding a baby gives a mother, Jenna lay back, fully intending to go to sleep. Instead, she got up to use the bathroom, and on the way back to bed, heard Kane's voice. He was talking to Jackson. She walked along the passageway and peered into the family room. Kane was on the sofa, with Jackson in his arms. Love overflowed seeing them together. Jackson was looking at Kane so intently, and Kane's head was bent, one finger wrapped in Jackson's tiny hand.

"I have a secret to tell you, and when you're grown, you'll know the truth of your heritage." Kane's voice was just above a whisper. "One day, when the world is a better place, you'll be able to claim what's rightfully yours. It's all there waiting and protected by the government." He touched the baby's lips. "For now, it's a secret to keep our family safe, but I named you Jackson Daniel because it's my family name. The name given to my great-grandfather, grandfather, father, and me."

Hand pressed against her chest, Jenna held her breath. She slipped without a sound back to bed. Heart pounding, she stared into the darkness. Speculation about Kane's real name had never been an issue because he refused to divulge it for her own safety. The sudden urge to Google the family came to mind and she squashed it immediately. The price on his head meant that his name over the internet would trigger anyone wanting to claim the bounty. For now, the terrorists believed he'd died in a car bombing seven years ago. If she made one slip of the tongue, he'd die. She wished she could take back the last few minutes, but how could she forget? Every time she looked at her baby, or spoke his name, she'd remember the touching scene. Should she tell Kane or keep the secret?

When Kane came back into the room and laid Jackson down in his crib, Jenna pretended to be asleep. As he pulled her against him and curled around her, she relaxed as the heat of his body washed over her. Life was good, and she could keep a secret too. If necessary, she'd deal with it tomorrow. She snuggled back against Kane and smiled into the darkness. *Tomorrow never comes.*

A LETTER FROM D.K. HOOD

Dear Reader,

Thank you so much for choosing my novel and coming with me on another of Kane and Alton's chilling cases in *Good Girls Don't Cry.*

I hope you enjoyed taking a journey through the past cases in my stories and finding the little Easter eggs of clues I hid for you along the way. It was a happy-tears ending for me with a little twist to add some intrigue. Don't for one moment believe that Jenna and Kane's story ends here. The next book will jump over their leave and see them back at work with the team and I do believe it's getting close to Halloween. My favorite time to set a story.

If you enjoyed *Good Girls Don't Cry,* I would be very grateful if you could leave a review and recommend my book to your friends and family. I really enjoy hearing from readers, so feel free to ask me questions at any time. You can get in touch on my Facebook page, X, through my webpage, or D.K. Hood's Readers' Group on Facebook. Here, we chat about books, have giveaways, and from time to time I offer members the chance to volunteer, to be an extra in one of my upcoming stories. Anyone who appears as an extra receives a special gold seal and an auto-graphed bookplate for their paperback.

If you'd like to keep up to date with all my latest releases, just sign up at the website link below. You can unsubscribe at any time and your details will not be shared.

www.bookouture.com/dk-hood

Thank you so much for your support. Until next time,

D.K. Hood

www.dkhood.com

facebook.com/dkhoodauthor
x.com/DKHood_Author

ACKNOWLEDGMENTS

To Helen Jenner and #TeamBookouture for making my stories great.

To Patricia Rodriguez, my talented narrator of the audio versions, who joined us in Book 3, *Follow Me Home*, and has become the voice of Jenna and Kane. She has brought my stories and characters to life. From the first book she narrated, the characters' voices I hear when I'm writing came through my earphones. It was and always will be a very special moment for me. Thank you, Pat.

PUBLISHING TEAM

Turning a manuscript into a book requires the efforts of many people. The publishing team at Bookouture would like to acknowledge everyone who contributed to this publication.

Audio
Alba Proko
Sinead O'Connor
Melissa Tran

Commercial
Lauren Morrissette
Hannah Richmond
Imogen Allport

Cover design
Blacksheep

Data and analysis
Mark Alder
Mohamed Bussuri

Editorial
Helen Jenner
Ria Clare

Copyeditor
Ian Hodder

Proofreader
Claire Rushbrook

Marketing
Alex Crow
Melanie Price
Occy Carr
Ciara Rosney
Martyna Młynarska

Operations and distribution
Marina Valles
Stephanie Straub
Joe Morris

Production
Hannah Snetsinger
Mandy Kullar
Ria Clare
Nadia Michael

Publicity
Kim Nash
Noelle Holten
Jess Readett
Sarah Hardy

Rights and contracts
Peta Nightingale
Richard King
Saidah Graham

Printed in Dunstable, United Kingdom